Present Tense

Book 1 of the Danny Sharp series

Time and Again

By

Yen Rickeard

To Jackie with Thanks

Yen Rickeard

Published by iron sword
Printed by Book Printing UK
Remus House, Coltsfoot Drive, Peterborough, PE2 9BF ISBN:
ISBN: 978-0-9956482-0-3

Foreword

With great thanks and appreciation to all those who helped in this journey of discovery, and with apologies to those whose excellent advice may not always have been followed as diligently as they might have liked, in preference for the needs of a good story.

Most especially
David Rickeard
Dr Peter Halkon of Hull University
All at Butser Ancient Farm
All at Castell Henllys
Drustan the Vain of the Dumnonii
Melistia of Dumnonika
The Megalithic Portal
The Cartographers Guild
BBC history sites
Druid Circle
Noble Warriors of the Brigante

Present Tense

Book 1 of the Danny Sharp series

Time and Again

Contents

Chapter 1 – Confusion.

It was raining. He was running.

The rain slashed hard and icy at his face. He was running as if all the hounds of hell were after him. Perhaps they were. He could hear the pounding of their feet behind him. He could hear their heavy breathing. He could smell their fetid breath.

His clothes were sodden, cold and heavy. They clung to him and slowed him down.

And now the long grass was matted with heather. He had to leap and bound, and they were better at it than he was. He could feel them getting nearer, louder, more eager. He could hear the snapping of their teeth behind his heels, closer and closer. His heart pounded. He was gasping. Any moment now the fangs would catch and ...

With a start he was lying in the dark. In the darkness he could see nothing. He dared not breathe, or move. Not a flicker that might attract – he didn't know what. He did not know where he was. He only knew with a horrid certainty that it was not his own room, or his own house.

From somewhere else there came a sound, muffled, familiar. Two straight lines of light suddenly appeared, and widened as the door opened, and Aunt Moira was there. He could tell it was her, though she was only a dark shape against the light. As she stepped into the room and turned on the light her familiar face became clear.

She said, in the old tongue, which was strangely disconcerting and yet reassuring *'Are you alright?'* Her eyes fully on him, alert and concerned.

He was still too scared to speak, to move, but he managed the smallest nod of his head, tense and tight.

She nodded back, and then, taking her eyes off him for the first time she looked round at the room. She looked at everything, the books on the shelves, the heavy curtains, his clothes scattered on the chair and on the floor, the picture on the wall, the ceiling, the light shade, every corner. If anything was wrong or strange she would have seen it.

Then she took the broom handle that was propped against the door jamb and she knelt down and looked under the bed. She had a good look. She hoicked his trainers out, then poked the broom handle into each dark corner efficiently but carefully.

Satisfied she sat back on her heels and turned her attention back on Danny.

Speaking normally now she said 'The only dangerous things in this room, Danny, are you and I. And I promise you that I will never knowingly do you any harm.' It was a solemn promise, he knew that. But it was less reassuring than he hoped. He didn't feel dangerous. Did she?

At any rate, it must have made her feel better, because she relaxed and smiled. 'Feeling better?' she asked.

This time he managed to nod properly, and to shrug looser the sheets that seemed to have tangled round him.

'You were dreaming,' she told him, as if he might not have worked that out. She stood up, as if that should be enough. As if the world was perfectly normal, with nothing to fear. As if she and he were really the only dangerous things here. Did she think he was dangerous?

She moved to the door, still watching him. 'I'm right here, in the next room,' she said. 'Call me if you need anything.'

'Can I have the light on?' the words rushed out of him.

She stopped. She was thinking about it.

'The dark isn't dangerous Danny. It's only things in the dark that might be dangerous.'

Which Danny thought was pretty much the same thing.

She went on, 'You should try and get used to it. Dark can be your friend.' She propped the broom handle by the door again. She was going to leave and shut the door, and turn out the light in the corridor. He knew she was. He thought fast.

'You have the dark,' he suggested, 'it's your friend. I'll be happy with gloom.'

Her lips quirked. 'Deal,' she said, and went out. The door closed, leaving the two thin lines of light, and he heard her go into the next room without turning off the corridor light. The two thin lines were enough. As his eyes got used to the gloom he could make out the darker shapes of things around the room. He could see what they were and where he was. And eventually, as time passed, fear left him, and he grew tired, and, before the dawn, he fell asleep.

Breakfast was in the kitchen, cereal, bacon, egg, beans, toast, orange juice – did she always have these things? Had she rushed out to get extra? Did she think he needed feeding up? He didn't want to eat, he didn't need to eat, but once he started he found that he was hungry.

When she had put the used cereal bowls into the sink and finished putting everything else on the table she sat down opposite him, and between mouthfuls she asked,

'Do you want to go to school today?'

That stopped him. That was a question.

She carried on eating as though it was normal. 'It's Monday,' she explained, as though that needed explanation. Her voice was warm. 'They'll understand if you don't want to.' She looked at him. 'Sometimes it's better to go on as if everything is normal. It gives your brain something to do.'

He didn't think his brain would work ever again. The same questions, the same thoughts over and over, round and round. And nothing made sense.

'You can stay here if you prefer. Or come to work with me.'

Aunt Moira worked in The Library. Not a library. The Library. The Very Special Library. You needed a pass to go into it, to touch the books, to read them. Most of it was underground, and it went for miles. You could get lost in there.

Above it there were lecture rooms, shops, roads, bookshops, cafes, pubs. People bustled about above it with no idea it was there, unless of course they were 'very learned'. It belonged to the university. Danny had visited once with his parents.

It was spooky.

Lights that came on above you as you walked down long dark corridors with nothing but racks of books and files lining the walls. So many books that the racks of shelves were stacked hard against each other, and you had to wind them apart, rack after rack until you reached the one you wanted and go down the narrow space revealed to find the book you were looking for.

There was no way he was going there today. And he wasn't going to stay here on his own, with nothing but his own thoughts for company.

She drove him to school the long way round, so they wouldn't have to go past his house. Or, where his house had been. As they neared the school she asked,

'Would you like me to go in with you?'

'No,' that was immediate. But then he remembered his manners. 'No, thank you. I'll be fine.' Would he? She didn't answer, and moments later she was pulling up outside the gates, slicing in where some other parent was pulling out.

'I'll pick you up at three thirty,' she told him as he slipped out of the door. And then she was pulling away.

He hoiked his pack higher on his shoulder and went through the gates with the others also arriving bare moments before being late. He could feel their glances, quick and away. He could feel their stares. They all knew. Or perhaps it was just that he was the only one not in uniform. He'd had some spare clothes at his Aunt's house, but not uniform. He was going to need a whole new set of – of everything.

And then there were Jamie and Grant, together, leering at him from a distance, pointing.

'Weirdo, whatcha gonna do today? Want some matches?' and laughing like it was a great joke, as if it was funny.

They kept it up through registration, until even Mrs Bridges had had enough and threatened to send them to the head of year, Mrs Maitland. They pretended to be scared and this was enough to keep them occupied until the class swaggered out to their separate sets for Maths, sending Jamie and Grant in one direction and him in another.

Mrs Maitland ambushed him between periods.

'Daniel, you poor boy,' she announced brightly as she appeared before him suddenly in the corridor, making sure that any of the other pupils who hadn't heard of his disaster would now have an inkling. 'How very brave of you to come to school today. We are all thinking of you, and of your parents. Dear boy, you mustn't worry.' As if worry were the worst of it. She went on in hushed tones, standing too close to him, 'If it all gets too much for you, or if you want someone to talk to, just come straight to my office. You know where I am.' She would be the very last one he would want to talk to. 'Such a terrible thing,' she went on, peering into his face as if she could suck out and devour his emotions, feeding on them with a bright unhurt curiosity, 'come and see me at break, if you need anything. Anything at all.'

He mumbled something that might have sounded like thanks, and hurried away.

He couldn't concentrate in French, or any of the following classes. The words seemed to blur and lose themselves in a vague and distant roar that made his head ache. No-one seemed to notice, and fortunately the teachers seemed to overlook his distraction.

At lunch he sensed eyes on his back as he sat hunched in a corner of the dining hall. He wasn't in uniform, that had gone with everything else he possessed, so he was easy to pick out. He wasn't hungry, and he left early. Not too early to avoid Jamie and Grant, back from the chippie conveniently close outside.

'Where you going?' Called Jamie, 'If it's the maths block, we can get some stuff to help it catch.'

He kept going, it wasn't worth answering them, but they were following him now.

'Nah, no-one in the maths block now. He's going for the IT, and get the geeks!' A girl's voice cut across their laughter. 'Oh shut up, you miserable slobs. At least they've got more than one brain cell apiece.'

'Oo-ooh.' they mocked, 'Look who it isn't!!'

'Is she your girlfriend now?' Grant wasn't going to let Danny go so easily.

'I'm no-one's 'girlfriend',' snapped Kelly, 'and I certainly wouldn't be seen dead with either of you!'

It took them a moment to find an answer, and Danny was almost out of hearing when Jamie came up with 'As if we'd fancy you.' But they did of course. All the boys fancied Kelly. She was slim and graceful, with dark hair and creamy skin. She was also top set in everything. In her little coterie of girls with brains, she stood out as the pretty one.

The one most likely to succeed. Top of the year. And she certainly didn't fancy ANY of the boys.

She could walk pretty fast too, because a moment later, it seemed, she was beside Danny. 'Flaming Cretins!' was her greeting. And while Danny was working out whether that included him, she went on in an only slightly softer tone, 'Haven't got a clue what the world is about. Hope your parents are all right.'

There was no answer to that, and he didn't know what she was after, so he just kept on walking.

'Don't let the idiots get to you,' she went on, as if he were answering her and they were having a conversation. 'They'll all stop talking about it as soon as your parents turn up.'

Which was alright for her to say, but what if they didn't show up? What if they were – gone. Forever.

'Danny?'

'Go away,' he told her. Which was hardly fair, she wasn't getting at him, was probably trying to help – but it wasn't helping. He stopped and turned to her, 'Just leave me alone. I don't want to talk.' It came out sharper than he meant.

'Well, just don't get feeling sorry for yourself, that's all,' is what she said, and she turned and walked away at an oblique angle, towards the IT block. So she had just been walking in the same direction, and taking the heat off him from the terrible twins.

Of course, it was Kelly who had first called them the terrible twins, Grant and Jamie, Tweedledum and Tweedledee. Because, as he now recalled, they had been making fun of a girl in the year below, who, like him, and just been taking their flack without response. Like him. That thought wiped the smile off his face, and he went into the library and buried his face in a book.

Somehow he got through the rest of his classes. Geography was almost over. The bell would ring and he would make it to the front gate and Aunt Moira would be on time. She was never late. For anything. Only minutes to go. And Mrs Maitland was suddenly there at the door, saying his name. For the second time, obviously, because everyone was staring at him, waiting.

'If you wouldn't mind,' she smiled, holding the door open, 'I won't keep you long.'

So he gathered his books in an untidy armful, and grabbed his bag, and went with her. They all watched him go.

Down the long corridor she warbled at him, meaningless words of condolences. He wondered if he could break and run, but of course he didn't.

There was a man by her office door, watching them come towards him. A lean dour man with watchful eyes.

'Detective Inspector Raynes' Mrs Maitland introduced them, 'this is Daniel Sharp.'

They were inside the office now, and Danny looked up into the dour face. This was not going to be good news.

The policeman was going to speak, but Maitland was fussing about seating and not to worry and she would be right there and such.

When she had finally finished, D. I. Raynes spoke at last.

'I'm looking for your parents Danny,' he paused, 'You don't mind if I call you Danny?' Danny nodded. Of course he minded. If DI Raynes had a first name it wasn't proffered. He went on, looking straight at Danny, 'Do you know where they are?' As if he could know. As if he would not be with them if he did know. As if...

'Danny?' The man's tone had changed, had lowered, was more friendly almost.

'No I don't know.'

'Have you an idea?'

The familiar dull ordinary everything, the school, Maitland with her soft smothering concern, the concentrated attention of the Inspector, all were swept away in sudden darkness and cold. The hollow sensation of that night, an eternity, but only two days, before, as he had realised he was alone, and had turned in the empty street to see...

The books tumbled from his arms. Maitland was on her feet, all fuss and bother. Raynes let her. He only watched.

'I'm all right!' snapped Danny, but he wasn't.

'Tell me what happened,' The Inspector asked quietly, patiently. But Danny didn't want to go there, to remember, to see again.

And then the door burst open and Aunt Moira was there, and angry words flew round him. Maitland was oozing sanctimonious care but Aunt Moira was crisp.

'I'll decide who is a responsible adult, thank you!' to Maitland and to the Inspector 'And you ought to know better!'

'The boy will have to talk to me sometime,' answered the Inspector quietly. 'The sooner the better.'

Aunt Moira looked hard at him, and made a concession. 'My house, six o'clock, after tea.' Then she nodded at Danny, and without another word they left. The books stayed on the floor.

Chapter 2 - Questions

At six o'clock precisely they heard a car door slam, and moments later, the doorbell rang. Aunt Moira and Danny were at the back of the living room, by the big window that looked out over the roof of the bedrooms below and across the wide valley to the moors.

There had been sausage, egg and beans, and crumpets with lots of butter, his favourites, but Danny hadn't been hungry. Still wasn't hungry.

His aunt lay a reassuring hand on his shoulder as she rose and went through to the front of the house, which overlooked the town, and the harbour, and where the inspector waited.

Danny heard their voices, muffled, working their way back through the house via the kitchen. She brought a tray with tea cups for three as well as the Inspector. They settled themselves, facing out towards the timeless landscape, and tea was poured.

'That's some view,' commented the Inspector, looking out, and then around, 'and quite a house.'

'Get to the point,' said Aunt Moira pleasantly.

The Inspector took note, and turned to Danny.

'I know it's hard, you need to tell me everything you can about Saturday evening.'

Looking at him and Aunt Moira, Danny could see they had something in common. A clarity of face, an intensity of attention, an openness of expression. But the Inspector was wrong. There was no point in trying to tell the Inspector everything. That would only give him a very wrong impression. Danny had tried it before, and so he knew better.

Mistaking silence for a difficulty in knowing where to begin, the Inspector said 'Start at tea time. You did have tea?'

'In the kitchen,' he said.

'With your Mum and Dad?'

'Dad was in the basement.'

'He didn't eat with you. Is that normal?'

'What's normal?' Danny wanted to ask, but didn't. He said 'He worked. A lot. For other people.' He did odd jobs. A handyman. People tended to ask him at odd hours. If something was badly broken or there was water gushing, or something might be dangerous, like broken shards or failing floors, he would go at once. He was like that.

'Did you get on, you and your Dad?' Past tense.

'He's my Dad,' said Danny, with all that that entailed. Only, he realised, seeing the way that the Inspector was looking at him, it wasn't the same for everyone. Bernie Bates' Dad was a drunk, and bashed his son from time to time. Grant's Dad was practically a psychopath; they all knew that. It was where Grant got it from.

Danny took a breath. 'He's my Dad, and he works hard, and he loves us and I...' There were no words to express how he felt, how much he felt. 'He's my Dad,' he finished lamely, willing the policeman to feel all the good that was in the words.

Inspector Raynes kept looking at him, waiting. Aunt Moira was watching the Inspector like a hawk, but he had eyes only for Danny, was waiting for more.

'He looks after us,' Danny told him.

'How do you mean?'

'He stayed behind while we got away,' was what Danny thought, but it was too much to say.

The policeman shifted position. 'He was in Afghanistan, your Dad, wasn't he?'

Danny nodded.

'That can change people, make them – harsher. Was he...?

'He's good, my Dad, he's not harsh – he's a good man!'

Aunt Moira cut in mildly, 'Tom's not a victim of traumatic stress, Inspector, he's not a violent man. He doesn't have to be. People respect him for what he is. A good, capable man who gets on with things.'

Danny nodded, that was his Dad alright.

'He was an explosives expert wasn't he? Did he ever have any in the house?'

'That's silly.' Danny needed no help with this one. 'He's not stupid or mad...' but it was definitely an explosion that had knocked him off his feet when he had turned in the street and seen...

'He left the army,' Moira added. 'I can't think where he would get explosives from.'

But Danny knew that if his father had needed something, he would get it, somehow. But why would he need it? Even if he did, he would never store it in the house.

'Did he have any enemies? Sometimes when men like your father leave the army they take private work that...'

'There's more than enough work for an odd job man in this town,' Moira intervened. 'And we don't lack money.'

The Inspector turned towards her, and beyond her, the view through the window, the far moors, and the pyramid skylight over the floor below them.

'I'm beginning to see that,' he said. 'The house in town was a bit grand, but this place – from the road it looks like all the other retirement bungalows, very ordinary. But in fact...' In fact from here he could see the glass pyramid that roofed most of the rooms below and behind the house. 'Where does the money come from Miss Halter?'

Moira smiled. 'My great grandfather used to farm most of this hill, mostly sheep, not very productive. After the war, they needed new housing, and when he had sold off the lower acres for a small fortune, he built the house that Tom and Freya live in. We grew up there, Freya and I, when this was all moor land. And later when they built this big estate Mum kept the top plot and built this. We didn't want it to look posh. We're not posh people.'

The house was at the very top of the hill, where the road turned and went back down again. The bungalows on either side had small gardens that went straight back from the road, which meant that this plot on the corner swept outwards on both sides. It was an upside down house, so the part that faced the road and looked like all the others on the street, was in fact just a hall and kitchen and this large living room. The land dropped away quite steeply behind, so there was room under the back of it for the start of the next floor, which was mostly bedrooms and a big study, lit by the glass pyramid roof. And below that, at the very bottom was the winter living room, small and cosy, nestled into the hillside.

Danny had always thought that the houses around it were small, like dolls houses by comparison. But now he had to admit, this was a big house.

The Inspector nodded and turned back to Danny.

'So, you'd had your tea. And your Dad was in the basement. What then?'

'I did some homework. On the kitchen table. Mum tidied. I watched some TV.'

'Dr Who?' suggested the Inspector.

'Wrong night,' and I don't watch the repeats thought Danny but he didn't say it. 'Some nature program. They had great apes. Orangutan. Then I played games on the computer for a bit, until bed time.'

'What was your Mum doing?'

'Working on something. Don't know what.'

'In the kitchen?'

'In her office.' She had been in her office, at least she had at first, when he went up to his room. He hadn't heard her moving about. But then he wouldn't have.

'She's an archaeologist, isn't she?'

Danny nodded.

'There were some really interesting things in the house I understand. Worth a lot.'

Danny shrugged. He knew that, here, the gladius on the wall behind the inspector had security wiring in case anyone tried to steal it, but as far as he knew they didn't bother with anything like that at his house – what had been his house.

'So, did you go to bed?'

'The electricity went off.' And somewhere something had started beeping. Some alarm. Remembering, the warm and open living room suddenly felt cold, and exposed.

'It was dark,' suggested the Inspector.

'We've got battery powered night lights on the stairs.' He'd been cross, because he had got to a crucial part of the game, and it probably hadn't got saved as the computer crashed.

'So what did you do?'

'I went out onto the landing.' The light had been soft and dim, the stairs seemed to glow. He called out 'The electrics gone!' It was a complaint. Obviously his mother knew that already. He was cross and complaining.

Somewhere below there was movement, and shadows flitting, but no reply, so he had gone down the stairs to the hall. And through the quiet house towards the kitchen and the door to the basement.

Then an explosion of sound, crashes and bangs, loud angry sounds, clashing and resounding. And voices, raised in anger. Loud cries, like orders being shouted.

Everything became confused in his mind, cut up into tiny scenes. His mother like a thrown spear dashing from a door. Blood flying like paint splattering.

A man's face like fury, brilliant blue, lurching violently towards him. A cudgel sweeping at him! Something from another direction knocking him flying, people fighting, his mother wielding a broom like a battle axe!

Her voice, 'Run. RUN!'

The front door that wouldn't open, couldn't open, and nightmare things behind him!

'RUN! RUN!'

And they were running. He was running, and she was running, up the street in the cold clean evening air.

And then she wasn't beside him. She was gone, and he turned to see, and there was no-one but him on the grey town street lined with cars. And no sound of pursuit, only the lights of the harbour far below. And then- And then ...

'That'll do,' said Aunt Moira softly but firmly. 'That's enough.'

Aunt Moira's living room was calm and ordered and ordinary. Just like always. Just as it always was. Ordinary. Except for the policeman watching him, weighing his words. Whatever words he had used. As though the shattering events had scattered his mind, like shards. And he couldn't remember what he had said, or if he had spoken or – or what had happened.

As if he could read minds, the Inspector said,

'When something like that happens, it's hard to take in. Your mind skitters. You've done well. But there's more...'

'Not now,' warned Aunt Moira.

'Not now,' agreed the policeman. 'But later, when you think about it you'll remember, you'll put things together. When you do, I'd like you to tell me. Can you do that?'

Yes, thought Danny, that would be easy. Like walking through walls. Like breathing water.

'Of course,' his Aunt was saying on his behalf. She stood. 'It may take a while, you understand.' DI Raynes transferred his gaze to her, assessing the elements of helpfulness and obstruction.

'The first few hours are the most important,' he told her, taking her cue and standing too. 'Every day that passes makes it harder for us to find them, if they are still alive.' He wasn't being nasty, He wasn't glossing over the worst, He was simply stating what was. Aunt Moira looked back at him in much the same way he was looking at her. She put her hand on Danny's shoulder.

'We appreciate that,' she said, 'we know you are trying to do your job, and it's our aim too.' Neither of them looked down at Danny. 'We'll let you know if there is anything that might help you.'

His Aunt was dismissing the policeman. His mouth twisted in amused acknowledgement before he turned back to Danny.

'Anything at all, let me know.'

Danny nodded.

'I'll be back with more questions,' he went on, 'soon.'

Danny nodded again, and his Aunt was moving the policeman out of the living room, into the hall. He could hear them talking but couldn't make out the words. He could guess. He thought he could guess.

Mrs Maitland would have told him. About junior school. About Black Dougal.

And sure enough, in the hallway Inspector Raynes was saying 'He seems troubled.'

'I'd have thought you'd be more concerned if he weren't.'

'Mrs Maitland said he was a troubled child.'

'She would.'

'Something about Black Dougal coming for tea'

Aunt Moira snorted. 'Not that old thing. He was nine. They'd had a re-enactment, and someone played their part too well. You can't blame a boy for believing his own eyes.'

'He became – very upset,' suggested the policeman obliquely.

'The teacher didn't believe him and the kids were calling him a liar. And his own parents had said it was Black Dougal himself. Of course he was upset.' She shook off some thought and went on 'They'd been drinking, high spirits after a party. They weren't thinking.'

Raynes raised an eyebrow. 'Lived in the underworld? Danced with fairies? Slew not one but three dragons? Even at nine you know the difference between myth and reality.'

'Stories get embroidered,' said Moira with a smile.

After the front door closed, and the car door slammed, she went back, to tidy the tea cups onto the tray.

Danny was no longer there.

When she had put the things in the kitchen she went and found him – in the library, with the TV on.

'You did well,' she said.

'He wouldn't have believed me,' muttered Danny,

The TV erupted into laughter, some game show. Neither of them were watching it.

'I will, Danny. When you are ready. I'll understand.'

And she walked out to wash up the tea things, as if everything was normal.

Chapter 3 - Deception

The next morning he woke late, saw the clock on his wall, and almost panicked. Aunt Moira was never late. She would never let him sleep in.

He had slept, he had let himself sleep, and the whole world had fallen apart. Again. He leapt out of bed and grabbed the broom handle.

He was afraid to open the door, but he had to know. With the broom stick held firmly. He turned the handle and opened the door.

The corridor was empty and unharmed. From the stairwell he could hear the radio playing, radio four. Aunt Moira's favourite.

He sidled along cautiously, broom handle at the ready. Going silently up the stairs he could hear movement, and smell toast, and bacon.

Aunt Moira was busy at the kitchen counter, putting things on a tray. She looked up at him and smiled, ignoring the broom handle.

'I was just going to bring you breakfast in bed,' she said, but you can have it here since you're up.'

'It's Tuesday.'

'I got the impression it didn't go so well yesterday,' she said as she transferred the tray to the table. 'I've taken today off work. If you still want to go to school, I can take you, they won't mind your being late.' She was laying out the breakfast things. The bacon was still in the pan, and suddenly he realised he was hungry. He needn't go to school. Not today.

He didn't even bother to go and get dressed first. His Dad liked him to get dressed first, ready for anything, but Aunt Moira didn't seem to mind.

When breakfast was over, before she had started on the washing up, Aunt Moira looked at him across the table. 'When you are ready, we should talk about what we are going to say to Inspector Raynes. You'll have to talk to him sometime, and you're right, the truth is probably beyond him. But he has to have something to go on. And so do I.

'Your mother is my sister, Danny. That could have been me – I think. But I don't understand – I don't understand what happened, how it could have happened.' She paused, 'Can you tell me?'

There was a moment's silence. Danny got up. It felt like his mouth was glued shut. He couldn't look at her, which was stupid. With an effort he opened his mouth and mumbled something about getting dressed. Going down the stairs, breakfast was uncomfortable in his stomach. He felt like a coward. He was a coward. He had let his Mother die, and he was still alive. His mother and his Father were both dead. No-one could have survived that explosion. They were dead and he was still alive.

When Aunt Moira finally came downstairs to find him he had stopped crying, but he hadn't got dressed. He was sat on the bed with his knees hugged to his chest, too cowed to even look up at her.

For a long moment she said nothing. Then she sat down on the bed beside him. After a while she said, quietly, as though words were uncomfortable in her mouth 'She's my sister, and I – I'm afraid for her too. Her and Tom.'

They both sat for a while. Then she went on, 'Whatever happened. We have to hope for the best.' She paused and sighed. 'There were things they didn't tell you. Things they didn't want to tell you yet. Secrets. Not knowing what happened...' she stopped abruptly.

Looking at her sideways he could see she was as confused as he was. He had never seen her look like that before.

'What things?' he asked.

She sighed again. 'Not knowing what happened I don't know what to tell you.' Then, her face changing to the more decisive look that was more natural to her, 'You get dressed and come upstairs and we'll talk. If you can tell me what you saw, perhaps we can sort out what happened.'

She looked at him then, sideways, like he was looking at her, only she had a confident conspiratorial air.

'See you upstairs,' she said, and walked out the door.'

Inspector Raynes had wanted Danny to come into the police station to make his statement, but Aunt Moira wouldn't agree. So the inspector was back in the living room, looking out over the rest of the house towards the moors.

He had listened carefully and asked few questions as Danny went through the story. He had listened but taken no notes. And then he looked out of the window to the clouds scudding over the hills with the threat of rain. For a while it seemed as if the clouds were of greater interest than Danny's story.

When at last he looked back, it was to Aunt Moira.

'You haven't been quite straight with me Miss Halter,' he said pleasantly. He glanced at Danny, 'Your mother may be an archaeologist but your Gran was the one. She's famous for it. That's where the money for this house came from. Gifted Gemma, they called her. Some of the greatest Iron Age finds ever.'

Moira smiled. 'We don't like to brag.'

He went on, "She would point and they would dig, and there it would be, some new wonderful find?'

'You've been reading Bernard Bradey's Book,' smiled Moira. 'He was besotted. He used to follow her around taking notes. It wasn't really like that.'

'There was some controversy, wasn't there? Wasn't she accused of stealing artefacts from Museums and burying them, ready to find later?'

Moira snorted 'They couldn't believe a woman could be better at finding old settlements than they were. When she laid bare the Beverly Edge site they had to admit she couldn't have planted an entire settlement. And then of course there was the Lansdowne Horde, with the jewellery. That was exceptional. No-one had never seen the like of that. They had to give her credit after that.'

'Priceless?' he suggested.

Moira just smiled.

'Over four million, back then, wasn't it?' he prodded.

'She gave it to the museum,' Moira rebutted him, then grinned, 'But she never had any trouble getting funding after that.'

'I'll bet.'

And still smiling he turned back to Danny, and in the same tone of voice asked 'Tell me about the blue men?'

Time stood still, jarred to a stop. He and his Aunt had agreed, that morning, no mention of the blue men. But here they were.

'Blue men?' Aunt Moira was saying, innocently, 'What blue men?'

But the detective's eyes did not waver from Danny's face.

'You mentioned them yesterday,' he reminded Danny

'Did I?' What else could he say.

There was an awkward pause.

'I don't remember that,' Moira said, looking puzzled. 'Were they wearing blue?' She was offering him a get-out, but he was too stunned to take it.

'I don't remember,' was all he could say. But all he could see, though he knew the detective was there, watching his every move, all he could see was the face, livid blue, the fierce eyes, the swinging cudgel. All he could hear was his mother's scream, not of fear or pain but of anger, of rage, of determination. A war cry.

Aunt Moira was saying something, something about remembering to breathe. The room crashed back around him with sickening familiarity, with a safety that was only wafer thin. He was trembling. They were both looking at him with an intensity that hurt.

'Just breathe,' said Aunt Moira. He breathed. The world seemed to settle, to become more firm, more real. He went on breathing, concentrated on it.

'They said at the hospital,' Moira was saying, 'that he had a mild concussion. That and the shock...'

'They let him go home with you,' D. I. Raynes replied mildly.

'Yes,' agreed Moira.

'Should we call a doctor?'

'I'm alright' muttered Danny.

'Should we call it a day?' suggested his Aunt.

Danny straightened his back. His mother wouldn't stand back. She hadn't run away.

He said, 'Things get jumbled up. And then – it's like I'm back there. And it was scary. Really...' no other word for it, 'really scary.' He was looking straight at the Inspector, to see if he understood. Raynes nodded, but didn't speak. 'I ran away. She was with me – my mother. She said run, and we both ran. She was there, beside me. But then she wasn't. She went back. She went back to try and save my Dad. And I didn't.' He blinked hard to stop the tears. He wasn't going to cry in front of the inspector, but his face felt taut with the effort of it.

'You said you both ran?'

Danny nodded.

'And then suddenly she wasn't there?

He nodded again.

'She didn't say anything?'

He shook his head.

'She wanted you to keep running,' the Inspector said, clearly. A conclusion. 'She wanted you to be safe.'

'And,' thought Danny 'she wasn't.' But he said nothing. The inspector was still watching him, but there was nothing hawk-like about it now.

'You're fourteen. You were her first responsibility. She got you safe first. Then she went back. Quite a woman, your mother.'

Danny took a deep breath. 'I should have saved her.'

Rayner leant back. 'You're fourteen,' he said again. 'Whatever was happening, you wouldn't be able to sort that out. Obviously she thought she could do - something. Maybe it wasn't as severe as you thought...'

For a brief second Danny saw again the face, the sweeping cudgel, heard his mother's voice, but the Inspector was still speaking and he concentrated on that.

'Maybe she had more faith in your father than she should have... Whatever. That isn't your fault. In a moment of crisis, you did what your mother told you. It was the right thing to do.'

It was like a tremendous weight lifting off his chest. He wasn't sure he could agree with the Inspector, but he no longer felt crushed.

The Inspector was still making conclusions. He leaned forward again. 'It was a strong explosion. My superintendent might have preferred to put it down as a gas leak but the crater walls are glassy from the heat. Then there's you. What you saw. My super would like to think you were an unreliable witness, what with the bang on the head and the shock.' He gave a grim smile. 'He's inclined to believe Mrs Maitland's opinion that you have a vivid imagination. I believe you. I believe what you say you saw. It might not be accurate, given the circumstances. It may need interpretation. What I don't understand is, what the two of you are trying to hide from me, and why.'

Danny was on the verge of blurting out 'Because you'll think I'm mad, barmy, a raving loony,' but something stopped him.

Moira said, 'I wasn't there, Inspector. I don't know what happened.'

'Everyone has secrets,' he told her. 'Every family. At least the ones I deal with. That's alright. The only thing I'm interested in is finding out what happened. What blew up the house. What happened to the parents. Whether it might happen again. Until I find out I am going to keep digging, and I will find out in the end. So you might as well tell me now and save every-one a lot of time and effort.'

'We don't have the answers to any of those questions.' said Moira, softly, getting to her feet. 'If we come up with anything which might help you ...'

This time the Inspector did not take the hint and get to his feet too. He looked at Danny. 'I believe that you had nothing to do with explosion. I believe that you were scared, and that your mother told you to run, and you did what she said. But there's more. If there is any hope of finding either of your parents alive, we need your help. Your full co-operation. It's no time for secrets.'

'I haven't any secrets,' said Danny desperately. 'I don't know any more. If I knew anything that might help, I'd tell you'

The inspector looked at him for a long moment, then got to his feet. To Moira he said 'I'm disappointed. I thought better of you.'

And to Danny 'I'll be back. I'll keep digging.'

As he and his Aunt walked to the door, Danny heard her thank him.

'What for?' the policeman wanted to know.

'For backing him up. For believing him. It's been tough for him, ever since he told them that Black Dougal came to tea. Nobody believed him. The kids called him a liar. And his teacher... she thought he was a bit crazy. It wasn't fair.'

'I know there is something you're not telling me,' he replied, 'probably for the good of the boy, but I can't make a proper picture unless I know it all.'

There was the sound of the door being opened. A heavy pause, waiting.

'Some pictures don't make sense,' is what she said.

Danny waited for her in the living room, with his knees tucked up to his chest, hugging them, head down, thinking hard.

When she came back she would be kind. He was tired of people being kind. Even Aunt Moira's type of kind, which was harder edged than most.

And he was tired of feeling guilty, even if he was. He didn't really accept what the Inspector had said, about him having done the right thing, but he couldn't change what he had done. He couldn't change that he had not even noticed his mother turn back, into danger.

But some of things the Inspector said did make sense. As Moira came back into the room he raised his head and said,

'Isn't it time you told me the family secret?'

She stopped. Then she sighed and came over to sit in her favourite chair looking out over the valley.

'It's not that simple,' she said. So there was a family secret!

'It's – complicated.'

He nodded. He supposed 'family secrets' usually were complicated. Although everyone knew Grant's Dad was a psycho and nobody said or did anything about it. So perhaps that was a public secret. He focused in on his Aunt and their secret.

'Freya, and Tom, thought – they want to wait a while. I think you ought to be told, but they say...' present tense thought Danny with a sudden surge of hope, 'well, they have good arguments-' She was finding this hard. It had to be really bad news.

'It's not some sort of congenital illness?' he blurted.

She laughed. It was relief. 'No, nothing like that! Much simpler, and much more complicated.' Suddenly it was no longer a source of burden for her, and so less so for him. She was going to go on, she was about to tell him, but the doorbell rang.

They both looked in that direction. The Inspector had hardly left, but now he was back again. What now?

Moira's face set. She turned and walked briskly towards the door. Danny didn't fancy the inspector's chances. But the voice that came as the door was opened was female, and light.

Chapter 4 – Normality?

Aunt Moira opened the door, ready to rebuff a policeman, and found a tall, pretty school girl of about Danny's age on the doorstep.

'Hello, is this the right house? I'm looking for Danny Sharp,' she said with a smile. 'We're having a maths test next week and if he's going to take it he might want to know what it's about.'

It was Kelly.

At any other time she would have been more than welcome. Now, while Danny was glad to see her, even with her load of books, there were bigger things on his mind. But well, she, Kelly, had thought of him. And she breezed in with a world of normality and a helpful mentality.

That and the fact that Aunt Moira had welcomed her in, and they were setting up at the kitchen table with a load of books, with a rush of information about Vectors and exams and being chosen for an early GCSE if they did well.

He looked to Aunt Moira, but she wasn't going to acknowledge his need for answers that she had been about to give. And anyway, he felt a warm glow that Kelly had brought him stuff, even if it was only homework.

So they settled down to Maths, and vectors, and more general geometry. The amazing thing was that Kelly made it sound easy, and she seemed to expect him to find it easy too. And it was when she explained, simply, with diagrams. Well, at least it was to begin with. After that he tried to keep up but it was more a matter of nodding wisely and muttering general agreement while trying to hold it all together in his head.

It was a surprise to find that it was six o'clock already, and Moira was starting to cook.

'Will you stay for supper?' asked Moira. Kelly looked at Danny.

He nodded agreement.

'I'll phone Mum,' said Kelly.

Listening – Kelly did not bounce off somewhere to speak unheard – Danny heard her answering all the questions his own Mum would have asked, where, who, when, what time will you, how will you? It made him feel strange – aloof, outside.

When Kelly gave the address of Scudmoore Crescent, there was a noticeable screeching from the phone, and Kelly made a grimace.

'Scudmoore not skidrow,' she explained patiently, then, 'It's a very nice house Mum,' looking round as if she had only just noticed quite how nice it was.

Then, 'It's Danny, he's in the same class as me.' Well for some of the lessons anyway, and then, 'No Mum, I'm staying for supper.' And then rather more firmly, 'Because I am and they're really nice.'

Moira offered to run her home but Kelly's Mum had already decided to come and collect her daughter, at half past eight.

'Sorry about that,' Kelly said as she put her phone away.

'Not at all,' smiled Moira, 'she's bound to feel protective.'

'Oh,' said Kelly, with a sudden embarrassment, and was going to say something else, but then didn't, and instead said how tomorrow Mr Greaves was going to go over other topics that would be in the test.

'Are you going to come in, or shall I bring you notes?' She asked.

'You explain better than he does,' offered Danny, and then pushing his luck 'perhaps we could do both.' She seemed pleased but whether it was at the prospect of both, or at the compliment, he wasn't sure.

Meanwhile Moira was cooking and in a scant half an hour, while Kelly had chattered on about school, maths and music, Danny's Aunt produced crab cakes with a stir-fry of vegetables on a bed of rice. Not what Danny would have chosen, but Kelly was well impressed.

They had hardly finished when the door-bell rang, and when Moira went to answer it, Kelly's Mum bustled in.

Seeing her hustle into the kitchen, Danny realised he had been expecting her to be rather different, more like her daughter. But Mrs James was short and fast moving, all hands and twitching features and darting eyes. It was only a few minutes past seven but she seemed to think that she was late.

'There you are,' she proclaimed on seeing Kelly 'are you ready, sorry we can't stop, thank you for having her, hope she hasn't been a bother, where are your books Love, oh it's been such a bustle, you wouldn't believe the traffic. The roundabout by Morrison's is choked.'

Kelly made no move to get up and get ready.

'This is Danny's Aunt,' she said, and Moira filled in, 'Moira Halter, pleased to meet you, Mrs James' and while they shook hands and Mrs James muttered how'de do's Kelly went on, 'and this is Danny.'

Mrs James turned to him with a fluster of hands, then recoiled in shock.

'But you're the boy!' she shrieked. 'The boy on the telly. The one who...' And she stopped with a gulp, suddenly silent. Her eyes rolled from Danny to Moira and then back. 'The boy who what?' thought Danny. At best, the boy had who left his parents to die. At worst ...

Kelly filled the gap nicely. 'The one whose parents are missing.'

'I've just made a pot of tea,' said Moira, surprisingly gently, 'would you like a cup?'

Mrs James just gulped, she looked like a rabbit who suddenly found itself in a den of stoats.

With extreme patience Kelly said, 'Sit down and have a cup of tea Mum, they're nice people.' And when Moira added, 'Milk and sugar?' there was nothing for it but for Kelly's Mum to sit down and confess to milk but no sugar.

'They've got a Rayburn,' Kelly confided. Her Mum looked and saw that the oven was indeed a wide range with six hobs and three heavy doors marking the various ovens. Her eyes opened wide, and she looked round the kitchen, seeing now all the benefits of space, and a kitchen table big enough to take all Kelly's books, with plenty to spare for several other people to do the same. She avoided looking at the boy-who.

'Nice kitchen,' she muttered, as if trying to fit this with a murder scene.

'I like it,' smiled Moira. 'I've got some cake somewhere...' which she had, and soon it was on plates. Mrs James eyes hers nervously. But Kelly bit into hers and said how wonderful it was, before going on to tell her mother about the test next week and how they would be allowed to take the maths exam early if they did well.

Danny felt he had to point out that he was unlikely to do as well as Kelly, which confused her mother by making her proud. Moira agreed that Kelly was obviously a very bright young lady, at which Mrs James began to look slightly less uneasy, and even took a tiny nibble of the cake.

To Danny's surprise, Moira was suddenly a cake expert, explaining how great the Rayburn was for baking, drawing Kelly's Mum into asking questions about relative oven heats, and which oven was best for what. Kelly was smiling, but she caught him looking at her and with a poke at her books said,

'Do you want to get some of this onto your laptop?'

'It's in the library.' It was an old one of Moira's. All of his things were gone, vanished. Every little thing he owned, gone.

'We're going to do some more work on the maths, Mum,' Kelly explained, standing up.

For a moment it seemed that her Mum was going to protest, but Moira said, 'Just down stairs. We can hear if they call,' and then offered more tea.

Moments later, books in hand they were away down the staircase to the lower regions. Danny opened the door. Twilight was still enough for the skylight to flood the room with vague light. A comfortable sofa faced the TV on one side, on the other was a small table to work on with chairs around it and a lectern to prop a book on if you didn't want the bother of holding it. Every wall was floor to ceiling book shelves, crammed full.

Kelly turned slowly taking in all the books.

'When you said library...' she breathed.

'Aunt Moira's a librarian.'

'So these aren't...'

'These are hers. Her own books. Or rather ours. She always says that.'

'Does she read them all?'

'Most of them are reference,' he waved an arm at a wall as he put their books on the table, 'so you can look up stuff.' Kelly moved closer to look at titles. 'A lot of history, from Gran,' explained Danny.

'But these are science,' murmured Kelly bending towards the lower shelves. 'Quantum Physics. Philosophy. Relativity.' She looked at him, 'May I?' and without waiting for an answer she pulled a thin volume from the packed shelf. 'A transitional analysis of temporal displacement,' by K. Wilcox. She flipped it open. Danny looked over her shoulder. As he expected there was a small paragraph of text, surrounded by lots of equations full of squiggles and subscripts and symbols he didn't understand. The text read, 'From which we can clearly see that given the temporal disparity there must be a singularity defined more generally by the following.' The following was another equation that filled half the page. As far as Danny was concerned it was all as clear as mud.

'Does she read this stuff' breathed Kelly, awe in her voice.

'It's from the university. Apparently she supports some of the research there. I guess they send stuff to show what they are doing.'

'She must be seriously smart.' Kelly was looking at him wide eyed.

'She doesn't do the research,' Danny protested. 'I don't think she understands that sort of stuff. She just thinks it's worth someone doing.'

'Why aren't you top set for everything?'

'Because I'm not smart, not like you. It's a struggle to keep up sometimes.'

She looked at him seriously. 'You're not stupid.'

'Thank you.'

'Well, you're not. You're – sensible. Practical.'

He was miffed, without knowing why. 'Maybe I should do Practical Technology,' he suggested tetchily.

Kelly snorted. For a moment she looked just like his Aunt when he had said something stupid.

'Maybe we should get this stuff on vectors onto something more 'technologically practical' than sheets of paper,' she suggested with a smile, looking nothing like his aunt Moira in any way.

They had plenty of time to get everything transferred in a way that Kelly was happy with. The equations in the book had moved them on to thoughts of algebra, and Kelly admitted that she had no idea what most of the squiggles in the book meant. Something to do with probability, and differentiation and – stuff.

By the time Aunt Moira called down the stairs they had moved on to computer games that they both liked, but apparently it was time for Kelly to go home. Her mother was fussing with keys and handbag when they got to the kitchen, still twitchy but almost smiling.

Kelly walked out of the door with a backward wave and 'See you tomorrow,' and it was as if she took the light with her. The foreboding was back almost as the door shut. Life was not just school and maths and easy stuff like that.

Chapter 5 - Reality

It was raining. He was running.

The rain slashed hard at his face. The ice in it stung like stones. He was running as if all the hounds of hell were after him. Perhaps they were. He could hear the pounding of their feet behind him. He could hear their heavy breathing. He could smell their fetid breath.

His clothes were sodden, cold and heavy. They clung to him and slowed him down.

And now the long grass was matted with heather, He had to leap and bound, and they were better at it than he was. He could feel them getting nearer, louder, more eager. He could hear the snapping of their teeth behind his heels, closer and closer. His heart pounded. He was gasping. And then this voice, his mother's voice, saying soft and secret in his ear 'Go left, round, not over, go round, not over' like an echo or a memory. And he veered knowing that the horror behind him would cut the corner, cut the distance. Any moment now the fangs would catch and –

He woke suddenly into darkness. His new room. His Aunt's house. Same old fear. Same old uncertainty. He lay still, his heart pounding. His mother's voice. He could still hear it, like an echo. Go round, not over. Whatever that meant. The blackness around him was severe. Anything could be there.

He knew that he had been dreaming, again. But that didn't mean that the darkness was not unsafe. The broom handle was by the door, five steps away. His bedside light was right beside him. He had only to free a hand and click, all would be revealed.

He would be revealed.

He could hear no breathing in the dark, except his own. Hear no heart beat but his own.

With infinite stealth he freed his hand from the tangled sheets, silently, silently. He reached and felt the bedside table, the hard, cool wood smooth beneath his hand. Found tissues, his glass of water, his pencil, some string, the bedside light. Softly, softly up the side, firming on the switch and ...

The room bathed with sardonic light. Nothing there. Nothing to fear. He breathed again. Nothing here. He looked round carefully, nothing had changed. He knew nothing had changed, but it was reassuring to see that it was so.

Under the bed was another matter, but he knew there was nothing there.

With sudden resolve he threw back the sheet and in four strides had the broom handle firmly clasped as he turned. Of course there was nothing hiding under the bed. No blue men in the dark.

When he had his breath back he turned, opened the door and stepped out. Nothing left, nothing right. He padded silently up the stairs into the quiet living room, where grey dawn light picked out the furniture. It was very quiet and still. A stray beam of light picked out the gladius on the wall in shining gold.

The clock on the other wall showed a shadowy 6.15. It was a stupid clock. It not only told the time, but the day of the week, the month, even the year. It was a clock for stupid people.

He felt out of place, unreal. Only the broom handle felt solid and real. He held it like a quarter staff, the way his father had taught him.

'In the right hands a quarter staff will beat a sword any day,' his father had said. That was when he was young, maybe seven, and his father had just left the army. They used to train together, in the back yard. The jab, parry, thrust, forward and back, the staff twirling, always in both hands, never swung wide. There are two ends to every stick, his father used to say. Danny hadn't practised in an age.

Did it work against cudgels? Would it have helped that night, if he had gone back, if he had a sturdy weapon in his hands?

He didn't think so.

He weighed the broom handle in his hands. A little light. A little thin. He held it before him, in both hands, shoulder width apart. He imagined his father beside him, talking him through it. The tap. One hand forward the other back, and one end swung with practised sharpness forward. The gotcha. The other end jabbed savagely back at an imagined attacker behind him. The trip. A hoik with the back end coming forward low down. The parry.

He hadn't practised for ages, but the moves came back smooth and swift. They weren't the proper names for them, but that was what he and his father had called them, in those far distant days, only a few days ago, when his father was alive.

No tears.

He worked through the whole set, slowly, making sure he was remembering them right, and then again, faster. And again. Sweat trickled down his forehead. Again and faster, his bare feet moving silent over the parquet floor, swinging him across the room like a dancer, faster and faster.

Until suddenly Moira was at the top of the stairs, watching him, and he stopped, self-conscious.

'You'll be needing a good breakfast then,' she smiled. 'Make it quick if you're going in.' The clear grey light of a cloudy day showed the clock at 8.02.

Hot and sweaty, he threw himself into a shower, failed to towel himself completely dry, so that his clothes caught against his skin, and arrived tousle headed in time to wolf down a bacon sarnie as Moira swung his back pack at him and opened the front door.

The direct route took him past his home, what had been his home. Like a missing tooth it stood out, wrapped in metal fencing with blue and white police tape to keep people out. There was some scaffolding, but no house. Instead a crater littered with debris. A chimney stack leaned out of it at an angle, above tangled sections of tiles. The scaffolding carried tarpaulins that hid what was below. It was unreal. Unbelievable. Then they were past. And now nothing seemed real.

The car swept to a halt and he was into the school and class, just as Mrs Middleton was about to close the register. She didn't complain. Kelly grinned at him as she went out the door, which wasn't lost on Jamie and Grant, but Danny found he didn't care. When they started making girlfriend noises it was as if they were in another world, removed, behind glass. Of course it wasn't true, but what did that matter.

Through the next few lessons he didn't take much in. Like an after image he kept seeing the place that had once been his home slide by, as if it was moving, not the car. No wonder the blast had knocked him off his feet. The houses on either side were boarded up. There had been workmen arriving at a house on the other side of the street. The front of it was pitted and scarred.

His mother had seen him safe, and gone back. Into that.

Aunt Moira spoke of them in the present tense, but she was mistaken. Must be mistaken.

Meanwhile everything else was going on as normal. The other kids chattered between classes. The teachers taught whatever they taught as if knowing things would change anything.

At the end of a lesson, must have been music 'cos they were in the music block, and everyone was getting their stuff together for the next class, so he did too. What else could he do? He didn't even know what class was next.

He might as well just walk. Walk out and away. Out of class, out of school, out. Away.

'Hey!' It was Kelly sudden at his side. 'I've brought a worksheet on Matrices. They're cooler than I thought. You can go 3D.'

He stopped. So did she.

'We went past the house today. My old house, that was.'

There was a pause.

'I'm sorry,' she said. Nothing else. He was glad of that.

He took a deep breath. 'They're gone.'

'We don't know that,' she said too quickly. Then more slowly. 'No-one knows what happened. We can't be sure.'

He actually weighed that for a moment. 'They're not super-human,' he concluded.

She shifted her bag on her shoulder, as though it were suddenly heavier. 'But we don't know. And it's too big a thing to just jump to.'

Yes, he thought, it was.

'So,' she put a hand on his arm, 'leave a little room for doubt. For hope'

That sounded reasonable. That sounded possible. She had turned him towards the maths block, and started walking, so he did too. There was, he thought, not much hope. So it didn't need much room.

He tried to follow Mr. Greaves as he went on about matrices, and then statistics. Cumulative probability. That seemed to be where Danny was, stuck with the overwhelming cumulative probability. And then, as if Mr Greaves knew what he was thinking he went on. 'Of course it is a mistake to think that because something is of low probability, it won't happen. In fact, it must happen sometimes, to make the numbers right. Somebody has to win the lottery. Someone does. It's just not very likely to be you.'

That was something to hold onto. If anyone could hold out against overwhelming odds, it was his father.

Chapter 6 - Investigation

His Aunt's parting words that morning had been that she had something to do that afternoon and that he should make his own way home. Kelly played chess on Wednesday. The club met in the hall so Danny went along too.

While Kelly took her place at the serious table, she was of course one of the top players, one of the sixth formers played against Danny. Danny could remember all the moves, he used to play against his father until he realised his Dad was making deliberate mistakes to let him win. The sixth former gave a running commentary on Danny's moves, saying what were the advantages and disadvantages of how he had just played. Towards the end this was often accompanied by the taking of one of Danny's pieces.

'Sorry, I'm not much good,' he murmured as the inevitable check mate came.

'Actually,' the boy said slowly, 'if you haven't played for a while, that wasn't bad.'

The boy Kelly was playing against looked up suddenly. 'How far?' he demanded.

'Fifty-nine.' Came the crisp answer from Danny's opponent, then he explained to Danny, 'moves. How long it took me to beat you.'

Kelly was beaming. 'Tariq is top of our league table. Nobody beats Tariq.'

'Not true,' Tariq replied modestly, but the way he said it told Danny it probably was.

'You have the makings of a good player. Would you like to play again?'

'No thanks. My brain is about to explode as it is.'

'Ah well,' muttered Tariq a little too dismissively, and moved off to another table where a group were gathered around a game.

Danny stayed where he was and thought. He thought about his house, all the things that made it home. The wide staircase, the slanting light through the living room window. His mother, when she was home, briskly defrosted some meal she had made earlier, but looking at him, listening to him. All gone. A crater and police tape. The roof in the basement.

He made up his mind.

Kelly was still playing her game. He picked up his bag, ready to go. He ought to tell her, but better not.

'Wait for me!' she called, followed at once by, 'Check and then its check mate in two!'

She was standing and grabbing her bag.

'No its not!' came an aggrieved response, but Tariq had moved over, and he laughed.

'Yes it is.'

'Witch,' muttered the other.

'Didn't see that coming did you?' she warbled as she followed Danny out the door. She had to run to catch Danny up.

'Hang on, what's the hurry?' she panted as she caught him up.

'You'd better not come.'

'Why not?' she was hurt, aggrieved. He would have to explain.

'I'm not going home. Not straight away.' He was still walking fast and since she had stopped, she had to catch him up again. But no recriminations.

'Where are you going then?

'Home. My real home. The old house.'

'It isn't there Danny.' She must think him an idiot.

'I know that!' She had sounded worried. He stopped. 'I'm going to look, to see...' what would he see? 'I'm going to try and work out what happened. What the damage is. How...' How could it have happened? The whole house exploded. Collapsed. Impossible.

She was looking at him, judging him. 'The police are doing that, they've got the technology. You might muck things up for them,' she told him. He knew that too. He had seen police shows on the TV. He shrugged.

'I have to see. For myself.' To face facts.

'I'll come too,' she said.

'You don't have to. We could get in trouble.'

'I'll be your witness,' she said, then with a grim smile, 'your lookout.'

'You don't have to.'

'Somebody does.' And with a hoik of her bag she was off, ahead of him, determined.

He caught her up and they walked in silence, down Bank Street, past the new shopping centre, then up the long slope of what had been his street. Not a word spoken.

There it was. The missing tooth. The hole, fenced in. Them fenced out. Things had changed since the morning. A crane lay hunched and compact at the side of the hole. The chimney stack lay shattered over the back garden, along with mashed up portions of the roof. Caterpillar tracks showed where the crane had stood and scooped them out. The crater seemed to gape wider.

Where were all the walls? The furniture? The paintings, the stuff? He hardened his thinking. If his parents were dead, where was the blood and the bones?

There had been flames. He remembered that. Behind the ambulance men leaning over him, there had been flames, an orange glow. That would have burned most of the furniture. Despite the days that had passed, you could still smell charcoal and ash, dead bonfire smells. There were blackened smudges, like soot, but where were the bent pipes and shattered walls that should have been left? It was mostly bits of roof as far as he could make out. As if the lower parts of the house had simply never existed. Wiped out. Vanished.

There were still bits of tarpaulin fastened to the scaffolding that jutted out of the hole, perhaps there was more to be seen there.

One of the sections of metal fencing jutted out a little. That would be where the workmen got in. He made for it.

'What are you doing?' Kelly asked, nervous for the first time. He had almost forgotten she was there.

'Having a closer look.'

'Is it safe?'

A lot safer than it had been. The fence grated as he widened the little gap, and ducked under the police tape.

'Be careful!' Kelly was looking up and down the street, but there was no-one out there. He dropped his bag and squeezed through the gap. Now he could see there was a ladder propped against the side of the pit that led down to where some of the tarpaulins were. He put a foot on it.

'Danny,' Kelly's voice was low, and urgent. He looked up. 'You don't know what's there.' She was pale. He understood.

'If they'd found my parents they would have told us.'

She nodded. 'Be careful. I'll be right here.'

Could she see his hand tremble, he wondered, as he took hold of the stake at the top of the ladder and lowered himself down? He hoped not. He stepped down rung by rung, telling himself there was nothing to be scared of. The wall that the ladder was leaning on, the edge of the crater, was neither jagged nor burned. It was a smooth glassy texture, brick coloured. He stopped and leaned closer. Not just brick coloured. He could see where the bricks had melted and glazed and run, covering the mortar between them. This was the outer wall of the basement, transformed, melted by intense heat.

He stepped onto the bottom, a thick crunchy layer of small particles, of dust and grime in an uneven layer over, he bent down to check what he had already guessed, over a glassy smooth surface of pale grey. This was about the level of the basement floor. It was the transformed concrete of the floor. There had been several walls down here, holding up the walls of the floors above. They were all gone. The tented tarpaulin was an enclosed space in a cavernous vault. He pulled back the thin sheet and stepped in.

A surreal sculpture of fused shapes twisted and swirled into an uneven column, as if some weird force had crushed then melted them into a single block. It was wide and tall. In the gloomy tent of tarpaulin, it caught light with a metallic shimmer, mostly dull but sparked in places with bright gold or copper tones. A stench of burnt plastic or rubber lingered in the air. There were occasional deep pits in the surface, pitted with black sooty stuff.

It made no sense at all. There had been nothing like that in his house. Not even remotely.

Danny walked round it once, his shoes crunching on the fine debris. He walked round it twice. It still made no sense.

He pushed his way through the tarpaulin at the back. There was more debris there, in big heaps. Big beams, from the roof probably, charred to narrow charcoal and burned to stubs. Broken and twisted tiles, some glazed in places, like the floor and the walls. And beneath that, a humped shape like a fallen column, perhaps like the one behind him. It was impossible to tell for all the junk that smothered it, but someone had cleared a little of it where it emerged into the clearer air, and the surface there looked the same.

He knew better than to try and scramble over the pile.

He went back and called Kelly. Once he told her it was safe she dropped her bag by his at the fence and climbed lightly down. They examined the first column together in silence.

At last Danny gave in and said, 'It's weird. It doesn't make any sense.'

Kelly adopted a more scientific approach.

'About two metres across at the bottom. Maybe – three metres, four metres high.' She sniffed at it. 'There was some plastic and other stuff, but that's all burned off. And look,' she crouched and pointed at some fine threads of red-gold copper that snaked across the surface, 'here,' she said, 'and here,' finding some more higher up. 'Like,' she proffered hesitantly, 'like wires.'

She circled the column slowly and stopped, pointing at a small patterned patch of glittering detail. 'That's silver,' she said, 'or maybe platinum, or,' more doubtfully 'or even titanium. And perhaps the bright specks are gold...'

'Or it's tin and copper,' suggested Danny.

'No, the copper is red, like that,' she pointed to a splurge of red-gold, smudged with black soot.' She stood back and looked at the whole thing again. 'Do you have lead in the roof?'

Not anymore. But, 'We did, I think. And in the pipes. Dad was replacing them bit by bit.'

'You know what I think? I think it's mostly metal. All the metal that was in your house. The wires and the computers, and the lead pipes. Everything electric. And all the plastic coatings, and the plugs, and the covers, that's all been burned off, here,' she pointed at a blackened pit, 'and here' at a curling gap that seemed to go deep and twisted into the core.'

'That doesn't make sense,' protested Danny. 'Everything metal? How? Why?'

She shrugged. 'How anything? Have they moved out loads of rubble? There should be so much more stuff. Like, a whole house into...' she pointed at the column, 'this.'

'I don't think so,' said Danny, 'they moved the chimney, but that's still in the garden.'

'That's the bit that doesn't make sense,' concluded Kelly. 'That's the weird. If this is the metal, where's the rest of the house?'

They both looked at the twisted swirl of junk.

'We ought to go,' Kelly suggested. 'We shouldn't be here.'

But something had caught Danny's eye. Something small and patterned, a circle of shining gold with swirls within it. He knew that shape, but from where? But just below it was another bright shape that he thought he knew. The pattern had melted a little, and been twisted, but as he looked closer he became more sure.

'What is it? Kelly asked.

'It's an earring,' he answered thickly. One of his mother's favourite earrings, with an intricate pattern.

'Danny?' Kelly asked, concerned.

He made himself answer. 'I can't remember. If she was wearing them. When –when it...'

A crunch of footsteps outside followed this revelation, Kelly whirled round guiltily. Someone else was here.

The tarpaulin was pulled back, and D. I. Raynes stepped into the tent.

He looked at them both. 'What part of 'Do Not Cross' don't you understand?'

'We were just looking,' protested Kelly. Danny just stood there.

And when the policeman didn't answer Kelly said, defensively 'We didn't touch anything.' And then 'It's his house.'

'All the more reason. You don't want to contaminate a crime scene.'

Kelly stood her ground. 'It's not like there'd be finger prints or anything. Look, everything's melted.'

'Or turned to dust,' agreed the detective. He had been watching Danny, but now he turned his attention full on Kelly. 'And who might you be?'

Danny came out of his trance to her defence, 'She's a school friend.'

But Kelly hadn't been about to take up on all the people she might possibly be. She said firmly 'Kelly James. I'm his witness. He wasn't up to anything.' And then as a quick after thought, 'Who are you?'

Detective Inspector Raynes flashed his warrant card at her, and said who he was. Kelly wasn't abashed.' May I look at that,' she asked, full of interest, and then explaining quickly, 'I've never seen one, and anyone could flip something at you and say...' She looked hard at the proffered card, and then nodded. Danny was embarrassed. He wished he could just fade out of the picture, but the Inspector didn't seem cross or offended. More amused, if anything. He put it away again.

He said to Danny, 'What have you found?'

Danny pointed. He had got over the shock. 'I think it's one of Mum's earrings. I'm not sure. I don't think she was wearing them.'

The Inspector stepped closer and peered at the twisted shape smoothly melted into the whole. Still looking at it he asked,

'What was she wearing?'

'Trousers and a jumper, probably.'

The inspector looked at him sharply. 'Probably?'

Danny shrugged. 'It's what she wore most of the time.' A sudden flash of memory. The blue face snarling, the swinging cudgel, his Mother her mouth open in a war cry, the dark green of her sweater. No earrings.

'Dark green sweater, no earrings,' he pronounced clearly. 'She wasn't wearing the earrings.'

'You just remembered that?'

He nodded, full of relief.

'Anything else?'

Danny shook his head.

Raynes turned to Kelly. 'Any more deductions?'

She shook her head.

'Then we'd better leave, before anyone else finds you.'

They clambered up the ladder one by one, Raynes last. Kelly was shouldering her back pack as he joined them.

'I'll take you home,' he said nodding at the car. 'Hop in.'

Danny looked at it. It was an unmarked car. In an empty street.

'I'll walk,' he said.

Raynes cocked his head a little. 'You, Miss?'

'I'm going with Danny.'

'How did you find us?' Danny blurted suddenly. There was that assessing look on the Detectives face, again.

'Have you been following me?' Danny demanded.

Raynes' lip twitched. 'I saw the bags by the fence. I put two and two together. I'm a detective.'

'How long were you listening to us?'

'Have you got something to hide?' But then, mildly, giving up the detective side, 'I'm like you Danny. I just want to know what happened.'

Not still looking for my parents then, thought Danny.

'Come on, I'll give you lift home, No questions.'

So they got in the car and he took them to Aunt Moira's House. No questions.

Kelly had not stayed long, her mother was expecting her to be home by eight, and would worry if she were not. Aunt Moira didn't come home until after Kelly had gone. Danny had looked at the kitchen cupboards and unfamiliar cooker and had given up any thought of getting himself a snack. Which was just as well as Aunt Moira came in with a big wrapping of fish and chips.

'I didn't know what you liked so I got a mix,' she said. So there was battered fish, and fish cake, and sausage and mushy peas and curry sauce and chips. Enough for a small army.

As they ate he told her about his visit to the house, or rather to the basement. He could tell she didn't like what he had done, but she said nothing, except to ask again about the columns. He told her what Kelly had said, about it perhaps being everything metal from the house. Somehow he couldn't tell her about the earring.

Chapter 7 - Facing up.

Another day at school. He was getting used to the incredible. The world was going on as if nothing had happened, as if everything was normal. Hardly anyone gave him a second glance now. Or at least, they wouldn't have if it wasn't for Grant and Jamie. And ignoring them seemed to be working, they got more reaction out of the teachers than him.

It didn't seem right that school should just continue, and expect him to work, and try to pass his exams, and go on as though this was his life from now on. A step change, but still just the same.

It wasn't the same.

It wasn't right.

He kept his head down, and tried to follow the lessons, and he could now. He listened to sustainable farming, and French grammar, and quadratic equations, but he couldn't see what good they were when your house could blow up and your parents vanish in a moment.

Even Kelly seemed to be living on another planet, the one where parents didn't vanish in a violence of smoke and flame, along with the whole house. A world where men with blue faces did not erupt from darkness.

He hadn't told her about them. The blue men. She would think he was mad. She would back off and leave him totally alone. Perhaps he was mad. But when he thought that, he got a flash of that scene. The door bursting open as if exploding, his mother flying across the hall, the fury of blue, the cudgel.

'Run! RUN!'

It wasn't just lighting, some effect of blue light. That face had been blue. But was it all the face? Could it have been paint? His father had been painting the Braithwaite's yard, but not that vivid colour.

'Hoi, weirdo, we got science next. Why don'cha do the science block? That'd go up like fireworks!'

'Yeah, do us all a favour.' Grant and Jamie were following him down the path, jostling against the flow of pupils coming the other way.

‘Go on weirdo,’ Grant was calling, ‘give us some fireworks.’ They were laughing as if this was a great joke.

Danny stopped. A sudden clarity fell on him, as if he had stepped out of his skin and was an observer, someone from outside, uninvolved. He turned.

There, some twenty feet away were Jamie and Grant, laughing, their faces made fat by wide mouthed jeering.

Danny started walking towards them. His legs were metronomes carrying him forward. Jamie laughed.

‘Look out Grant he’s coming for you!’ A big joke. Grant was laughing too, but Danny’s legs were carrying him towards them at a steady fast pace. He could see something change in Grant’s face, something brutal woke in his eyes. They were close now but Danny’s pace did not falter. He felt a fierce cold rage building up like a pressure in him. He saw Grant’s fists bunch, but before he could raise them Danny was there, still moving forward so that their chests collided with force, and Grant had to take a step back to steady himself.

Nose to nose almost, Danny spoke, his voice quiet but fierce. So quiet that even Jamie at Grant’s side had to listen hard.

‘My house blew up. My parents are missing. They may be dead. You find that funny?’

Everything seemed suddenly quiet. Some other part of him was aware that everyone on the path had stopped, that eyes were turned their way.

Grant’s face twisted in a sneer and his voice was pitched to hurt, ‘Just having a laugh,’ he said. ‘Where’s your sense of humour?’

‘If you think any part of that is funny there is something seriously wrong with you!’ snapped Danny, furious, but still low pitched. And as he said it he saw in Grant’s eyes something different and deeper that quelled his anger. He went on even quieter, the anger still there, but subdued now ‘I’m sorry about your Dad. You don’t have to be like him.’

He turned on his heel. As if in slow motion he saw a gaggle of first years, a group from his own class, some year tens, all motionless, all watching as if time had slowed down. And over their heads, by the office, Mrs Maitland, eyes fixed on him.

Then he was walking away. His back felt broad and unprotected, despite the backpack. Any moment now Grant would be on him like a ton of bricks, fists flailing, bearing him down to the floor. Any moment now, but he would not turn to look, though his ears strained to hear Grant's pounding feet.

But no. Here was the science block, and he was through the door unscathed and Grant and Jamie were still in the distance. It was Jamie that Grant was giving a shove to before walking away.

He felt a sudden triumph, not over Grant or Jamie, but over himself.

Inside the Science block they had seen nothing. As he walked in nobody turned to look at him. But as he took his seat at the back of the lab there was a buzz of whispering from the newcomers, and eyes turned his way. He ignored them as the teacher started to explain something about light waves and then turned the big screen on. They watched a video on light waves, and the transmission of energy. He could see how the wave ran along, but he couldn't see how that transferred energy. No doubt it was simple for someone like Kelly, but in this class he felt he was not alone in his ignorance.

As the teacher turned his back to write the main points on the white board, a paper plane arced its way onto the table in front of Danny. He ignored it but Jamil picked it up and smoothed it open. Then she jabbed him in the ribs.

'Good job Dan' said the anonymous note. Jamil looked a question at him, she obviously had no idea what it was about, but he ignored both her and the note. He remembered the look in Grant's eyes, the hidden emotion under the brutal. He reached out a hand, turned the paper back over and tried to concentrate on the terms being written on the board.

Wave length, frequency and speed. He couldn't see energy anywhere in the equations.

Chapter 8 - A Squall

Walking home alone, feeling separate from the world, he deliberately avoided the street his house was on. It was good that Aunt Moira was not coddling him, racing to pick him up when she had work to do. It showed she trusted him to be sensible.

He hadn't seen Grant again, or Jamie. He wasn't sure how Grant would take their brief encounter, now that he had had time to digest it. Danny's guess was that he would react badly. Still he had faced them, and was still in one piece. He felt good.

That feeling evaporated as he reached the top of the hill and saw a familiar car parked outside Aunt Moira's house.

As he walked up the path he could see there was no-one in the living room. He opened the front door as quietly as he could and stepped in to the sound of voices. They were in the kitchen. Maybe he could sneak past and go downstairs without being noticed. Their voices were muffled by the closed door, but it didn't sound like an interrogation. In fact, Aunt Moira was laughing. Not the sharp little laugh that meant she thought something was stupid, a proper little laugh of amusement.

He stopped. He felt let down. Her sister vanished, his home destroyed, his father gone, and everything turned upside down. How could she be amused? To be laughing? Come to that, how could he have been feeling good that he had faced off Grant?

He tried to take hold of his feelings. He should feel good that she could feel happy. But he didn't.

The door from the living room to the kitchen was open, and he would have to cross it quickly, and hope that he wasn't seen. But as he approached he could hear what they were saying.

Moira was thanking the policeman for something. She sounded quieter than usual, less crisp.

Raynes was answering, 'Well, it's sort of my job. He's looking for answers, that's all. I shouldn't be telling you, but, well, it's not impossible that he could make some sort of bomb, given the right stuff in the house, but I don't think Danny is in the picture. As far as I'm concerned Danny's alright, or he will be.' His voice changed, becoming softer, 'You on the other hand...'

Moira giggled.

Danny was shocked. He couldn't believe it. Aunt Moira did not giggle. He would have sworn to anyone that she couldn't, wouldn't be able to, didn't have the gene for it.

He moved forward a little. Through the crack in the door jamb he could just see them, a thin slice of them, standing close together.

The policeman was saying softly 'You're still keeping something from me, and you know I'll find out in the end.'

'I've told you everything that...'

'You don't know what might help me. Can't you trust me to tell the difference?'

'Yes,' she said, 'You know I do.'

Danny's blood ran cold. She was going to tell him. She wouldn't tell him, Danny, but she was going to tell this stranger. Somehow the policeman had got under her guard and ... He didn't know whether to stay still and hear the secret, or...

He found himself stepping into the doorway. 'I'm back!' he announced, and Moira took a guilty step away from the policeman. Danny made himself look surprised at seeing the Inspector. 'Oh', he said accusingly, 'it's you.'

The policeman only looked amused.

'How long were you listening to us?' he asked mildly, and Danny recognised his own words from yesterday. But they were immediately followed by 'And yes, I'm still making enquiries. This was more than a gas explosion, and we can't tell what,' he lifted an eyebrow 'Any ideas?'

Danny couldn't tell whether the man was mocking him or not. 'You're the detective,' he said.

'And you're the one with inside knowledge' countered the policeman. 'Did your Dad keep anything, anything at all, that might be explosive in that basement? Stuff that might have some other use, but when heated...' he let that hang.

Was he trying to blame the whole thing on his father? Or just trying to find out what might have happened? None of that fitted with the blue man; even if he hadn't been blue, he had been there. Danny had seen him. Unless he imagined it. Unless the concussion had given him hallucinations. All these possibilities jarred in Danny's mind, along with the question of something which when heated, might explode. How would he know what things might do that?

Aunt Moira said, 'I can't think of anything, but if we do we'll let you know.'

Raynes hesitated, then, 'If we can't find a reason for the explosion, it's a murder enquiry. We don't give up on those.'

Moira looked at him sharply. 'You haven't even found a body.'

'You've seen the crater.'

Neither of them looked at Danny.

'I would need a body,' Moira said softly. 'We don't give up that easy.'

'Nor do we,' he countered, but moving now, getting ready to go. 'You've got my number,' he finished, looking at Moira, 'Any time.'

She nodded and then he was going, and Moira was seeing him to the door.

Danny was angry, and hurt. She was saying goodbye to the policeman, and she hadn't even said Hello to him. She was going to tell the policeman the secret, when she wouldn't tell Danny. She needed to see the bodies, she had given up on hope.

He had to admit, it was only a very small piece of hope that he was hanging onto. And only because Kelly had told him to. He had thought he could rely on his Aunt Moira, but it seemed he was wrong.

He turned and stamped down the stairs to his room, pulled out his phone and called Kelly.

Half an hour later they were down on the sea front, with a brisk wind in their faces, heading out for the seawall. There had been time for a brief shouting match with his Aunt before he left. Only he had to admit, she hadn't done much of the shouting. She had been annoyingly calm. 'He's only doing his job,' and 'Don't be childish. He's trying to help us.' That man had certainly got under her skin.

Kelly listened in silence. Even to his silences. The sun was trying to burn its way through the cloud, and water sparkled. Boats groaned and clattered as ropes hit masts in a flurry of fury, and men worked silently at whatever needed doing on the fishing vessels waiting for the tide. Sea gulls screamed. The wind blew everything clean and fresh.

At the end of the sea wall there was no wall, just an abrupt finish to the stone and a long drop to the sea. A car could drive right the way up to the edge, or over if it failed to stop. He and Kelly stood at the very end, looking out to where there was nothing but sea.

There was nowhere else to go, but back.

Kelly said, 'What makes you most angry?'

'Everything!'

'What about everything? What in particular?'

He shrugged. 'We hardly even know him. She's hardly spoken to him.'

A seagull landed on a bollard and observed them, looking for potential food.

'She didn't strike me as fickle,' murmured Kelly. 'Not, light.'

No, Aunt Moira was not light.

'She won't leave you in the lurch.'

He felt as if the stone beneath his feet had vanished and he was falling. Emotions boiled. Including anger. But Kelly was pointing across the harbour to a shallow beach, where sometimes tourists paddled.

'The Vikings used to land over there, Miss Hadly says. And tied their boats to that rock. Do you reckon there could be any signs of that?'

'I don't care about the bloody Vikings!'

Kelly turned to face him. The wind blew strands of hair across her face. 'But you have to hang on to the normal,' she said calmly, 'It'll see you through.' The wind took his breath away. And most of his anger.

'You sound like Aunt Moira.'

'I'll take that as a compliment,' she said, turning her back to the wind and putting her arm through his. 'Let's go and get a drink, over there,' nodding to the line of cafés that faced the wharf.

Somehow in walking back the world seemed to settle to a calmer place, and even the wind was less strong.

‘The worst thing,’ Danny concluded, when they had finished their drinks, ‘is that now I have to go back and say I’m sorry.’

Kelly looked at him in alarm. ‘Can boys do that?’ She asked with a teasing sparkle in her eyes, ‘Say they’re sorry?’

‘They do if they’ve got an Aunt like Moira.’

‘Not everyone is that lucky,’ said Kelly getting up. ‘Shall I walk back with you?

‘Won’t your Mum be worried where you are?’

‘Mum’s always worried. It doesn’t matter what I do, she’ll worry anyway.’

Danny was about to say, ‘That’s what Mums do,’ but it stuck in his mouth.

So they walked back up the hill mostly in silence, though sometimes Kelly commented on a corner shop that sold art materials, or a line of ordinary houses that had just been listed as being of architectural importance, as an example of the normal.

Chapter 9 - Hidden Secrets

On Friday afternoon they had PE, and they had been told to expect a long distance run, out to the crags. But Mrs Maitland was there with the PE teacher to tell them that the weather was too wild to be out on the crags, so they would be running round the sports ground instead.

It was not the first time Danny had seen Mrs Maitland that day. She seemed to have been everywhere, in every corridor, passing by as they filed into every class or glancing in at the window in every lesson.

'You're getting paranoid,' Kelly told him as they jogged side by side round the pitch.

'I'm not. She's never turned up in PE before. AND,' cutting off Kelly's reasonable response, 'the weather's no worse than it was yesterday when they sent the 8th year out there.'

For once Kelly had no answer and they jogged on, lapping a gaggle of slower runners.

'Look,' Danny nodded his head towards the path beside the field, 'there she is again.' As Kelly looked, Maitland vanished behind some shrubs, and did not reappear. He wasn't sure if Kelly had seen her, but she said,

'Let's give her a show then,' and, just as they were lapping for the second time a couple of girls who were just walking and chatting, she burst into a full run. Danny had to work hard to catch her up.

'Only a couple more turns round the field,' she panted, 'let's come first for once.'

No chance of that. Danny had never come anything like first. And anyway, Paul was a Harrier, he ran for the county, there was no passing him. But trying to keep up with Kelly, they passed most of the year group, including Grant and Jamie, who made up in muscle what they lacked in technique or determination. On the last lap Kelly pulled away from him, to come in third after Paul and Jamil. Danny was almost as surprised as the PE teacher to find that he had come in the first twenty.

He walked home tired but pleased with himself, with the promise that Kelly would come over on Saturday morning to go over the maths before the exam.

It was a surprise to find Moira already home and beginning to cook.

'I've been neglecting you,' she said, 'so I thought we'd have a proper meal.' Danny eyed the pile of vegetables that she was chopping.

'I don't like broccoli,' he blurted. Nor aubergine, he noticed, but perhaps it would be going too far to mention that too.

'Try it and see,' said Moira with a smile. 'You can leave the rest if you still don't like it. It's all food. I'm making a risotto, so you'll get all the vitamins anyway.' He wasn't sure that was an advantage, it would mean he got all the taste too.

Instead he told her that he was in the top ten per cent of long distance runners. Where long distance equated to an hour and a quarter of running. She was pleased.

'Well, it's hardly surprising. Your Father's pretty fit. He can make a good turn of speed with a full load.'

Danny noted the present tense. 'You still think they're alive?'

She looked at him. 'It's possible. I know it looks bleak, but – well, not knowing how or what...' She put down the knife. 'Freya, she'll want me to look after you like she would. I can't just...' She sighed.

And then her phone rang. She was pleased for the interruption. 'Hello Ken,' she said with a smile, turning her back.

Danny wandered away, through to the living room, in time to see a white van with markings on its side stopping outside their house. Then it moved on. He went closer to the window to see where it was going, but it had stopped just a few doors down, and now people were getting out of it in a hurry, with cameras, big video cameras. It was a TV News Crew. His heart seemed to miss a beat.

What did they know that he didn't? Was this just background on the unexplained explosion, or had something new been discovered?

Moira came through, still on the phone. 'But that's ridiculous!' she cried angrily, looking out of the window, down the road towards the town. 'How could they even...'

Then she saw the television van.

Danny had seen fury once before. He recognised it now.

'Thanks!' she snapped, turning off the phone, 'thanks very much!' She didn't sound thankful, and she was speed dialling someone else.

'Danny, come away from the window!' retreating as she spoke 'Downstairs living room!' she commanded.

Last time he had done as he was told, and look what had happened. But looking out of the window all he could see was a group of people with cameras now trained on the house. And now further away down the bottom of the hill, the sparkle of blue flashing lights. No sirens.

'Now!' snapped Moira, and, then, with less of the fury, 'It's only the police. And they are NOT going to arrest you! Not on camera, they're not.'

He followed as she powered down the stairs, talking on the phone now. He could catch the odd words. 'Yes,' she was saying, 'my house, with full press coverage!' and then 'No, we won't be in!' Then 'Please! Now!' Not so much a plea as a command.

They had reached the second set of stairs, and were going down into the darkness of the winter sitting room. Danny clicked on the lights. Set deep under the house, it was a small cosy room, with a stylish gas fire that looked like a real one, and, of course lots of books and a few cosy chairs.

'What's happening,' he demanded.

'Some idiot at Police Headquarters has decided to arrest you.' She opened a cupboard at the back of the room and heaved a pile of cushions and blankets half out of it.

'Raynes!'

'He's not an idiot. Arrest you, with full media coverage!' She was angrily pulling out the vacuum cleaner that sat in the other side of the cupboard.

'What for?'

'For the sake of it!' She snapped as she climbed into the cupboard.

He watched with a growing sense of gloom. 'We can't hide in a cupboard. They'll search,' he began.

She turned to him in the confined space of the cupboard, and the fury transformed into the mischievous grin of a teenager.

'Oh yes we can!' and as she spoke, the back of the cupboard swung towards them revealing a space filled with darkness.

There was a secret room in the bottom of her house!

From far above them came the sound of heavy knocking on the front door.

'We can't stay there forever,' protested Danny. Moira was grabbing the cushions and blankets, and tossing them into the darkness.

'We won't have to,' she assured him. 'We'll just be 'out' until my lawyer sorts them.' She slammed the cushion side of the cupboard closed with her foot and went into the darkness of the hidden room.

She beckoned him in, and he went. She lifted the vacuum cleaner after them and closed first the outside door, then the hidden door. As it closed there was a click, and the lights went out.

It was cool and dark, until Moira switched on a small torch. They were in a small space. The back wall of the cupboard was covered in quilted material, pinned to it. Above them bare rock curved down and out to enclose a narrow space with a rocky floor. Moira arranged the cushions and blankets and they both sat and leaned against the rock wall. She put a finger to her lips for silence, and turned off the torch. A velvet darkness enfolded them in silence. In the inky dark there was only the very faint sound of their breathing.

Time seemed to stand still. They waited.

Eventually a muffled voice called, 'Clear!' and a door slammed.

'What -?' Started Danny, but from the darkness Moira hushed him.

They waited some more. Danny was half afraid he would fall asleep, and if he slept he might dream the nightmare run. But then, every time he woke from that, he never shouted or screamed, he was silent. So there was nothing to fear in falling asleep. He drew the blanket closer and snuggled on the cushions.

They waited some more.

Suddenly there was noise. The cupboard door, the ordinary one from the room, was being opened, there was some sound of things being moved, and muffled voices, an instruction. And then there was banging on the back wall, so close to them it made Danny jump. But the quilted fabric deadened the sound. It must have quelled the hollow sound of the wood too, because a voice, surprisingly close, said.

'Nah, there's nothing.' And then as things were being put back into the cupboard. 'I ask you, who has hidey holes nowadays. Not like it's a castle with priest holes.'

And the door shut again. A short while later another door, the one to the stairs, also closed with a muffled thud.

They waited some more.

'How long…' Danny started to ask, and was shushed again.

Why did Aunt Moira have a secret hidey hole? It was a good question, he thought. How come they were hiding out in it?

He reached out a hand and felt the rock against which he lay. It was uneven, and hard edged and even sharp in places, totally unlike the fused glass of what had been the basement of his house. It was cool and hard against his hand. His fingers found a crevice and explored. Cracks and crannies. Like a cave. Had they found it when they dug out the foundations of the house? Found it, and used it to make the winter sitting room, nestled at the bottom of the house. Or had it been quarried out specially? It didn't feel quarried, it felt, well, natural.

He tried to imagine the cave, and how they would build the walls of the room into the shape of the cave, maybe chiselling rock away to form the corners, maybe filling in walls leaving gaps between the plasterboard and the rock face.

But why a secret door, so well concealed? Why would Moira need a hidey hole?

He thought about it, and he imagined Raynes, sitting in one of the easy chairs in the room outside, perhaps also in the dark. Sitting and waiting. Waiting for them to come out.

He woke suddenly. It took a moment to realise where he was, and why Aunt Moira was a silhouette against warm light. Moira was out in the cosy sitting room, the light was on, and it felt like the dead of night.

'We'll have a cup of chocolate, in a mo,' suggested Moira as she fired up the computer in the corner of the room.

'Why did we hide?' Danny demanded as he came out into the room. 'You only run away if you've done something wrong.' he went on, peevishly, as she continued to work the computer. She looked up at him then.

'We've done nothing wrong. But since they're stupid enough to think you might have caused that explosion,' she was choosing her words with care, he noticed. But then she always did. 'they would have been pretty harsh with their questions. I don't want that for you. It's bad enough for you living through this without ...' She had found what she wanted on the computer, and now she read it out. Or at least parts of it. 'No material evidence, circumstantial – 'suitable adult' inadequate and biased. - Fishing expedition - Denied all knowledge of media informant – improper and invasive –have agreed an interview at a place of your agreement tomorrow at 3 p.m. I suggested your house but at your discretion.' She's seen them off all right!'

'Who?'

'My lawyer, the police.'

'You've got a lawyer who'll turn out at a moment to...'

'We're an important client, and I had her primed.'

'Primed?'

Moira sighed.

'Hot chocolate,' she said, 'and buttered toast, and explanations. Should be safe to go upstairs.'

He followed her upstairs with a heavy heart. The house was gloomy despite the starlight that glowed above the glass roof. It was past midnight he saw as they reached the kitchen. Closing the door to the living room behind them, so no light would spill out where it could be seen from the road, at last Moira turned the lights on.

A nasty smell of burned vegetables showed that she had left the burner on under the food when she had answered the phone earlier. Fortunately someone had turned it off, but the proposed dinner was ruined. Moira threw the lot into the bin, and the pan into the sink, and set to making drinks.

He sat at the table and watched her, heating milk and putting powder in mugs as though nothing had happened. Like his father when he came back from stopping someone's house from flooding because they didn't know where the stop cock was. All in a day's work.

'Stay calm,' his Father had told him, 'see what the problem is. Then fix it.'

'Why is there a secret room at the bottom of the house?' he asked abruptly.

'Luck!' replied his Aunt promptly, pouring hot milk into the cups and stirring vigorously. Luckily she continued 'When your Gran had the house built, there was this curious little cave, and rather than fill it in, they turned it into a hidden room under the house. You know your Gran, she can be fanciful. She was going to make the whole room a secret space, but it was just too nice in the winter – never too cold, and so cosy. So she made a secret cupboard instead. We used to play in it when we were girls, Freya and I.'

'Very convenient,' Danny muttered, 'for hiding from the police.' Moira carried the mugs to the table.

'We've never done that before. Hopefully never again. It was convenient, wasn't it?'

'Tell me again, why we had to hide?' He wasn't buying Moira's story, somehow it just seemed wrong, but he couldn't see why she would lie to him.

She took a long sip of her drink, holding it with both hands.

'I think its politics,' she said at last. 'That's all I can think. You know Ken, D. I. Raynes, knows you aren't responsible for what happened to your house.' The 'Ken' startled Danny. The policeman really had got under her skin. She was going on, 'But his Super – Superintendent – needs some sort of resolution. I shouldn't be telling you this,' she added quickly, 'so pretend you don't know. The Super's wife–,' a little hesitation, 'she's got it into her head that you are...' she shrugged, and gave into the inevitable 'mad and out of control, basically. Don't worry,' she tried a girlish grin but it was more of a grimace, 'no-one else does.'

Except – thought Danny, thinking of the laughter and jeers that had followed the Black Dougal incident, except perhaps everyone. He took a breath. Stay calm, think what the problem is. Heaven knows how he could fix it.

'So, why did we have to hide?'

'Well,' Moira was thinking now, no prepared answers, 'quite apart from the fact that you are innocent, and that a period of interrogation, however short, wasn't going to do you much good, there was the TV van. Someone had tipped off the media. Your arrest would have been on the TV news. Your reputation would be damaged. No matter how soon you were released, and it would have been soon, believe me! It would be – well, like that thing with Black Dougal, only much, much bigger. Much worse. I couldn't let that happen.'

Danny could see that. That made sense.

While he was digesting that Moira went on, 'So arrogant! Tipping the balance, telling the media. I've talked with our lawyers. I think you should meet Patricia, she's very sharp.'

'Sharp?'

'She doesn't miss a thing. I bet she ripped their warrant to shreds – logically I mean not practically, although...' and she smiled to herself.

'You said 'primed'...' was she expecting him to be arrested?

'Of course. I spoke to her soon after I got you out of A & E. Your parents are missing, and I'm the registered guardian in that case...'

'My parents made a registered guardian?' whatever that was precisely. They had planned for what might happen if ... He felt as if his head was about to explode.

Moira's voice was calming 'Of course they did. Gran is – far away, and your Dad, he's still a reservist for the army, and your Mum travels a lot, and some of the digs are in difficult places. Anything could happen. It's a wise precaution.'

This was not his life. This was not the world he knew.

All right, his Mum did go away, but never for more than a few days, unless they all went together, mostly in the summer. And his Dad, his Dad was always there, fixing things, looking after stuff, just there. They didn't need hidey-holes and secret doors and lawyers and guardian status. And then his mind hit the ultimate, the explosion, the house gone and both his parents – gone.

His whole life, gone.

His whole life, blind and stupid. He had thought they were ordinary, just like everyone else. Or that everyone else was just like him. But the truth was, they weren't.

All right, he had known that they were well off, that other people did not have the money to do whatever they wanted. But now, looking with new eyes, looking afresh at this house, and his own house, before, yes. They were rich.

How could you be rich and not know it?

Because they had tried very hard to be ordinary, to look ordinary, to do ordinary things. The normal, as Kelly might put it.

Moira was watching him from across the table. She looked concerned. He coughed, as though clearing his throat might clear his mind.

'You have to tell me the secret.'

She nodded. 'I will. There's just one thing I have to do first, to make it right.'

She raised a hand to quell the protest that was coming. 'Tomorrow. I promise. And then we'll get Patricia in. She'll be your 'responsible adult' when the police come. And don't you say anything to anyone without her being present.'

He wanted to shout, to rage at her, but he was too tired, and too confused. And everything was just – too much. So he went to bed like a good boy, but inside he was seething with determination. Tomorrow she would not put him off. Not again.

Chapter10 - Vanishment

Danny had expected to spend the night in a turmoil of thought. He was surprised to wake up and find that he had slept the rest of the night away, and woken up refreshed if uncertain.

When he ran upstairs it was to the sound of female voices talking, and he slowed on the stairs, trying to hear who it was.

'I should go and wake him,' Moira was saying, decisive as ever. The reply was too quiet for him to hear properly, but Moira snorted. 'Don't believe all you hear, boys don't need that much sleep and anyway, he's had plenty.'

No point being found loitering on the stairs, Danny bounded up the last few and burst into the kitchen just as Moira was about to exit to fetch him.

It was not the promised lawyer Patricia. To Danny's surprise it was Kelly, set up at the table with a half drunk mug of coffee. She gave him a big smile. 'Hello sleepy head,' she said. He looked at the cooker timer. It was nearly eleven.

'Why didn't you wake me?' he demanded.

'I thought you needed some sleep,' replied his Aunt. But Danny thought it more likely that she didn't want to have to tell him the facts. As if she read his mind she said, 'Get yourself some toast, I've just got that one thing to do downstairs. It shouldn't take too long.'

It wouldn't have to, thought Danny. At three the police were going to come, and he guessed the famed Lawyer Patricia would be arriving before that. Not much time to talk before-hand then.

He wondered whether he should tell Kelly he was too busy to do maths with her, but it would hardly wash, having got up so late. Instead he asked her whether she would like some toast, but of course she had long since had breakfast.

'Your Aunt said you had a late night,' offered Kelly as he popped some bread in the toaster.

Should he tell her about the police raid? No, because then he would have to explain how they hid, and that would make him sound guilty. Of what was another matter.

Instead he found himself saying 'I've been having bad dreams.' That made him sound like a wimp, and he wished he had not said it.

But Kelly said, 'It's not surprising. It's a terrible thing to have happened. My Mum has nightmares all the time, and nothing bad has ever happened to her. At least, not as far as I know.'

Her Mother did seem very jumpy, but Danny didn't think that would be the right thing to say. So he found himself saying, 'The police are coming round this afternoon, to ask more questions. I've already told them everything I can remember.'

Kelly looked at him, hesitant. 'Were you really there?' she asked.

He nodded dumbly.

'You got blown up?'

'No, I was on the street when that happened,' he didn't want to talk about it, to have to explain how it was he was alone on the street and his Mother had gone back. Raynes had been wrong about that. Instead of things coming back to him, they seemed to be fading away, like a dream half remembered. He was no longer sure of anything.

Somehow he found himself telling her that instead.

'Horrible,' she said. 'I can't imagine how you must feel, Danny. It's just...'

'Anyway,' he said, cutting her off, 'Maths exam. Tuesday. The normal.'

They went through the open door to the sitting room, where they could spread the books on the coffee table and look out over the valley, where everything was normal. But he couldn't concentrate, not properly.

Kelly was well into the maths, spreading Venn diagrams across the table and somehow tying them to matrices. But then she looked up and saw him staring out of the window. By the time he realised she had stopped talking she had her phone out.

'Have you seen this?' she asked, and showed him a video clip. He recognised the music but it was being mimed by a group of kids, and they were seriously mocking the whole thing. He guessed it would be hilarious to anyone else in his class, even he had to smile at the strutting and the posing. Kelly's laughter was infectious, but he wasn't capable of catching it.

She swept the books to one side. 'It's only a maths exam,' she said. 'It won't change the world if you don't do well this time.' But that wasn't the way she normally looked at things, he could tell. Only she was right. Things weren't normal, not for him. Still, he had to try, to somehow go on.

He said, 'You'll do well. You always do.'

'I have to work at it too!'

'Maybe that's the secret,' he smiled. 'You do work at it.'

'Yes I do. Goodie two shoes, that's me.' Why did she sound hurt? He thought he'd said something nice to her. She was dialling up another video, 'How about these?' she asked.

It was the same group of kids taking the mickey out of something more soulful, but somehow this was less funny. Perhaps it was the sadness in the music. Perhaps that's why Kelly liked it.

Make an effort, he told himself, and racked his brain for a song that was in the charts right now. She had them all on her phone. In the cloud. At her fingertips. And a whole load of other ones he had never heard of. Lively, different, sometimes quirky, the sort of thing that made you smile, that even made him smile.

For a while the load lifted off him. Then his tummy rumbled. He looked up.

And saw the time.

The clock said 13.55. How had that happened? It didn't seem they had been here that long.

They hadn't had lunch, and the police would be here in just one hour. The lawyer should be here by now. And what was his Aunt doing?

'What's up?' asked Kelly seeing the look on his face.

'The time,' he told her. 'The police will be here in an hour and ...' Best not to mention the lawyer, 'Aunt Moira's been gone ages. She said she wouldn't be long.' That was three hours ago.

'She's probably deep into something and forgotten the time,' said Kelly. Probably right.

'I'll go and remind her. Won't be long,' Danny called as he started down the stairs.

Her office was at the end of the corridor, next to the back door that opened onto a patio. He knocked. She didn't answer. He opened the door. She wasn't there, so he nipped back to the library. She wasn't there either. He felt a frisson of disquiet. She couldn't have forgotten and gone out?

But looking back at the outside door he could see that the bolts were still home. She couldn't go out and bar them after her. So she had to be in her bedroom.

He knocked, then called her name, then opened the door.

The bedroom was tidy, it smelt of her perfume, but she wasn't there. This time he stepped inside and looked behind the bed, but she wasn't hiding or lying unconscious.

Alarmed now, he stepped back into the corridor. There were two other bedrooms, and his own. None of them contained his Aunt.

Kelly and he had been in the living room at the top of the stairs all the time. They had been deep in conversation, but she couldn't have slipped past them, surely.

A horrible feeling of dread was growing inside him. He walked to the bottom of the stairs. Kelly was standing at the top of the stairs, no doubt wondering what was taking so long.

'She hasn't come past you, has she?' he asked trying to sound normal.

'Isn't she there?'

'I can't find her.'

'In the toilet?' suggested Kelly ever practical.

'Wait there,' he said and went back and checked the bathroom, and then the en-suite in Moira's bedroom. Everywhere was as quiet as the grave.

Kelly had come down the main stairs and was waiting there.

'Is there another way up?' asked Kelly. 'Another staircase?'

'No.' But there was one going down.

'Then she must be down here somewhere. Unless she's gone out.'

Danny looked down the corridor. The bolts were still in place on the back door.

‘French windows?’ suggested Kelly, ever helpful.

There were, in Moira’s office. But when he went back they were firmly shut and locked and the only key was hanging on the hook beside them.

Kelly was beginning to look as puzzled as he felt, but not nearly as alarmed. He took a deep breath. Keep calm.

‘I’ll check again’ he said, and while Kelly waited in the corridor he went through every room on that floor again, looking inside every cupboard, checking under the beds, a thorough search.

The door to the stairs down to the downstairs living room loomed ever larger in his mind. Winter living room. Hidden spaces.

But it couldn’t be denied. She wasn’t anywhere else.

‘This is seriously weird,’ said Kelly, as if he wouldn’t know that.

‘She must be downstairs,’ he said trying to sound normal. ‘Just make sure she doesn’t – erm – come past you.’

He bolted down to the winter sitting room.

There it was, all neat and tidy, just as the police must have found it. The cushions and blankets were in the cupboard, the cleaner was in its place. Behind him he could hear Kelly’s feet on the stairs.

‘This is nice,’ she said in surprise. ‘I was expecting a basement.’

‘She isn’t here.’

‘Well,’ said Kelly thoughtfully, ‘this is an impossible situation, isn’t it? She came downstairs. We both saw her. All the outside doors are shut, and she didn’t come up, or we would have seen her. So, either we went into some sort of trance so we couldn’t see her, or, she’s still down here.’ She sounded as if it was a clever puzzle set to test them. One that she felt sure she could crack.

Danny stood with the open door to the cupboard behind him, like a gateway to disaster. Kelly had put it exactly right. Moira had vanished, just like his mother.

But also, Kelly had put into his mind the possibility that perhaps, on that night, only a week ago, he might have been in some sort of a trance when his mother shouted ‘run’ and he ran. Perhaps she had never been with him on the road. Perhaps there had never been the shouting and the face impossibly blue and insanely furious. But to think that was madness.

The open door was still behind him. Kelly was facing him and it. Moira hadn't even told him about the secret room, not until she felt they had to use it. It was after all a secret. But there was, after all, no other place she could be. They had looked everywhere else.

Kelly was still looking at him, still looking puzzled.

'There is one last possibility,' he said at last. 'Only you have to promise not to tell a soul.' Of course she promised.

It took them minutes to find the catch. Moira had reached up with her right hand. The wood was good oak, with grain and knots in it, smooth to the touch. It was Kelly who pressed on the small knot in the corner, and felt it give. But no door opened. Danny tried it, remembering how Moira had stood, and moved. He poked a finger hard on the knot and it gave way. Wriggling it around, he felt it click, like a switch. With a sudden click the door came free. As he withdrew his finger, the dark wood of the knot slid back into place. He ran his hand over it, and couldn't even feel it was any different from the rest of the wood.

'You've got a secret passage!' exclaimed Kelly in delight.

'It's only a hiding place, a secret compartment,' Danny explained, going into it. In the gloom, there was no trace of his Aunt. 'She isn't here.'

Kelly stayed outside, in the room. 'Can you close the door?' and then rather fast, 'and can you get out if you do?'

Danny thought about this for a nano second, located from the inside the button that had opened the door, and then pulled the door shut on himself. A moment later the button gave way to his touch, and the door opened again, to show a much relieved Kelly.

'I was scared it was going to be one of those disappearing cabinets' she said, 'like magicians use.'

Danny was surprised. 'They aren't real, you know.'

'Of course not. They've got secret compartments, or a hidden door so that the person can get out without being seen.'

'Not this one' Danny told her 'this is solid rock.

Kelly put one foot into the space so that she could reach out and touch the rock. It was solid enough. She stepped back out into the winter sitting room and looked about her.

The cupboard had been set back into empty space, so that the front of it was level with the walls. So here there had been space between the walls and the rock. Danny wondered whether there might be other gaps, other hidden spaces. But everywhere was shelves, and books.

'Book-case door?' suggested Kelly. It didn't seem likely, but they had a go. Kelly picked up books and looked for hinges. Danny tried shaking the shelves to see if they moved at all. Time was passing. In half an hour the police would be here. How was he going to explain that his Aunt too had vanished, though without violence and explosion?

Chapter 11 - Impossible

Kelly was standing in the middle of the room, looking thoughtful.

'Misdirection,' she said suddenly. 'It's what magicians do.' She stepped back into the cupboard with a purposeful air.

Danny watched.

First she ran her hands over the surfaces of the cupboard. The she entered the still open compartment, and looked about her.

'Ah-ha!' She proclaimed. Danny poked his head in to see.

'Look,' she showed him. 'At one end the rock slants forward to the edge of the cupboard, it looks like it is going really close to the wall of the room but at the other end...'

At the other end the rock was still some distance from the back of the cupboard, and the small gap had been walled off in wood. Danny was sceptical.

'If that's a door it going to be a really tight squeeze to get through.'

Unabashed Kelly was examining for knot holes, but there were none. However, the rock was uneven, especially near the top, and the wood had been cut to fit the contours, but it wasn't exact. Soon she found one cranny she could push a finger through, then another. It was the fourth one, nearest to the back of the cupboard, that finally made her eyes light up. She fiddled around for a bit, and then there was a satisfying click. But nothing moved. They were both in the hidden room now, pushing at the end partition wall, but it didn't budge. And a few moments later there was another click, perhaps a little more solid in sound. Again nothing happened.

Kelly took stock. 'Perhaps one of us had better be outside the cupboard' she suggested.

'Why?' Danny couldn't help but feel a little aggrieved. It was his house, in a manner of thinking, his secret compartment, but Kelly was making the running.

'We'd feel a bit silly if something happened and we got trapped in here.' Or one of them disappeared, thought Danny with sudden concern. Everyone was vanishing. How could he explain his Aunt – or his Aunt AND Kelly

'You go out then,' he said, 'let me try.'

For a moment he thought she was going to argue, but then she clambered out into the room, and he took a turn at feeling through the narrow gap. It was a little harder to find, but yes there was a switch, or a button on the other side. He pressed it. Again the click, but this time followed by an exclamation from Kelly.

'It's the end of the cupboard!' She exclaimed. He pulled himself back into the shell of the cupboard, and there, sure enough the end wall of the cupboard, the side as you looked at it from the front, had clicked very slightly out of place. But even as he put his hand out to pull it open, it clicked shut again.

They very soon found that within seconds of being clicked open it would close again unless you opened it wider.

But with it at last open they could both see that the rock face revealed curved unevenly towards the wall of the room, although here it was gloomier, and almost lost in darkness. Just another hidden compartment.

So much trouble for so little gain.

But turning Danny saw that here, in the so cleverly hidden compartment there was another switch. He pressed it, wondering where in the house some other door would open. But all that happened was that a light came on. One small rock-mounted mesh-covered light, right towards the far end of the compartment casting bright light and deep shadows.

The disappointment was so great he could have wept. She wasn't here. She wasn't here. She had vanished. She too had vanished.

Kelly was crowding him by standing in the cupboard to peer into the now bright room.

'Go right up to the end,' she commanded.

'What for, there's nothing there.' He could see there was nothing there.

Kelly was impatient. 'We're talking magic boxes. Nothing is what it seems. Go and feel.'

The police would be here any minute, there was no time for this. But Kelly was blocking the way out and the easiest way was to take the three or four steps down to the end.

He didn't have to feel. From here he could see. The dark shadow at the end was a deep fissure at an angle to the main space. He thrust his arm into it and felt empty air. And now that the light was behind him he could see that, although it would be a tight squeeze, the cave continued. It was as though a huge boulder had been thrust into the side of it.

Beyond lay darkness.

Kelly was practically jumping up and down. 'A false secret compartment and a real secret passage!' she proclaimed.

'We'll need a torch,' said Danny.

'We'll need to know we can get out again,' said Kelly.

Danny ran upstairs to get the torch from his bedroom. Still twenty minutes until the appointment. This might not be where Moira had gone, but it was the best lead they had. He picked up the torch, and as he left, he saw the broom handle by the door jamb. A moment's hesitation, better safe than sorry, and he was on his way down the steps, torch in one hand, stout wooden stick in the other.

Kelly was waiting impatiently. She looked a little surprised at the broom stick, then her face brightened, 'You're going to prop the door open!'

It was an idea he hadn't thought of. A moment later he had discarded it. There might be better uses for a weapon. And he didn't like the idea of leaving the door open for anyone to find. He didn't want Raynes thrusting his nose into Moira's secrets.

If they weren't going to prop the door open, Kelly insisted on his going into the tunnel, closing the door and then opening it again from the inside. She wasn't going to risk being trapped down there. Once that was done they moved into the passage.

Danny went first. The first little bit, squeezing into the hidden gap, was the hardest. His own body cut off the light from behind him, and the torch only made a little circle of light. But the cave soon opened up into a curved passage, with uncomforting recesses and bulges to be avoided. The ground was uneven and he shone the light back to show

Kelly where she could put her feet. The air was cool and still, the rock held a faint moist-metallic smell.

He had only taken a few steps, but his eyes were become used to the gloom. Ahead of them was a faint bluish glow that made silhouettes of the rocks ahead.

Danny handed the torch to Kelly. He wanted to be sure of the broom handle, that he had both hands free to use it. He regretted now the amount of conversation they had had when they first found the passage. The sound would have echoed down this short distance. If there was anything nasty there, it would know they were coming. And the blueness of the light was unnerving. In his mind now, blue meant danger.

Suddenly the passage opened into a wide cavern filled with a glowing light. He would have to jump down a few feet to the floor of the cave, but in the centre of the room was a bonfire of blue. But as his eyes grew used to the light, not a bonfire. Flickering pulsating flames hung suspended in the air. From about a foot above the cavern floor to the same distance from the roof. Taller than it was wide. Not much brighter than his torch light, but enough to reveal the whole cavern, with its cracks and prominences. Enough to reveal that Moira was nowhere here.

He felt Kelly come up behind him and look over his shoulder. He could hear her intake of breath.

'What is That?' she whispered with mixed awe and excitement.

What indeed?

He stepped down carefully, coming closer to the flame. There was no warmth from it, no sound. Kelly dropped down beside him. The flames went on flickering and twisting. Danny took a few careful steps to his right, finding flat slabs for his feet.

It looked the same from there too.

'Where's it coming from?' asked Kelly. 'What's feeding it?'

Good questions. Not quite as good as 'Where's your Aunt Moira?' but maybe just as important.

'I'm going round it,' he told her, and started off. It was not a big cave, but he could not see the far side of it properly through the haze of light.

As he moved away she said tightly ‘Be careful!’

‘I am,’ he assured her.

From the far side of the cave, just twenty feet away from Kelly, it looked the same. There was nothing holding it place, supporting it, feeding it. It just hung there, a cool flickering glow. There were no other passages, hidden doorways or anything but rock. Kelly was still vaguely visible through the blue haze and flickering light. He went on round until he was back with her.

Back up the passage, where they could neither see nor hear it, a timer reached the end of its five-minute wait. Both doors swung shut with a heavy thud. The light turned off.

Neither of them noticed the absence of the extremely faint glow that showed where the passage entered the cave. They were intent on the light.

Kelly held her hand out towards the flames. ‘That,’ she said breathlessly ‘is cold light People would give millions to know how to do that. Billions.’

Danny reached out a hand to touch the flames, but Kelly knocked it back with an alarmed ‘Don’t!’ and then ‘You don’t know what it is. It could be dangerous.’

Danny shrugged and then swift as lightening swept the tip of the broom through the edge of the flame. He felt a sudden shiver in the wood, but the tip was unharmed, not scorched, not scratched. He touched it and it was neither hot not cold, nor in any way he could feel different to any other part of it.

‘It’s amazing,’ Kelly breathed, staring at the fire. ‘That is energy. A cold energy source. Your family has access to a cold energy source!’ She could tell Danny wasn’t so impressed because she went on ‘Do you realise what this means? What this could mean to the world?’

No he didn’t. He could only see the trouble that had been taken to hide this thing. And that they hadn’t found his Aunt. The police could be knocking on the front door even as they spoke, and his Aunt had vanished. Like his parents. Or unlike.

Kelly was going on about energy conservation and self-sufficiency. He stuck his hand out suddenly and swished his fingertips fast through the outer flickers of flame, like you could through a candle if you were fast enough. There was a slight tingle. Nothing more.

Kelly had given a little yelp, and was now telling him not to be so stupid.

'It's perfectly safe!' he snapped, and thrust his whole hand into it.

Cold closed round it like a vice and pulled it further in, tugging hard on his arm. He tried to withdraw it, but it had a firm hold on him and was dragging his arm slowly further in.

There was nothing to push against to resist it. He thrust one end of the broom handle against the rocks beneath the flames, so he could push against them, but the tip grazed the flames and was yanked forward into them.

Kelly was shouting at him, but he was trying to drop down, to use his weight against the pull inwards. It only hurt his arm more, and it was hurting quite a lot now.

'Take it out!' shouted Kelly. But he couldn't.

Kelly grabbed his other arm, and threw herself back against the rocks, but the cold was dragging him deeper and deeper into the flames. Up to his elbow now, and despite all his struggle it was drawing him further in. Kelly had grabbed a hand hold in the rocks and was pulling on his other arm with all her strength. He felt as though he was being stretched out, being pulled apart. His shoulder was nearing the flames now. He had one foot against a rock below the flames and was heaving with all his might. His shoulder screamed against the strain.

Then his knee touched the blue glow and he felt the pull there too. He bent his head away from the flames that were consuming his shoulder.

'Let go!' he screamed at Kelly, he couldn't stand much more of this pain that was bursting into his chest. But Kelly wasn't letting go. She was at full stretch now, clinging to the rock with one hand, holding determinedly onto his arm with the other.

'Let go!' he screamed, the pain was intense. His face was turned to hers beseechingly, but she could see him. Where he had gone into the flame, there was no trace of him. The fire was consuming him completely.

And then her hand was not strong enough on the rocks to hold. Suddenly she was flying free towards him, and Danny was vanishing into the flames, and her hand, holding his arm, went with him.

She felt the grip, she felt the force, she felt the cold. The echo of his scream was still in the cave, but he was gone completely. Vanished away. And the force was pulling her after him.

She made a lightening decision.

Kelly jumped in after Danny.

Chapter 12 - Lost in Space

Kelly jumped in after Danny.

She leapt straight through the flames and landed on top of him, in a tangle of arms and legs. He was groaning as she rolled off him. Her whole body tingled with a strange electric feeling, but apart from that she felt fine.

Danny was curled up and whimpering. But he was here and alive, not consumed. Kelly tried to roll him further from the flames. He beat her hands away, crying out with pain, but he did roll further from the fire.

She kept calling his name. At last he unwrapped himself a little. Shuddering he sat up.

'Are you all right?'

'No.' He eased his shoulder and moved that hand, clutching and releasing. 'It really hurts.'

'Still?' She was feeling fine, but she had only been in the fire for a second.

'Not so much.' He tried to stand up, but Kelly had to help him. The broom handle had been thrown onto the rocks but was within his reach, and he used that to lean on.

'What hurts?' she asked.

'Everything,' but in fact the effects were fading. Only his shoulder and his right hand, which had been drawn first into the fire, still hurt with a hard, deep ache. He looked at the blue fire. Whatever it was, it wasn't good. And they hadn't found Moira.

'We'd better go back up,' Kelly said.

He was still pulling himself together. It felt as if he had been pulled apart. What was the point of that?

'I thought we'd be dead,' gulped Kelly. He looked at her, bemused.

'You were vanishing. I couldn't see you. I thought – I thought…' It had clearly rattled her, but Danny felt a leap of hope. Vanishing? Becoming invisible? Is that what had happened to the others? Were they still here, but no-one could see them? Then Common Sense added, or hear them? He looked down at himself. He was clearly visible now, whatever Kelly might have thought she had seen.

'We'll go now,' Kelly said again. She wasn't hurt, but she was clearly unsettled.

'Okay,' there was no point staying down here, with the strange fire.

Now Kelly looked for the passage way, and found that the faint glow that had come from the light in the secret compartment was gone. She looked around for the torch.

The blue light from the fire was diffuse and not strong, it was hard to pick out details, and there were lots of nooks and crevices. She couldn't see the torch, but it could have fallen anywhere. She crouched down to see better. 'Where's the torch?' she demanded.

'What?' demanded Danny. Even though the pain was receding, it still hurt. He felt as though he had been crushed by some heavy weight. Kelly explained what she was looking for.

'I can't see it anywhere.' She felt her pockets, and became alarmed. 'And my phone. It must have dropped out of my pocket.'

'I think we were on the other side,' mumbled Danny. So they worked their way around, Kelly on one side and him on the other, checking all the way for the torch and the phone. They didn't find them.

Dark shadows were everywhere, a thousand little crannies that could hold a torch or a phone.

Kelly was for keeping looking, but Danny knew that time was passing.

'We'll come back with a lantern, from the camping kit.' He said. 'We have to get back. It isn't far.'

Looking carefully, they found the rocks where they had climbed down, and from there the narrow passage. The darkness was daunting, but as Danny had said, it wasn't far. Ten feet, perhaps fifteen and they would be back in the hidden room.

Kelly went first this time, Danny could not trust the feeling in his right arm. Feeling their way, they moved away from blue light into darkness, only knocking shin or shoulder now and again. It seemed a long way. They found the turning point where the passage way turned into the little room behind the wall.

With one hand on the rock face and the other before her, Kelly made her way towards the door and the light switch.

After a bit she stopped.

'Have we come the right way?'

'There isn't any other way.' Danny was right behind her. She could feel his breath on her hair. The air around them was black as ink.

'That's what I thought. There weren't any other turnings off.'

'It just seems longer in the dark.'

'That must be it.' She inched her way forward again, carefully, less sure.

They kept moving.

'Ouch' Kelly's foot struck rock. There was an obstacle in front of her, almost knee high. There had been no step up or down in the passage way.

Now she felt around. The rock face was still to her right. Where the wall of the sitting room should have been, to her left, only open space. Ahead of her she could feel the top of a rough boulder. There was no door.

'We should have spent longer looking for the torch,' she said, refusing to be scared. 'This isn't the way we came.'

'Just a bit further,' suggested Danny.

'There's a dirty great boulder in front of me!' And it didn't smell right, not the close-enclosed back-of-a-cupboard smell. This smelt of dirt, earth and decay. Now that they were standing still the sound of dripping water was distant and clear.

Danny put a hand on her shoulder. 'There's light,' he said. 'Over there.' Pulling on her shoulder to turn her leftwards.

Like a memory on the retina, there was a blur of grey amid the black. It seemed far away, and high up. Not the downstairs living room then. It took a while for the realisation to sink in.

Kelly gave a little cough. 'That could be in the...' she paused to find a suitable word, 'in the roof.'

'It's not that high. Let's go that way.'

'But then,' she paused, 'but then we'd lose the rock face. We wouldn't find our way back.'

‘I don’t want to go back,’ Danny said, moving his shoulder to ease the ache. It was getting better, but it still hurt. ‘There’s nothing there that we want.’

‘But…’ she didn’t want to lose the wall, and the way back ‘but we know where we are, there. We must have taken a different passage.’

‘I don’t think so,’ Danny countered. ‘And once we get out we can get a torch and come back. If we want to.’ So saying his broom handle tapped out the terrain to his left. ‘Come on, keep close.’

Reluctantly Kelly put a hand on his back and they started towards the light, clambering carefully over rocks, keeping together, the wooden rod testing what was before them all the way. The ground sloped unevenly upwards towards the light. The closer they came they more they could see.

It was not so very far to go, and the path they took became easier as they approached the light. Rocks began to take form for the eye as well as for the foot. The exit from the cave was small, and low, a narrow horizontal slit, the light was filtered through the leaves of shrubby little plants.

It was a very natural cave, and a very natural cave mouth.

But just inside, tucked against the other wall of rock, was a rather unnatural shelf. And on the shelf were neat stacks of things in plastic bags, and a lantern with an unlit candle in it.

They both paused, pleased to have some natural light, but uncertain of the outside.

This should have been the inside of Moira’s house.

There was no knowing what was outside.

By mutual silent assent they went to the shelf, and, with some trepidation, Kelly opened one of the bags.

It seemed to be a bag of rags, hessian or coarse wool, and some twine and cord, an old pair of woollen leggings

They exchanged glances. Danny opened another. Neatly folded, a woman’s jumper, and tailored trousers. He stuffed them back in. The third held a flowery dress in heavy material, the fourth another jumper and trousers.

'It's a wardrobe,' he whispered with a nervous laugh, pushing them back into the bag. Kelly stayed his hand. She touched the soft material of the jumper.

'Isn't that what your Aunt was wearing, when she went downstairs?' she whispered. Danny looked again. What had Moira been wearing? He couldn't remember. It had been a jumper and trousers. That was what she usually wore, sometimes with a suit jacket over the top. It was the sort of colour she would wear.

He looked at Kelly, she seemed to think it was. Then she stepped back. In the gloom under the shelf they could now see a range of shoes. Ordinary shoes. One man's three women's.

'Her shoes,' declared Kelly.

Hope blossomed in Danny's heart.

Wherever they were, it was not Moira's house, but here were her clothes and, his heart began to race, those could be his parents' clothes. A gust of wind blew in from the cave mouth, bringing with it the scents of heather and gorse.

Danny turned, ducked low and burst out through the entrance, sweeping the low plants out of his way.

Chapter 13 - Seeing is Believing

There he was on the hillside, looking out over a strange valley, filled with strange trees. No main road cutting through the hillside. No houses. No houses on either side. No house belonging to Aunt Moira. He turned and looked up to the top of the hill, just a short way above them. Nothing but heather and herzleberries. A strange country.

Kelly joined him, and looked about too.

'How did we get here?' she asked. 'We haven't walked far. What, fifty yards into the cave, at most, and then, maybe double that coming out. Where's your Aunt's house? Where are we?' Around them the heather shivered its branches and the gorse shook under the cool breeze. Cool, but not cold.

Danny eyed the horizon. That curve of the hill, that rocky outcrop. A sense of unreality grew inside him, like a cold dread. He had sat in the window of Moira's house often enough. He knew those hills, those rocks. There could be no other terrain quite like it. But the woods in the valley, where had that come from? And what had happened to the main road that should be scouring the hillside?

And there just thirty feet from them was the rocky knoll that should be marking the end of the lower patio of Moira's house. He knew it well. He had climbed on it as a child, jumped off it onto the smooth paving of the terrace. Impossible that it should be there, but not the terrace.

He turned and looked up the hill to the top. There it was. A few rocks where the house should be, and the summit where Scudmoor Road should run. Impossible that it should not be there. He turned and would have run up, bounding over the heather, but Kelly clutched at his arm.

'We'll get lost!' her voice pinched by fear. 'We'll never find the cave again.'

Danny looked at her, her face pale with fear and shock. She was right. They were standing right next to the cave mouth but it was so well covered by heather and herzleberries you couldn't see it was there.

He looked down the hill to the little rock he knew so well, then up the hill to the band of rocks that lay just this side of the ridge. He judged how far he was from each, he lined up one of the rocks above with his own old friend below, and judged his position along a line that connected them.

'No we won't,' he told her, trying to sound confident. 'I know how to find it. I know where we are.'

No he didn't. Where they were was impossible. But it seemed to calm her.

'Come on, I'll show you.'

He took her arm, and they started to walk together towards the summit. Only the bushes were so obstructive they were soon each finding their own way to the top.

No flat tarmac. No Houses. No town. They moved down, out of the wind.

There it was. No town.

He stood at her shoulder and pointed out the impossible. Overlooking the sea, Gamma's Rock. Rock of the Old Person in the old tongue, the rock his Grandmother had been named after. There the crags. Hardnose Point. All the familiar landmarks. No port. No houses, no shops, no town hall where his great Grandfather's house had stood. Just the sloping hillside.

Where the shopping mall should be, were green fields

And there, where the harbour should be, so smudged by mist-like smoke that at first he had not seen them, the mounded thatch of some round houses, tucked in against the base of the hill.

'No,' said Kelly clearly. 'That's impossible. 'No. We're dreaming. I'm dreaming. It's not real.'

The wind buffeted them. 'Does it seem like it's a dream?' asked Danny, but she shook her head and moved away from him, as though it were all his fault, as if he were the one that was doing the dreaming.

Danny knew how she felt. It was how he had felt ever since that day, a week ago, (only a week ago?) when his world had exploded, and nothing since seemed real or possible. Only he had got used to it. He had had to accept it. And this, this was no more impossible than that.

Only, it was impossible.

He pointed them out again, the undeniable landmarks that made this their home town, only without the town.

'No,' repeated Kelly. 'You can't just – 'nothing' a whole town. It can't just...' she shivered, and then more firmly 'Anyway, it smells all wrong. Gorse and heather don't smell putrid, like a dead animal'

From behind them came a voice *'Well now, there's beautiful, then,'* in the old tongue. They whirled.

Sitting up in the heather, brushing leaves and twigs from his hair was a young man. And such a man. His scruffy hair was long and plaited on either side, his strong face tanned and weather beaten. He had a woollen shawl wrapped round his shoulders. He wasn't much older than them, but his face was weathered, his nose skewed and one eyebrow was interrupted by a scar.

He got to his feet and brushed off his tunic of beige, trimmed in blue, to go with leggings strapped in place with leather strips criss-crossed round. It was Kelly his eyes were fixed on. Instinctively Danny took a step to come between them, thankful that he had the broomstick in his hands, and that the man was no taller than he was, even though a few years older, and rather stockier.

To Danny's relief the man held his empty hands out to either side in a universal gesture. The woollen shawl was stained in places, a reddish brown, like dried blood. But his face looked friendly enough.

'Steady on,' he said, *'just a greeting. She takes your breath away though, doesn't she?'*

Danny took a deep breath. He didn't look at Kelly. He recognised the old tongue. His mother had schooled him well, not just in the language but in etiquette. He had never dreamt he might use it. It was totally unreal but –

'Greetings friend,' he replied. The stranger cocked his head as if this was unexpected and needed thought.

'You're to come with me,' was his reply, moving towards them and gesturing towards the distant houses. He brought with him the smell

that wrinkled Kelly's nose, unwashed body, dirty clothes, sweat, a goatish smell.

'What's he saying?' Kelly asked, stepping closer to Danny.

Danny stood his ground. '*Who are you?*' he asked, keeping his tone polite.

The man smiled. '*Sorry. I am Tasgo. I am sent by the Old one to show the way.*'

'*You were expecting us?*'

The man threw his hands wide in a gesture of helplessness and dropped the formal tone. He grinned. '*I don't know what I was expecting. It's been a bit strange.*'

'You're telling me,' thought Danny, 'You don't know the half of it.' He was dredging for his next words. '*In what way strange?*'

'*You'd better ask the Old one.*' He gestured towards the houses down below, and added, '*There'll be food. Don't know about you, but I'm famished.*'

'What's he saying?' demanded Kelly again. 'What language?'

That drew Tasgo's eyes back to her, with obvious admiration. Danny saw that amongst the things that dangled or were strapped round him was a longer shape wrapped in animal hide. The hilt was obvious.

Thinking fast, Danny said, firmly, '*She's a chieftain's daughter*'

Tasgo laughed, seemingly delighted, '*A real catch!*' he said, and then with a conspiratorial glance of dismay at Danny '*Just my luck.*' Then, '*Come on, I'm hungry!*'

Kelly was getting hacked off with this by now. She started to demand again to know what was being said, but Danny got in first. 'He really fancies you, and he wants us to go down to the huts.' The first bit stopped her in surprise, and she looked at Tasgo again. His smile transformed him. He became almost handsome.

'What language is that?' She demanded, all irritation dropped.

'Old' said Danny, then '*And if we don't want to go with you?*'

Tasgo seemed surprised. The smile was still there, but faded. He turned his attention full on to Danny. It was challenging. A thrill of fear shivered through Danny.

'That would be a pity,' he said. Threat or dismay? Danny couldn't tell. But then the grin was back, *'I'd be in real trouble with the Old one. And the food's good, believe me.'*

He sensed Danny's reluctance. *'Come on,'* he urged, *'a shame to come all this way and then not visit after all.'* All this way, noted Danny, before translating this for Kelly, adding 'He sort of seems to have expected us.'

'Not possible,' concluded Kelly.

Tasgo gave an open handed shrug, *'Where else is the little princess going to spend the night? On the cold hillside?'*

Danny didn't like the 'little'. Kelly was at least as tall as Tasgo, but Tasgo was stocky and he looked strong.

'It's the cave again, in the dark, with nothing there or,' how to put it, 'risk going with him to the huts.'

Kelly hesitated. 'What do you think?'

'Decide.' Danny wasn't taking his eyes of the stranger.

'Not the cave,' said Kelly.

'Lead on,' said Danny. Tasgo's face brightened, he seemed really happy, and he started to bound down the hillside, then stopped and looked back at them. With a big grin he gave Kelly a little bow, and offered her his arm. Kelly ignored this and took her own path through the heather. Danny took a line between the two, using the broom handle like a long walking stick, and keeping their guide always in full sight.

Here where they were walking, should be Scudmore street, though the angle was slightly wrong, and they would be cutting through first the gardens, and now the houses. The view to Gamma's Rock was unobstructed. The sounds were not of distant traffic and humming machines, but only the wind through heather, and distant birds. And since Tasgo was down wind, the scents were of broom and peat.

The bones of the land lay revealed, the rocks, boggy patches where water drained into tiny rills, everything that was invisible under the town. But Tasgo knew every dry path and easy ground. It was easier to follow in his footsteps then find your own way. Soon he was leading, and Danny and Kelly followed together behind him.

'This is mad,' muttered Kelly. 'How did we get here?'

There was only one answer. Danny's brain hurt with the struggle of believing it. They were still exactly where they had been. But here was Tasgo, who spoke the old tongue. There were the same rocks and skylines, only the modern had gone. And there, becoming increasingly clear, were the thatched roundhouses of ancient times. Laid out, Danny realised, almost exactly as in the model in the town museum. One large building, three smaller here, and a bit further off a couple more, closer to the shore.

Tasgo gave a hailing shout, and far ahead a young figure appeared from among a cluster of sheep. The child took one look, and was off, vaulting a gate and vanishing into a dip. Minutes later he reappeared, smaller and more distant, racing down a track towards the huts, arms waving in the air. The young voice reached them later, a trilling warble that held no meaning.

By the time they passed the sheep in their pen, people were gathering in the track, half a dozen figures looking up the hill towards them. Tasgo turned with a grin.

'Hope some-one is opening the ale flagons. You must be thirsty, too.'

That was the least of their worries. Kelly caught Danny's arm, and drew him to a stop.

'We can't go there,' she said in whisper, as though Tasgo might understand. 'We don't know who they are. We don't know...' her voice broke with all the things they didn't know.

'We know where we are,' he told her. 'We don't know when. Kelly, we've gone back in time. Hundreds of years. Maybe thousands of years.'

'Grow up! We can't time travel. That's just silly stories. No-one can...'

'Those are iron age huts, maybe earlier.' He wished he'd paid more attention to his mother's work. 'Tasgo's speaking ancient English, the old tongue ...'

'Like you're fluent in that!' she snapped.

'Not fluent, no, but I speak it. My Mum speaks it.' Moira speaks it. His Dad, not so good but – things were whirling in his head. That television interview, the other man shaking his finger at his mother, with a superior smile 'But this is mere speculation Mrs Sharp. No-one knows how it must have sounded...'

'How could that be? How could that be?' Kelly was shaking her head.

'Kelly...' but Kelly was backing away.

'I'm not dreaming. I've gone mad,' she wailed 'It's not possible.' Wailing she threw herself to the ground and sat, head in hands weeping.

Tasgo had stopped and was looking at her with obvious concern. '*What's wrong with her?*'

Danny didn't know what to do, what to say. Tasgo took a step towards her, but Danny put up a hand.

'Let her be. For a minute, let her be.'

Tasgo looked at him hard then. His hand had come nearer to the hilt of that sword. *'Tell me,'* he demanded. *'What is she to you? Is she with you willingly? Is she a Bride price? Why are you here?'*

Whoa, this was getting way out of hand.

'NO, NO, nothing like that. She's a friend.' How to explain? *'It's been a long journey.'*

'What is her name?'

For some reason Danny did not want to tell him.

'Give her a moment,' he said. *'She knows no-one here, and she is a...'*

'Chieftain's daughter,' finished Tasgo grimly. *'You lie badly.'*

So much for that pretence then.

Danny was more worried about Kelly. Some people were coming up the track towards them, and there was Tasgo to deal with.

'Kelly, Kelly, it may not be all right but it's where we are, and we have to - to deal with it.' He wanted to put his arm round her but it would feel awkward, and Tasgo was watching, thinking who knows what.

'Kelly, look around you, this is what we've got. You're not mad. It's the world.' He grasped suddenly at the way she saw things as puzzles. 'We just have to work it out. Look at it, it's all we've got. We've got to work out what's happening and how to deal with it.'

Kelly gave a big sniff, and pulled a hanky out of her pocket. She blew her nose, and then looked up at him, eyes red with crying.

'Danny Sharp, I hate you!' she said with vengeance. Then she stood up, brushed the dirt off her jeans and looked about her, finishing with Tasgo, who was once again smiling at her.

She pointed her finger at his chest. 'And you can back off right now too!' she snarled. A message that seemed to get through to Tasgo well enough.

As Kelly started to march down towards the track and the people, Tasgo gave an appreciative shrug. *'Perhaps she is a chieftain's daughter after all.'* He conceded.

'You'd better believe it,' Danny told him, as he started after her.

Chapter 14 - Arrival

They stood together on the track, waiting, an authentic group from pre-history. Danny recognised the clothes from re-enactments. His mother would sometimes take him along with her when she gave advice on clothes, tools, or weapons. But the re-enactors had all looked clean and freshly laundered, their clothes new and precious. The real thing was less romantic.

The man stood leaning on his stick, his tunic frayed at the edges and grimed into several shades of neutral. It was patched, but had rubbed so thin in places that you could see the outline of his scrawny body through it. His gnarled feet blended into the earth of the track without the benefit of shoes. Could he be 'the old one' they were being taken to? The women were obviously better off. Though well worn, their tunics were neatly mended and possibly newly washed, leather footwear on their feet, stout sticks in their hands. Not the most welcoming of committees.

Behind them children had scuttled to safety but were watching from behind the low wall, the cart, a barrel, and the doorways of the huts.

Kelly strode towards them with a desperate abandon. She clearly didn't have any faith in reality any more. Danny was having to move faster than he liked to catch up with her. Her last words to him were still ringing in his ears. 'Danny Sharp, I hate you!' She meant it.

Meanwhile Tasgo followed on, whistling some tune as if he had not a care in the world. He broke off to shout over their heads in the old tongue '*It's all right, there's only the two of them.*'

'O yes,' thought Danny, 'we were expected all right.' After all the uncertainty, and the fear, after all the impossibility, he was beginning to feel angry, like a pawn in somebody else's game. It did not help that the someone was probably his own family. That because they had not trusted him, he had no idea what to expect or how to react. And the last thing that he expected was for the greeting party to bow deeply.

One of the women actually went down on her knees. That stopped Kelly in her tracks.

The old man, head still bowed, eyes averted said '*Welcome. If we knew you were coming, we would have prepared a feast.*' It was put as a compliment, but he sounded peeved. Looking at him, Danny thought feasting would be beyond them. It looked like they would need all the food they could get for themselves.

He translated for Kelly, even though she hadn't asked him to. She probably wasn't talking to him. He was about to reply, trying to find a polite way to decline, but Kelly stepped forward, motioning for the woman to get up, for them all to stand up straight.

'No' she was saying, as if they could understand her, 'get up. It's all right. You don't have to...'

They retreated, beginning to look worried, even scared. One of the children behind the wall turned and scurried for the safety of one of the huts.

'Kelly, don't! Stop! They don't understand...' He had no idea what the right thing to do was. Probably to accept graciously.

Kelly didn't spare him a glance. 'Tell them!' she said angrily. 'You tell them.'

'Stop looking angry, you're scaring them.' And then taking a deep breath. '*Please don't, don't, please.*' He wished he knew more words, he wished he had listen to his mother more. '*We don't need a feast. Really, it's not needed.*' Although he couldn't help feeling that being treated with such respect was a lot better than some of the other possibilities.

Tasgo came up from behind Danny, walking straight past almost with contempt. '*She's the daughter of a chieftain, that's all,*' he said to the little group, '*Don't make such a fuss.*'

Yes, thought Danny, a feast would be better than that. The old man scowled at Tasgo, but Tasgo shrugged and turned to Kelly reaching out a hand in invitation.

'*Come Princess,*' he said, '*come and rest a while.*'

Kelly straightened her shoulders. 'In for a penny,' she said, and walked towards the group, ignoring the outstretched hand. To Danny's surprise she dropped something like a little curtsey to the old man, and offered him her arm. Alarm spread over his features.

Kelly didn't press it. Some of the women smiled. One of them made a movement of the hand, of the whole body turning, inviting Kelly towards the huts, and that's where Kelly went. Danny was left to follow after, Tasgo grinning at him as he fell in beside him, bringing the stench of dirty clothes and unwashed body with him.

There had been chickens clucking round the huts when they were walking down the hill, those had all vanished. There were signs that some people had been working out in the open. Straw, wood shavings, a pile of logs newly split, even a group of vertical weaving looms, weighted with stones. No-one was working them now.

Like a nightmare gathering momentum the little group were ushering Kelly towards the largest of the huts. Their eyes were bright with expectation, but no-one was smiling now.

Kelly moved determinedly on, towards who knew what. No-one was paying any attention to Danny. He would have to run to catch Kelly up, but he wasn't going to do that. Not scampering about after others. He was aware of Tasgo, keeping beside him pace for pace. No trust there, not either way.

The hut was beginning to look impressive. The ground in front of the door had been swept clear and level, the walls rose to nearly head height, painted white, while the doorway was framed with an intricate pattern of red and of blue.

Inside was darkness.

Their welcoming party held back, indicating the doorway, and Kelly was about to step in without even checking whether there was a door which could shut behind her. Danny called out, 'Wait!' his voice sharp with anxiety.

She still didn't look at him, but she stopped, as if suddenly aware of the uncertainty in the gloom. Danny got closer, with Tasgo still at his side.

Danny's turn to stand back. *'After you,'* he told Tasgo, *'You can introduce us.'* Assuming there were people inside. People such as 'the old one.'

Tasgo gave a twitch of a smile, and a sardonic bow. He went in and, without waiting for Danny to explain, Kelly followed. Danny tagged on behind, and the others crowded in after him.

It was warm and gloomy in the smoke filled room. It smelt of fire and smoke, and of people. There were no windows and the gloom seemed to stretch forever. New wood had been thrown onto a fire in the open space, but it was only just catching. The little flames reflected in a large metal pot that hung over it but were hardly enough to light the room as people began to fill the doorway.

Further back all manner of things seemed to be jumbled around, posts with things hanging from them, blankets draped from beams, wooden furniture of varying sizes. But Tasgo was moving past the fire into the gloom.

There was a big chair there, with a high back, but no-one was sitting in it. Instead, to one side of it, were a gaggle of children, some apparently cuddling chickens. Behind them was a larger figure sitting on a low chair. It was to this figure that Tasgo went, standing to one side out of the way. *'These came, Gamma, no-one else,'* he said.

She stood, an old woman with white hair that seemed to glow against the darkness. The children moved aside to let her come forward into the little light of the fire, and it was obvious that she was important. People had moved away from the doorway, and either this made the light better, or Danny's eyes were getting accustomed to the gloom. Now he could see the gold jewels glistening in her hair, the large brooch clasping her shawl, the intricate pattern in her clothes. The re-enactors would have been proud of her showing.

Despite her age she came forward lightly, but suddenly stopped. She looked surprised, and puzzled. Then she spoke.

'Danny? Is it really you?'

Danny was stunned. How could she know his name? Was she some sort of seer? And she was speaking modern day English. Impossible.

'My Darling boy!' she went on, delighted, 'It's about time, too.' She was holding out her arms as if expecting him to rush into them. Just like his Grandma did.

And slowly it dawned on him. Despite the place, despite the time, that's who she was. This was his Grandma, his own Grandmother. Who was supposed to be in India, looking for ancient artefacts in the Hindu Kush.

It had taken him so long to work this out that Grandma had dropped her arms and was looking beyond him, past Kelly, to the door. Now she sounded concerned. 'Where's your mother Danny?'

His throat tightened. It was hard to open his mouth and speak. 'Was hoping you could tell me that,' was all he could get out.

She cocked her head slightly, looking at him with that total interest she always had. Then she smiled at Kelly. 'And who is your lovely young friend?' she asked, as if they were sitting at home and she had just come back from India, and Kelly was just visiting. As if it were all perfectly normal. Danny couldn't take it in. It was all beyond him. Perhaps Kelly was right, they were mad. Some sort of shared hallucination. Or just his hallucination. Maybe he was at home, in his own home lost in some sort of ...

Kelly said, 'I'm Kelly James. I go to the same school as Danny.' No more 'we're in the same class.' That was long gone.

Gran said, 'Something has happened hasn't it? Come and sit by the fire and tell me.' Then without pause for breath '*Eles, make our guests comfortable, the best. Drustan, some chairs please.*' Slipping effortlessly from one language to the next, as the old man put low stools in place, 'You are quite safe here, and we'll make sure you're looked after. Come sit...' Switching her attention again to their surroundings '*Aed, are you strong?*' She was talking to Tasgo.

He grinned '*Always.*'

'*Would you go back up the hill, for me? Not all the way perhaps. I can give you another draught before you go.*'

'*I'd rather have ale.*'

She smiled. '*Have both, you've earned it.*' And then, turning, she was all concern for Kelly making sure she was seated comfortably, that the fire was not too hot for her. The new wood had caught and it was setting up a fine blaze now. The dim recesses of the hut were resolving themselves into chests, and piles of furs, tools, even shelves of things that Danny could not recognise.

Finally, as they were brought beakers of some drink, and Tasgo took his and moved away from them, she turned back to Danny.

'You look as though you are in shock boy. Come sit down, take a drink, and tell me what has happened.'

The drink was watery but both sweet and sour, and slightly musty. Danny guessed it was ale. Tasgo was across the room now, gulping down his beer, but also being handed a small beaker of something else. Danny heard the old man speak to him, using the word Aed again. Was that the man's name? Had he lied when he said he was called Tasgo?

'Danny. Tell me what happened. Why are you here on your own?' Gran brought his attention back to her.

So Danny told her. Everything.

The blue men, the explosion, his parents both vanished, and how could they possibly be alive, the hospital and Aunt Moira taking him home. The words fell out of him. His total bewilderment, how insane it was to be at school, the policeman and his questions, the suspicion and the hiding. Kelly sat huddled over her drink, staring into the fire, saying nothing even when he was talking about her, and how Moira had vanished too, and how they searched and found the second secret room and the blue flame. The agony of being sucked into it, and their total bewilderment at finding themselves here, wherever, or rather, whenever here was.

Gran hardly had to say a word. It all flowed out in a rush, the fear, the frustration, the loss. He ended it all up with 'No-one told me. They never told me anything. The secret passages, the flame, here. Nothing. You're supposed to be in India. You all lied!'

There was a long pause. The fire crackled. Everyone else was silent, listening first to his tirade, though he supposed they could not understand a word of it, then to the silence.

'I'm sorry,' his Gran said eventually. She looked at Kelly, still staring at the fire. 'I'm sorry you've ended up here. How did that happen, I mean how did you get involved?'

'She didn't!' growled Danny. 'I didn't! It just happened. What's going on Gran? What is all this? Where are we? Where's Mum, and Dad? What is this?'

His Gran sighed, then she smiled, settling her hands in her lap. 'Very well, I'll try to explain. It's a long story.'

Kelly gave a little cough. 'Can we hear it outside? Please?' she asked, her voice small, not like the Kelly Danny was used to. 'It's dark in here, and very smoky.'

For some reason this seemed to make Gran think for a brief moment. 'Of course,' she agreed, 'let's take our stools out into the light.' And then, once again, she gave a few quick instructions to those about them, and then led the way out through the door.

Chapter 15 - An old story

The sun was still glimmering behind scudding clouds. It seemed too high in the sky, too early in the day. Danny was trying to piece together the hours, the minutes since they had gone down into the basement living room to search for his Aunt. It wasn't working out. The sun should have been behind the shoulder of the hill by now.

His Granny was settling herself into the chair that the old man Drustan had brought out for her. Already some women had gone back to the looms and were threading shuttles through the hanging threads. Tasgo, if that was his real name, was walking out past the low wall heading towards the hill, and children had emerged from hiding, and were now hanging about listening to the talk they could not possibly understand, staring unabashed at the new-comers in their strange clothes.

When they were settled on the low seats, Granny began.

'When I was young, younger than you are now, I lived on my Dad's farm. He farmed, mainly sheep, and though we owned a lot of land, we didn't have much money. I used to help out on the farm, bringing in the lambs whose Mums had died and feeding them by the fire, and sometimes helping round up the sheep for dipping or shearing.'

Danny knew all this. It was family history, but he could see that his Gran was going to take her time, and make a story out of it. Kelly kept her eyes fastened on his Granny's face, as if by ignoring the world about them she could make it go away. Gran was going on.

'He showed me the places to shelter should the weather suddenly take a turn for the worse, including the little dip on the far side of the hill.' she nodded towards the hill behind them, where the town should be and, at the top, Scudmoore road. 'Well, one day I found a lost lamb, and the weather did catch me out. I couldn't see over the hill, the clouds just poured over it, thick and wet, and in minutes you could hardly see a hand in front of your face. But I found the little dip, and we hunkered into it, the lamb and I, as close as we could, and huddled out of the wind.'

Danny wished she would just get to the point, but he knew there was no stopping his Gran once she got going. It would just provoke more explanations.

'At any rate,' his Gran went on 'The lamb was more inquisitive than I, and she nosed about, and vanished behind the little tufts of plants. So I went in after her and found the cave. Even my Dad hadn't noticed it, and he'd been shown all the shelter places by his Dad. And even now it's not easy to find, believe me, not even when you know it's there.'

She smiled at Kelly, ignoring Danny's impatience. 'I used to like playing with my dolls. We lived more simply then. Even the TV hadn't reached us. Even if we'd been able to afford one. Anyhow, I brought a couple of dolls up there and played house in the mouth of the cave. And then, I suppose I'd been reading Famous Five or something, whatever, put it into my mind, I got to thinking that maybe there was treasure hidden deep in the cave.

'So one day I stole a couple of candles, and a lantern, and came up to explore. And I guess what happened to me was what happened to you. I found the fire and got pulled into it. I fell on the floor, and lost my lantern, and had to find my own way out. I was dead scared I was going to be late for me tea, and me Ma would be so cross at me. I was always being late for me tea. So I ran up over the top, and the farm wasn't there. Not the farm, nor the harbour wall, not the boats, not the town at all. I was dead scared, believe me.' She had lost the posh accent she used for talks, and television interviews. She was back with the accents of her youth.

'But these nice ladies, picking herzleberries, they found me greeting, and they were so lovely to me. They fed me berries, even though I thought it was the wrong season and there shouldn't be any berries. They talked so soft but funny, I couldn't understand a word they said. But they took me down to the huts, these huts, and they fed me, and got me some proper clothes. These sort of clothes,' she gestured at her own clothes and those of the people nearby.

'Well at first I couldn't understand a word they said. But they treated me nice, and I learned quick. But I missed home, of course I did. So one day I made me a torch, and took it up the hill. And when I was sure no one was watching I went back into the cave. And back into the deep cave. And back into the fire, hoping it would take me home. And it did.'

Kelly leapt to her feet at that.

'We can go back through the flame? We can go home?'

'Yes my love, you can.'

'That's what we should do! Right now!' She turned to Danny. 'We can go back!'

'What about the explanation?' Danny didn't think his Gran had told them anything new, apart from being able to go back. He wanted to know what was going on, where they were, or when, and how, come to that. 'Don't you want to know what's happening?'

'Of course I do!' she was still cross, but now that she knew there was a way home, she no longer seemed quite so mad at him. 'But we have to get home! What about the police? And your Aunt? And the exam on Tuesday? My Mum is going to be crazy with worry!'

'Don't you think this is a bit more important than all that?' he asked. He was aware they were being watched, that people had been startled by Kelly's outburst. Kelly looked at him. And then she looked about her. It was as if she was only just seeing it all. As if, now that she knew there was a way out, she could begin to take in where they were properly.

Gran said, kindly, 'It's all right Kelly. Another few minutes won't matter.'

'You don't know my Mum,' said Kelly, but she sat down again. 'And,' she went on thoughtfully, just as Danny's Gran was about to say something else, 'it may be important. There's the police – they were expecting you to be there, and your Aunt. When they find you aren't there, again, and they look around,' she was gaining confidence and speed 'they'll find my bag. And,' the conclusion was hitting her hard, 'they'll call my Mum.' She stood again. 'We have to go. Now!'

Gran turned to Danny. She was looking alarmed too. 'Tell me you didn't leave the hidden doors open Danny.' Her voice had come back from the accents of her youth to something sharper and less relaxed.

Danny couldn't remember. He was thinking hard, but it was all a blur now. It was Kelly who said, 'The cupboard door was open,' in a small voice. Gran turned her eyes to the hill, as if searching for rogue policemen emerging over the top. There was no sign of Tasgo on the hillside.

'Never mind,' said Gran, turning back to them, 'it can't be helped now. You didn't prop the secret door open, did you?' She sounded as though she was sure he hadn't.

Now Danny remembered Kelly suggesting it, and was thankful he could tell his Grandmother that at least he had not been that stupid.

'Then it shouldn't matter,' she said settling herself placidly.

'You don't understand,' Kelly urged. 'I have to go back. Now. My Mum...'

'Mothers worry about their children,' Gran interrupted, 'that's natural. Children don't have to worry about their parents.'

'I do,' burst out Kelly. 'I really do. I look after her.' Gran was looking at her with a surprised incomprehension. 'I have to,' Kelly was near tears again.

Danny remembered how Kelly's mother had looked when she came to the house, all darting eyes and over-excited hands. How nervous she had been, and how Kelly had settled her at the table with so little fuss. How could he have missed that? It all made sense now. But it couldn't be that bad surely?

'But Kelly, she's all right, I mean, she's got a job and everything. She'll be okay.'

'She's got a routine.' Kelly countered. 'She takes pills, she – she needs me.'

'Perhaps it will do her good, to have to do without you?' Said Gran.

Danny realised she had no idea what Kelly was talking about. When he thought of his mother, or Moira, they were, he suddenly realised, formidable. Like his Gran. That was Gran's world. That was how they viewed life, how they lived. Gran fitted perfectly into this world where everything had to be done yourself, sink or swim. Apparently it was very different in the James household.

Kelly was trying to explain, but Danny realised she was finding it hard to do so without saying anything that would give a bad impression of her mother. Gran obviously didn't understand and was finding her rather stupid.

He took a deep breath and cut across the jagged flow of words. 'Kelly,' he said, 'is very clever. The cleverest. Just explain what all this is about, and then we'll find Aunt Moira and go home.'

His Gran smiled at him. 'So simple,' she said, and then to Kelly, 'Would that do? After all you can't go back and tell your mother you don't know what happened, can you?'

Kelly wavered for a moment and then sat down again.

'Now, where was I?' began his Gran. Then looking at Kelly she said 'Perhaps I had better cut the story short. Everyone had been worried about me, but they thought I was making up stories about the hill. Grandad told them there was no cave up there, and he wouldn't even go up with me to see. So I almost began to believe I had dreamed it all.

'But then we began to learn about the old days, at school, and it all made sense, so I went back again, just for the day. And it was all still there, and the ladies were glad to see me. So I took to going back, just for short whiles, and then for weekends. I never told anyone of course, because they wouldn't believe me. The village was turning into a town, and I got a job there. I could stay longer when I came, whole weekends and sometimes weeks, so I learned the language. And I read a lot of books of course.'

'Anyway, it gave me the evidence to place when we are. We are trading finished goods for iron bars, that Madog works, but we're still using bronze, and copper. The Romans haven't got here yet, but we know that they are a strong presence over the water. So before the first century AD but probably not more than 200 BC. '

She gave a little laugh, 'I tried taking back a short sword, but it wouldn't come through the flame. Moira calls it a time portal, she's the brainy one. I did bring back some pottery, but people thought it was a fake, because it had only been made a few years ago, according to the carbon dating. So then I had to bury things where I knew I could find them later.'

'That's sort of cheating isn't it?' muttered Danny.

His Gran cave a careless shrug. 'Maybe,' she said. 'It was the only way people were going to take me seriously. After all, I had plenty to tell them about this age, if only they would listen.'

'Why didn't you just tell them about the – the portal?' asked Kelly. 'Then they could see for themselves.'

'What, after the way the treated me the first time?' scoffed Gran. 'And besides,' she confessed 'I liked being the only one in the know. You wouldn't believe how stuffy some of the academics could be! But then I realised, how dangerous it would be, if others got to know.'

'Dangerous?' asked Danny.

'They'd want to come back,' explained Gran. 'They'd want to see for themselves. Can you imagine them, dozens of them, coming down here, poking at this, peering at that, bringing modern day ideas and constructs with them, behaving the way they do in the twenty first century, here in the past?'

'They'd change everything,' murmured Kelly thoughtfully. 'They'd change history. They'd change the future.'

Gran looked at her with more respect. 'Exactly!' she said. 'I learned to be careful, very careful, what I said, how I behaved, when I was here. The more I learned, the more careful I became. It's only a small village, but if I dropped some modern technology back here, well, they go to market in Cynmar, and Dugal, well, he's a respected man...' As she said it her eyes strayed to the track, and her lips set in a determined line. Then she caught herself and turned back to them.

'As Kelly said, it would change everything. So while you are here, you have to be careful. Say nothing,' she told Danny 'nothing about the future. Watch your words. Try to fit in, and don't react when they do things differently here.'

Danny was still trying to get his head round it. 'So,' he said feeling foolish for saying it, 'we have a time portal in Moira's house.

And we don't tell anyone about it.' He said slowly. 'How did that happen?'

'It didn't happen, it simply is. I found it, that's all.'

'So there could be others?'

Gran looked at him, startled. Had she never thought of that herself?

'I don't think so,' she said dismissively. 'I mean, what are the chances of a lone person coming across it? And in the past, not knowing what it was, surely they would have made a big fuss about it? I'm sure we would know about it if someone had found one.'

But no-one knows about this one, thought Danny to himself. The sun had at last begun to sink into the shoulder of land, and the air felt suddenly cooler for the lack of it.

'So, are my parents here then? And Aunt Moira?' He asked, carefully not mentioning again the explosion, the total destruction of his old home.

For the first time since they had sat down here, his Gran looked troubled. 'I don't know Dannaigh,' she said. 'It all sounds – very strange. Moira's house, that is all right, is it? Nothing happened at Moira's house?'

'Except she vanished,' he said. Which should surely mean that she was here.

'When exactly was this?'

Danny didn't know for sure. 'This morning,' he said, trying to gauge the hours between, the hours they had spent here. So much had happened. His shoulder and his wrist still ached from the agony of the fire. That in itself had seemed to last for hours, though he guessed it was minutes, or maybe less. He shrugged. 'This morning,' was the best that he could do.

His Gran looked grave. 'We had some trouble,' she said, 'this morning. Up on the hill. Some horsemen. That's why I sent Aed up there.'

That settled it. Danny said, 'He told us his name was Tasgo.'

Granny grinned. The same sort of grin that Moira had given when she showed him the secret room. Then she gave a short laugh. 'Aed is a good name, a strong name, but he'd like something stronger, something he has earned. Tasgo is good. It means –

'Badger,' Danny filled in the word before she could. She nodded.

'A badger is wise, and strong. What it has, it holds. It is a good name for him.'

Danny remembered him, up on the hill, when he had first appeared out of the heather and herzleberries. It was a good name, he thought, for warning strangers off.

'He was there to deal with them, the men?' he asked.

'They seemed to be gone. He was more of a look out, in case they were still about.'

Danny didn't think much of him as a look out. 'I think he was asleep when we came,' he said.

Gran only smiled. 'It doesn't surprise me.' It seemed Tasgo could get away with anything.

And then a child came racing down the track. From the wild gait and waving arms, Danny guessed it was the same one that Tasgo had sent running ahead of them when they arrived. Only this time they could hear his joyful shouts.

'They're coming back! They're coming back! All of them! They're coming back'

Chapter 16 - Warrior's Return

Instantly the village was in motion, the women left their looms, children were running out towards the track, chickens were clucking and running around excitedly, other folk appeared from within the hut or from further into the village. Gran was on her feet, her face suddenly full of joy, and she too ran towards the track, abandoning Danny and Kelly completely.

Round the knoll came two horses, pulling a chariot, in the swaying body of which were two forms, one dark haired and solid, with furs over his shoulder, spears upright beside him and a heavy brooch holding his cloak in place, sparkling in the evening light. The other was Tasgo, looking triumphant, though he could only have joined them when they were almost home. Soon after them came two more chariots, and a dozen horse, some with two men on their backs.

The children had run out to meet them and now ran recklessly around the hooves and wheels, laughing and shouting out. Somewhat behind came men on foot, and they all carried spears.

The first chariot pulled into the open space within the low walls, wheeled and stopped. Gran flew like a young girl into the arms of the dark-haired man, who held her to him as if they had been parted for years. With a shock Danny recognised the man she was cuddling up to and whispering in his ear.

'That's Black Dougal!' he told Kelly.

She looked at him sideways 'Really?' she said. It was obvious she still didn't believe him.

Meanwhile Tasgo had hopped off and came round to see to the horses, removing their harness and letting the shafts of the chariot fall. One horse shook its head and jerked away from him, ears back and teeth showing.

To Danny's surprise his Gran was calling to him 'Danny, hold that horse!' As if he knew anything about horses. But he got up and made a tentative move towards the animal, which was obviously in a foul humour, tramping its feet and moving with restive anger. It wasn't big for a horse, but he didn't like the look in its eyes.

'It doesn't like the smell,' Kelly said sharply, moving past Danny. 'Tell Tasgo to move away,' She was already making an imperious sweep of her arm to Tasgo as she stepped up to the horse and took a firm hold of the bridle. Danny didn't have to relay the command, Tasgo was only too quick to retreat.

Almost as soon as he was gone the horse was quiet, flicking its ears and making gentle inquisitive bobs of its head at Kelly as she patted its neck and spoke soothingly to it. It was a changed animal, quiet and friendly.

'What should I do with him?' she asked Gran.

'Follow Marrec,' answered Gran, indicating a tall man who was approaching with two other horses. He could have been handsome if it were not for a large bruise over his cheek and chin. He gave her a wide grin, showing two missing teeth. Unlike Tasgo he smelt of horses and hay, and his clothes were at least halfway clean, and his hair neatly braided.

For a moment she hesitated, her eyes met Danny's, but he had no more idea whether she should or not than she did. But since it was his Gran telling her, he shrugged, and nodded. Away she went, her horse quite ready to walk on with the others.

Black Dougal and his Gran were walking towards him now, hand in hand. The man was looking him up and down with approval. '*It's been a while,*' he said, as if it had been yesterday. '*You've filled out well. Welcome!*' And letting go of Gran's hand he swallowed Danny in a bear hug that threatened to squeeze the life out of him.

'*Welcome!*' he cried again in a loud voice, letting Danny go, making sure that everyone could see and hear how pleased he was with the new arrival. And then, more matter of fact, taking Danny's arm as they continued to walk towards the hut, '*I hear you have had some troubles. Let's see what we can do. But first I have to wash, after the journey.*'

Drustan had run out with a beaker of ale, and Black Dougal knocked it back, glugging it all down in one go, little dribbles running down his chin. He handed it back saying *'Some for our guest too Drustan, and my other tunic. I'm for the river.'* He was looking round at his domain, making sure that everything was as it should be, and that all his men were now here.

Where had they been, all the men? Danny wondered as Dougal clamped a hand on his shoulder. *'Eles will look after you,'* and calling across the now crowded space, *'Eles, see that our guests have everything they need.'* With that he was off. And Danny was left standing.

He looked round for his Gran, and there she was with Tasgo. He was making some sort of earnest entreaty and she was smiling on him. A gust of wind brought her words over. *'Of course you can, but first let's ...'* The woman Eles appeared at Danny's side with a jug of ale, ready to fill his beaker again. Danny didn't think he needed any more to drink, but he wasn't sure it would be polite to refuse. He looked around, but there was no sign of Kelly and the horses. He was about to ask where they would be, when he saw his Gran was tugging Tasgo's tunic over his head. And then he couldn't help but stare.

Tasgo's left shoulder and chest were rainbow painted, but more likely with a hammer than a brush. Purple and black, surrounded by green and yellow, with a livid red slash through the upper section. Even from here he could see where the wound had been sewn together. With a wound like that Danny would expect to be in hospital, but Tasgo had been out on the hills, walking and talking and – keeping watch.

Tasgo was raising his arm and swinging it in a slow circle at Gran's command, and as he turned his eyes caught Danny gawping, and held them in a gaze that was both proud and challenging. Danny closed his mouth with a snap.

With a satisfied smile, Tasgo turned back to Gran, who was probing the edges of the wound with delicate fingers. Whatever she was saying was very pleasing to him. The smile burst into a big grin, his whole posture lightened, and grabbing the tunic from her with a whoop of joy, he turned and skipped away towards the smaller huts as if unhurt.

It didn't help that Eles was watching too, with a happy smile. She was much happier looking after the departed Tasgo than she was telling Danny where to find the horses.

When he went to find Kelly, she was already walking back towards the main hut, with gap toothed Marrec beside her, burbling away, trying to impress her with his knowledge of the horses and to flatter her with compliments on her own handling of the mare. What he was making of her silence Danny couldn't tell, because he broke off when Kelly greeted Danny by demanding to know what the man was saying.

'He's being nice to you,' Danny told her.

Kelly didn't look at the man. She frowned at Danny. 'You really do,' she said, 'you understand them. You speak...'

'Yes,' he said. He had always thought of it as a bit of fun, when he had thought of it. At home they spoke a private language, that no-one else could understand. They did it a lot, especially when he was young. He thought it was a game, fun. So now, while he wasn't fluent, he could understand. Because his family had a 'time portal' and they used it.

More than that. Kelly was obviously in total denial about where and when they were, but there was a familiarity for him. Now that the shock had worn off, it was getting to feel, well, comfortable, to him. Maybe it was just the re-enactments he had been to, and his mothers work that spilled over into their home life, but he had a suspicion he had been here before. When he was very young. He would ask his mother when, or was it if, they found her.

'We should go home,' Kelly said quietly. The light was already fading. The hill behind them was shadowed and indistinct. He thought of the rills and rocks. It would be dark before they got there. Marrec was standing there, watching them, as though there was nothing more interesting in the world. Danny turned to him.

'Thank you for walking her back,' he said, and then told Kelly, 'Just being polite.' And back to Marrec *'Where have you been, all of you?'*

Marrec seemed surprised. *'Cynmar,'* he said, and seeing no recognition in Danny's face *'the big river*?'

'Ah,' said Danny, as if that meant something. With all the spears, he wondered if they had been fighting, but they hadn't look damaged when they arrived, or victorious. More tired, but happy.

'*What is her name?*' asked Marrec, looking with doting eyes at Kelly. Danny wondered how many times he was going to be asked that.

'*He wants to know your name,*' he told Kelly.

She sighed and squared up to Marrec, looking him straight in the face, with no smile. 'Kelly James. We go to the same school.'

'*Kelyn-aimes,*' smiled Marrec and put the palm of his hand on his chest and said his own name.

'Pleased to meet you,' said Kelly with gritty politeness.

'*She is very good with the horses,*' confided Marrec to Danny, as if it was to be a shared secret. '*They like her.*' Which was obviously the biggest compliment he could think of. Danny passed it on., adding 'Where did you learn that?'

'Riding school. I'm a stable lad,' said Kelly, then 'We should be going, it's getting dark.'

Already it was gloomy. Danny looked up at the big shadow of the hill. 'We'd need candles,' he said reluctantly. 'And – I want to know what Gran meant about trouble this morning. I want to know where Moira is, and my parents.' He could see Kelly resisting the logic. 'I need to know, Kelly. I have to find them.'

Kelly was still looking longingly at the hill. 'But, my Mum. I have to get back to her Danny.'

Gran's voice came from behind him, 'Not tonight, Kelly my dear. It's not safe on the mountain.'

'We'd be careful,' began Kelly turning towards her. 'We could pick our way...'

'It's not the rocks and streams I'm worried about my dear. There were horsemen there this morning. And they weren't friendly.' Gran was smiling and moving towards Kelly, holding out a hand. 'We'll have to wait until the morning, now.'

'But,' protested Kelly, 'someone could go with us, to look after us...'

'Not tonight,' Gran said gently, 'The men are tired after their travel, and there's food to be had. Let's go in.' And to Marrec, '*Could you fetch some straw for us please Marrec, they'll need a bed for the night.'*

Kelly looked to Danny for support, but he could see that his Gran had a point. And really, the thought of going back to face D. I. Raynes without his Aunt was daunting. After not being there twice, they would never believe he had nothing to do with all the disappearances. The horror of that night still haunted him. He felt cold just thinking about it.

He said, 'I'm not going up there on our own in the dark. Not 'til we know what's going on.'

She didn't like it, but she gave in. What else could she do?

Chapter 17 - A Small Feast and a Big Story

In the gloom of the main hut Gran was setting up a place for them to sleep. In the far recess, enclosed by walls of hanging cloths, was Gran and Dougal's bed, covered in furs and looking quite comfy. Danny and Kelly's beds were made up on either side, rough baled straw, covered in cloth and then with piles of furs. The skins were not quite as supple as the fur rugs Danny was used to at home, but when the beds were made they looked quite cosy by the light of the open flame lamps.

All the while Eles had been coming up to his Gran with questions, and going away with a short answer.

'A chicken?'

'Too late for that.'

'Eggs?'

'We need them to hatch.'

'Turnips?'

'If you must.'

'There's that bit of gammon… '

At last Gran turned to face her. *'I told you to throw that out. The maggots would be tastier. And no! Don't even consider that. Eles, you know how to cook.'*

'But,' Eles was wringing her hands, *'it should be a celebration, what with…'*and she shot a glance at Kelly who was helping to tuck cloth tighter round the hay.

'We have a lot to be grateful for,' agreed Gran, *'but it isn't a celebration. Make sure there is enough for the men, is all.'*

Eles moved away grumbling to herself, and then Black Dougal was back, his dark tunic replaced by a cheerful yellow and blue one, wet hair hanging loose round his shoulders.

He put an arm round Danny's Gran, and kissed her, drawing her into the main area of the hut, then turned to Danny.

'Now, Your Grandmother tells me you have had some troubles. Tell me what happened with Freya and her man. Come.'

He went over to sit in the big chair that Danny had noticed, pulling up a stool next to it. Danny took the stool. He wasn't sure where to begin and what to tell. And it was difficult putting it all in the old tongue. There weren't the words for so many things that he took for granted. He kept it simple.

'Some men painted blue got into our house. They fought my parents. They destroyed our house. Everything – went away. Including my parents.'

Gran had come over while he spoke, bringing Kelly with her. Kelly sat on the other side of Dougal, looking at the preparations for the meal, trestles being set as tables, different pots of food on the fire, a quiet bustle. Gran began to comb Dougal's hair, using a scented oil to help get rid of the tangles.

Dougal was after the details. *'How many men? How did they get in?'*

'I don't know.'

'You know more than that. How many men did you see?'

Danny thought back. He tried to ignore the fear, the uncertainty. There had been one, attacking his mother. The cudgel coming at him meant there was one attacking him. Through the open door to the kitchen there had been other figures, moving fast. One for sure, perhaps two, perhaps his father.

'I saw four,' he said, *'but - our house has many - places. There may have been many more...'*

'I have been in your house,' said Dougal, reassuringly *'once when you were young. I have been into the hill and seen your country. It is very beautiful, and I know your house. Your father was there?'*

'Yes.'

'He did not get out?'

'No.'

'Your mother, Freya?'

'She did, she went back.'

'She went back,' echoed Dougal, firelight reflected in his eyes as he looked at Danny. He didn't say the obvious, that Danny had been out as well, and that he had not gone back. Instead he nodded with

approval. *'She is a fierce woman, your mother. You should be proud.'*

Danny swallowed. *'I am,'* he said, realising it properly for the first time. Proud of his mother, ashamed of himself.

Dougal leant forward, dragging his hair from Gran's hands, and looking hard into Danny's eyes. *'You are something very special,'* he said, *'for her to have left the fray to save you.'*

It was like a body blow. Like the world falling away, turning upside down. Like he had felt on the pier when Kelly had said Moira would not abandon him.

He felt his arm grasped in a vice-like grip, but warm, and steadying. Dougal's eyes were still fixed on his. *'Believe it,'* he said. *'You are something special. For Freya to save you before Toma.'*

With an effort Danny found his voice. *'I'm her son,'* he said, thinking that's what mothers did, for their sons, however unworthy. Kelly heard the change in tone and turned to look at him.

'Yes you are,' agreed Dougal, taking it differently, *'You will see, when the time comes.'* He sat back and in an aside to Gran said, *'Thick braids please,'* carrying straight on, *'So, how did they get into the house?'* While Gran began to divide his hair into locks, ready to plait it.

Danny began to say he didn't know, but stopped himself. He went back in his mind to his descent of the stairs, when all was silent and half lit, before the first shouts began. As if he had travelled back to that time and place he heard the sounds from below, deep in the house.

'Through the...' there was no word for basement, *'the cave under the house'*.

'There is a magic fire there too?

'No. No there isn't.' He didn't think there was. Could there have been? But Dougal was pressing on.

'An ordinary door?'

'No.'

Dougal nodded thoughtfully, and Gran pursed her lips at him for stopping her plaiting.

'And when the house was destroyed, where did they go?'

Good question. *'They went with the house. There was nothing left.'* Well, next to nothing.

'With the house' pondered Dougal, and then swiftly, *'We will say nothing of that. When I ask you, say only what you first said.'* He was looking over Danny's shoulder, and when Danny turned he was surprised.

Swaggering towards them was the sturdy figure of a handsome young man, in a fine tunic of bright yellow edged with blue, his red-gold hair a mass of fine plaits, a sword strung across his chest, topped with a clean and shining version of the face that belonged to Tasgo. He was hardly recognisable. He was grinning, pleased at the effect he was having.

'Well,' announced Dougal, *'that's an improvement.'*

'When there is a pretty girl in the house, you have to look your best!' Tasgo gave a glance to Kelly who was still not quite sure whether to believe the transformation. Then with total lack of bravado he turned to Gran, *'Thanks Old one, I think I would have cut my own throat if I wasn't allowed to wash.'*

'Don't go wrenching the wound open again, showing off, is all,' Gran said, still plaiting.

'I think we'd have cut your throat for you, if we had to sit with that mess for dinner,' Dougal smiled. *'So just as well. We need you to mend fast Aed. Rest. Don't drill the young ones tomorrow morning. There may be action soon enough.'*

In one swift movement Tasgo/Aed hoiked a stool closer with his foot, drew it up to Danny's and sat. *'Gorbed?'* he asked, eagerly confidential.

'They may ride with us,' was Dougal's answer, to Tasgo's obvious surprise.

It was then that Kelly got up and began to walk away.

Gran called to her, 'Where are you going?'

'Out,' said Kelly, still walking.

'Dannaigh, go with her,' was Gran's response, she was still plaiting Dougal's hair, and Danny saw now that she was weaving ornaments into the plaits.

He would rather have stayed, and heard what was being said, but he felt responsible for Kelly, having got her into all this.

She was already at the door by the time he caught up with her. Outside it was dark, a darkness intensified rather than relieved by big torches set about the open space.

'That was a bit rude,' he said as he joined her.

She looked around, rather than at him. 'So is everyone jabbering on without a word of explanation.' He was obviously still in her bad books.

'Sorry.'

'And,' she was still looking about her, and seeing only the flaring lights, she lowered her head and her voice, 'I need a pee.'

'Oh.' Now there was a question. A question not often answered he thought, going through all the things he had heard his mother say. He was beginning to think it was just find a quiet spot and do it, but then remembered the Yorvik museum.

'Hang on a mo,' he said, and then as he turned away, not knowing quite what mood she was in. 'Stay here, I'll be right back.' He nipped back inside.

Tasgo and Dugal were still in conversation, but other men had joined them now. Danny avoided them, going round to his Gran, just finishing off the last of the plaits, now with the shining metal brooches tied in.

He explained why he had come and Gran sighed. 'Modern day folk. I'd better come and show you both.'

Kelly was not outside the door, but he spotted her some distance away, looking at one of the chariots.

'We have two toilets,' Gran explained, as she led them into the darkness, 'because we do a lot of work in the village. Out in the open, just keep away from the streams. The women mainly use this one, because it is close to the looms, but you can too Danny, it's not uni-sex.' She was leading them past the torches and the looms into the inky dark. 'They're earth closets, and we move the seats to a new place from time to time, and use the soil from the much older ones for fertiliser.'

Fortunately she had brought a light with her, though its flickering flame was not nearly as good as a torch. Ahead of them was a small wicker fence, about shoulder high, with a gap in it. She held the light so that they could see a low wooden platform open to the sky, with 3 holes to sit over. 'There's your toilet,' she said moving her light further over, 'and the moss is your toilet paper.' The moss was stuffed in a wicker cage on the far side. Kelly was wrinkling her nose, but Danny thought it smelt better than the toilets at school did at times.

All Kelly said was 'Three?' and Gran laughed.

'We're very communal,' she said, resting the light on a shelf. 'Come back soon, food's nearly ready,' and she walked away. Danny, after a moment's hesitation, followed, leaving Kelly in the dark with the one flickering light.

It was easier walking from darkness towards light, you could see where things were. He stopped before they got to the first flaring torch. Perhaps his Gran sensed it, for she looked back at him, waiting, silhouetted by the light behind her.

'I'll wait for Kelly,' he said, 'she isn't finding this easy.'

'You wouldn't be thinking of trying to go up the hill by yourselves?' she asked suspiciously. 'That would be a big mistake.' Her tone softened. 'You'll understand more after we've had food.' And she walked on into the light, and beyond it.

He waited in the darkness. He saw men and women and children making their way to the main hut. No-one seemed to notice him, in the dark, on his own. He heard their voices talking, the old language. He felt very much an outsider. How much worse must it be for Kelly, who could not understand a word they said. It became quiet. There was a faint murmuring from the hut, many voices talking quietly. He began to think he should go and see if Kelly was all right, but she probably wouldn't appreciate that.

Suddenly there she was, walking with the little lamp, coming towards him.

'Are you okay?' he asked. There was a pause as she came nearer.

'Thanks for waiting,' was all she said. Her voice was husky, as if she had been crying.

'You're not okay?' he tried.

'Of course I'm not okay!' she snapped, looking at him for the first time. 'We're here and we should be there! You can tell what's going on but I can't! And my Mum will be out of her mind with worry! And...' she stopped suddenly.

'Oh. Right,' was not an adequate answer.

Then she went on, firmly, but no longer angry. 'And my shouting at you doesn't help anything. We're here now. We have to make the best of it.'

That was a change. 'Right,' he said.

'So how about translating for me?'

'I'll try, but I don't understand everything they say. It's...' difficult, but that wasn't the point. 'I don't understand it all anyway. I don't know – much more than you really. But, like you say, we have to make the best of it.' He was thinking that, if it hadn't been for the disaster that had brought them to this point, it was really quite interesting, intriguing. There were his parents to think of though. Hard to make the best of that, but he tried.

'Dougal seems to think we can find the rest of my family. That would be good. We should go in, they'll have started supper without us,' he finished.

But they hadn't.

As they ducked under the door lintel, the warmth and chatter and smell of food hit them. A long table now ran down one side of the hut, surrounded by people standing around or sitting and talking to people across the table. As they came closer, a silence seemed to spread ahead of them. Everyone turned and looked. Dugal sat at the far end and he stood and beckoned for them to come to him. By the time they got there the hut was in silence, so Dugal hardly had to raise his voice to be heard.

'Everyone, while we were away Danaigh and Kelyn have come to visit. They are Kith and Kin to our own Gamma, and although they do not know our ways well, they are dear to me. I know you will make them feel at home here.'

There was a murmur of response, and as they took their seats on stools next to Gran, Danny muttered to Kelly a brief version of what had been said. Already the hum of conversation had grown again, and baskets of wheat cakes – a sort of unleavened bread- were being passed round. Their own bowls were pottery, but he saw that further down the table they were mostly using wooden bowls.

Eles and a couple of other women were ladling stew from the cauldron into big bowls which were passed down the table. Other bowls held vegetables, though it was hard to distinguish what exactly they were in the limited light. The taste didn't help much either. Although blander than Danny had expected, they tended to be slightly bitter. Vegetables, was the most that Danny could come up with, when Kelly tried to work out what they were. Everybody used their fingers, or stabbed the bit they wanted with a knife. Gamma and Dugal, and Tasgo had spoons he noticed, as well as a few others.

The stew was rather better, with a meaty taste, though he only found one small mouthful of meat in his bowl. A jug of ale went round and people filled their own beakers, or those of the person next to them. The unleavened bread was useful for mopping up the stew, and when that had been eaten, big dollops of soft white cheese were brought to the table, and the bread was used to smear cheese onto it to be eaten.

Kelly stopped eating when she saw bread going straight from mouths back into the cheese for seconds.

The chatter was incessant, but Danny was aware of Tasgo, sitting on the other side of Dugal, watching him. He tried to ignore him, translating some of the chatter round them for Kelly, but it seemed to him that there wasn't much being said, some talk about sheep, or the weather. Still, there was a tingling feeling of something being about to happen, some tension in the air. People kept throwing glances their way, or at Dugal himself.

Then a couple more jugs were brought out, and people emptied their beakers ready for this new drink. Dugal took one of the jugs and, standing up, made a little ceremony of pouring some for Gran, then a small amount in Danny's cup, then Kelly's, then Tasgo's and another man, before filling his own cup.

Silence rippled down the table. Dugal raised his cup.

'To old friends, and new ones,' he said. Danny repeated it for Kelly before he and she joined everyone else in tasting the sweet warming liquid. Danny knew the taste of mead, and made sure Kelly knew to take it in sips, as the chief continued to stand, looking down the lines of faces turned to him. Even the children bickering under the table grew silent.

'Well, you all know where we have been, and that we're back without blood shed. But we all need to be aware of what has been happening. These are serious times. So let's go over it.

'Just a few days ago, no more than seven, on the very day of the landslide, Cunedag was watching over the sheep. Cunedag, where are you? Show yourself!'

There was a scrabbling at the far end of the table, and a child suddenly appear, wide eyed for being called on.

'Cunedag, what happened that day?' demanded Dugal.

Cunedag stood up tall, as tall as a nine-year-old could. *'I was watching the sheep,'* He said, looking round and seeing everyone looking at him, some of them smiling encouragement. *'There were some men, and they were chasing some of our sheep around.'*

'Villagers?' asked Dugal.

'Strangers,' said the boy.

'What did you do?'

'I went to ask them what they were doing with our sheep.'

'And?' smiled Dugal.

'One of them pointed his spear at me, and when I didn't go away, he ran at me with it.'

'And what did you do then?'

The boy was beginning to enjoy being the centre of attention. *'I knew that Margan and Pinner were in the top wood, collecting for the charcoal burn, so I ran down to them. I wasn't scared!'*

'Good lad!' Dugal turned to one of the men and gestured for him to get up. *'Margan, what then?'*

Margan was an older man, with a thick moustache, which didn't hide his leathery skin with numerous little scars. He was matter of fact. *'I sent Cun over to Aed where they were stacking the wood, and Pin and me, we went up the hill.'* He was frowning, as if remembering was not easy. *'I hadn't got a weapon to hand, but we'd saved a couple of staves that might do for spears, so we took them instead.'*

'What did you find there?'

'A couple a folk, strangers, trying to herd sheep, very badly. They weren't having much joy of it.' A ripple of laughter jostled about. *'When they saw us, they left off chasing sheep, and took a stance.'* He shrugged, *'We walked towards them and hailed them reasonable enough, but they shook spears at us. I asked them what the'* Danny didn't know the word he used, but could guess, *'they were doing with our sheep, and they made a charge at us.'* He shifted a shoulder, uncomfortably.

'Well, we don't want them thinking we're easy, so we stood. We was low down, by the wood, and we knew others were on their way. Least wise, we hoped they were.' Another ripple of good natured laughter. Everyone was enjoying the tale.

'Then Aed, he burst out on the higher ground. Fast foot flying fury he was! An' they took one look, and they ran too, t'other way. Mind you, Marrec and Madog weren't far behind him, carrying shields and spears, so they did know they was outnumbered.' Outright laughter this time.

Dugal turned to Tasgo, no need to ask him to get to his feet, he was already there. *'So, what next Aed?'*

'I always have my weapon to hand,' Tasgo boasted, taking up the tale to a gust of laughter, as if it was a communal joke. He went on *'We chased, they ran. At the least, we should know who they were and why they thought they could take sheep from us at will.*

'It settled into a jog up the river. Them putting on a spurt and slowing down to get breath when they thought we'd given up, then running on.' He gave a short laugh. *'You could almost think they were waiting for us to catch them up. We went right up, round Grim Shoulder, heading for the ford.'*

'That's a fair way,' Dugal acknowledged *'A long trek. The sun would be getting low.'*

Tasgo shrugged. *'Still light. We knew we'd get them at the ford.' He paused.*

'And?' prompted Dougal.

'It was a trap.' This time it was a shocked intake of breath that echoed through the room. Danny thought that everyone must know what had happened by now, but Dugal and Tasgo were making a show of it. Or maybe it was entirely for his benefit, his and Kelly's.

'There were twenty of them lying in wait for us.'

'Twenty?' asked Dugal as if in disbelief.

'Twenty,' proclaimed Tasgo, showing with his fingers as he counted, and pointed to the positions as if they were now all there, and could see the landscape with its hidden fighters. *'Five on the other side of the river, with bows and slings, five behind Ninian's rock, four dropped under the ledge where the track turns by the riverside, the two we were chasing, and four down by the ford, waiting. They were painted. A war party.'*

'Twenty against the five of you,' said Dugal.

'If they'd done it right, they'd have had us,' conceded Tasgo. *'If they'd hidden better, and waited till we passed them before coming at us, we would have been in range of the archers, and surrounded. But they weren't hidden well enough, and once we'd seen them, they had to come at us.*

'And hiding down from the track under a ledge? That's a stupid place to launch an ambush from. Pin and Madog knocked them down like flies.

'The others leaped at us from behind the rock. I took the first on my shield and Margan, he ducked a spear and cut the thigh muscles of that one, so he was down and gone. Marrec was there right beside Margan. So now it was three against four, while Pin and Madog were finishing off their share. Those liked the fight so well they ran, all expect the one who thought he could wade the pool under Ninnian's rock.' Some laughter at this. *'Whether he made it across in the end or the river took him to sea,'* Tasgo shrugged.

'But the others?'

'They fought. I would not be here now if Madog had not reached us in time. We were two swords to four, but,' he was looking down the table to where the children had gathered round Cunedag and he spoke now as a teacher giving a lesson, *'a good spear used well can prevail*

against a sword.' Leaving the children, he went on. *'So now it was our five against their four, and we despatched two from battle, but then,'* he sighed and looked sad, *'then there was this great hulking brute running down on us from the ford. His hair was dark, his skin was pale, the earth shook with his every stride, and he had a long shafted, heavy, two handed, curved blade axe!'*

Suddenly Dugal was a huge figure swinging something overhead, and the huge axe slammed into the table top, splintering wood, the sound deafening, echoing from the rafters. The broken table shuddered and settled under the weight of it.

There were shocked gasps from all sides, not just from Kelly.

'This axe,' exclaimed Dugal, and everyone including Tasgo stared at it for a moment. Then Tasgo shook his head.

'Really,' he said with all the sorrow in the world, *'it is a useless weapon. Yes, the blow is hard enough.'* He looked down the table to Madog, *'thanks for bringing me the shield, mate. I'd be dead without it! But honestly,'* he looked again at the axe, *'you have to use two hands to swing it, it's so heavy it slows you down, and when you swing it over your head, your chest, your arms, your belly, your groin, they're all exposed. He was dead before the axe hit me and shattered my shield.*

'The others, they were coming up from the ford, but, I think they had put great store by this big man and his big, useless axe. When he fell, they stopped, and the others, they hobbled back to join them, back where the archers could send their arrows.

'So there we were. The archers were useless if we stayed out of range, so nine against five now. We weren't stupid enough to go down to them, and for some reason they weren't too keen to come up to us.' He stopped and smiled, remembering the stand-off.

'But Marrec, he had a sling shot, and he started picking up pebbles. And Madog, well Madog?' He gestured down to Madog, who got slowly to his feet looking at the axe.

'Well,' he said, *'it's an axe, isn't it? It's a blade. So I picked it up. Just to look at it. Nice work. Couldn't do better myself. Bit big, but...'* he shrugged. *'So I looked around for something to try its bite on. And there's this big bloke with the dark hair just lying there. Tasgo, Aed,*

he's right. Too big, too heavy. Hard to handle. Takes a head off clean though, I'll give it that.'

Danny felt a cold wave douse over him, as if all the blood were draining from his body. Some of the young men seemed to find it funny. He didn't look at Kelly, and he didn't translate. Fortunately no-one was looking at them. But Madog, he was going on.

'And then I looked down at the others near the ford. I hefted the axe. The axe is heavy. Hard to wield, but... Pin, he picked up my shield, and he came by me, and hoisted it to his shoulder. It looked a good bet against the archers. Then Marrec, he started to swing the sling, and the enemy, they were backing off.'

His arms spread wide in a gesture of surrender to fate. *'But well, there were archers, and Margan, he said we should back off while Tasgo was still walking. So we told them what we thought of them and their pissing ambush, and we left. I was going to bring the head back,'* he said regretfully, *'but in the end some-one had to carry Tasgo, so we left it behind.'*

Danny's mind stumbled over that. Tasgo needed carrying? All he had said was that the axe broke his shield. Danny looked at the axe, and the shattered table. He looked at Tasgo. Tasgo was looking back straight at him, watching him.

Kelly jabbed Danny in the ribs. 'You've stopped talking,' she complained quietly. 'It can't be that bad.'

Tasgo was still standing there, watching Danny, seeing his expression, just one week later. Could it have been that bad? He remembered the rainbow shoulder, the wound still stitched together. Kelly leaned closer and whispered, 'They're bragging. It's all for show.' He took his eyes off Tasgo and looked at her. She was looking out into the crowd, watching the faces, reading the reaction with modern civilised eyes.

'It was a skirmish, Kelly. At least two people died.' She turned to him. She looked into his eyes, and saw there the weight of what he had heard.

He saw her confidence in the bragging waver.

But Dugal had asked another question, and Tasgo turned to answer. *'Yes'* he was saying boldly, so that everyone could hear. *'Despite the paint, I recognised one of them. I met him at the market at Cynmar last summer.'* An angry murmur ran round the hall, and Tasgo raised his voice over it. *'It was Gorbeduc. From Cynmar. Those bastards…'*

Dugal's voice cut through *'…are our bastard allies,'* he finished. *'We owe allegiance to Cynmar. We have a pact with them. They've been honourable bastards, so far. They rely on our fighting force, they have always respected our warriors. So if that was one of their raiding parties, it is a serious matter.*

'Once we were sure that Aed would mend, and when we had gathered the farm folk, we set off to see what they thought of us now.'

Now the whole room became hushed. They knew their kinfolk had returned, safe and sound, but the whole story had yet to be put together.

'Gorbed lead his men out.' His smile was wide and wicked. *'They muster eight chariots, now, all two horse. We had better up our game.*

'But he was demanding blood money from us, for Gorbeduc's injuries after we attacked him for no reason. So I asked him if he counted sheep stealing and a baited trap as normal behaviour. You'll be glad to hear he doesn't.

'Gorbeduc had come back injured after being away some weeks. He said he had been set on by us when only passing through our area.

'When Margan and Marrec told how it really happened, Gorbed knew it for truth. Especially as Gorbeduc was not there to answer for his actions. When he heard we were on our way, he took one of the horses and ran'.

Dugal lifted his mug. *'So instead of trading blows we drank ale and mead and traded toasts.'*

It may have been a happier ending, but it was still an anti-climax. Dugal let it settle on them, but when they saw he was still standing, waiting, they settled down again.

'Gorbed feels let down by his son. And he has seen you fight Aed, so he is doubly angry your shield should be shattered. So,' he beckoned and Druston tottered forward with a shield incongruous in his arms, *'He has sent you this one. Light to carry, because he knows you are fast on your feet. Also, two iron bars. He thinks well of you. And for Marrec,*

with his missing teeth, a whole sack of wheat to make something he can swallow.' There was some laughter at this. He let it die down.

'Here,' he said, *'is where the news gets bad.'*

They leaned in, all ears. This was more like it.

'Gorbeduc is Gorbed's youngest son, and a trouble to his father. He mixes in bad company, he goes his own way. In the latest case on a horse that was not his own, and to the North and West. It seems Kuillok has been whispering in his ear, making him promises of a bright future.' A frisson ran through the crowd and the mention of this new name. The good humour of a tale well told vanished. Danny noticed glances thrown oddly at himself, eyes that darted away nervously.

'We are fortunate,' Dugal looked round at them all, gathering them together in his gaze. *'We have Gamma, to mend our wounds, to soothe our pain. Since she first came to us we have prospered. Even the Druids, when they visit, call her wise.*

'Kuillok is a creature of another sort. And it seems Gorbeduc is in his pay.'

Margan's voice called out, *'Bad judgement on both sides then!'* which drew a few sharp laughs.

Dugal let that ride, and when they were still, went on *'But this is more serious than that. More serious than a sneak attack on us. More serious than a local battle. This was more cowardly than a sneak attack. It was to make sure that we here were busy.'*

To Danny's surprise Dugal turned to him.

'Dannaigh, on the day of that attack, seven days past, what happened, Under the Hill?'

It was totally unexpected. He felt empty, outside it all. He didn't know what to say. When he just sat there, Dugal made a gesture for him to rise. So he stood up. He looked round. All eyes were on him. Then he remembered their conversation from earlier that evening. He took a deep breath so that his voice would not shake.

'Men painted blue attacked our house. The fought my parents. They destroyed the house.' He was unsure of the next bit, but took a leap of faith. *'They took my parents.'* As he said it, it felt good. Not dead, taken. If only it were true.

There was a deep silence. A stillness. Only the fire crackled, and flickered. Dugal held Danny in his gaze, motionless.

Somewhere at the far end of the room someone coughed. Then a voice came, apologetic, '*Underhill is – not for us.*' And from somewhere else '*We don't mess with...*'

Dugal said quietly, '*Tell them who your parents are Dannaigh,*' and again it was silent, as if something momentous was happening.

'*Freya,*' he said, his mouth feeling full, but knowing now that it was names they were after, '*and Tom*'. It felt as if the world were rolling away from him. If it had been silent before, there was no word for what it was now.

Across the table, Tasgo's face was changing. That confidence, the challenge, were fading from his face. It was a new Tasgo staring at him, with something close to disbelief.

Whatever was happening, going on in people's mind, what they were making out of this, was beyond Danny. He broke free of Dugal's gaze and looked at Gran. She nodded at him. She looked proud of him. What had he done?

Out of the silence Dugal said, '*There is more.*' He turned back to Tasgo. '*Aed, Tasgo, you were on the hill today, despite your wound. Why?*'

'*Cunedag and Bahee, and some of the small folk were keeping an eye on the sheep. They saw men on the hill.*'

'*Cunedag, always in the thick of it,*' said Dugal approvingly, '*Cunedag, tell us...*'

Cunedag was ready, eyes ablaze, with words almost faster than he could speak them. '*Round by the Ash grove. We saw men. Like the other ones. Two of them. They were running up the hill. I sent the girls back to Gamma, to tell her. They'd gone, the men, gone up the back of the hill, so I went round, a bit, so I could see, without getting close. Then there was another one, with horses. And the first ones, they were coming down fighting with someone, a woman. She was shouting a bit. And biting, and kicking, cos they had her arms. And then one of them hit her, and she stopped fighting, and then they carried her. And then Tasgo came and, Aed I mean, came and I waved, but they were running into the woods, they had her, the woman, over a horse, and they were two to a horse, and riding and...'* he had to pause for breath then. He would have carried on, but Dugal thanked him and turned to Tasgo, who continued for him.

'I saw them go into the trees. Mounted. I didn't see the woman. There may have been more in the wood, impossible to tell. And you had all the horses at Cynmar.'

'And you are not yet ready for fighting one against three, even if you could catch them,' agreed Dugal, turning to Danny again.

'Any guesses to the woman?' he asked calmly.

But Danny knew. It was no guess. *'That would be Moira,'* he told them.

From down the hall a fierce *'Bastards!'* broke the silence. And then the hall erupted. Everyone was shouting at once. Anger was a savage beast that filled them all. Fists shook. From nowhere it seemed, spears had appeared in hands. Men and women alike were on their feet.

Part of Danny felt cold and apart from it all. This was a war party in the making. It was madness in the making. He wanted no part in it.

The rest of him felt hot, and excited, and strong. They knew who had Moira, and they were going to get her back!

He felt Kelly get up beside him and take his arm.

'You're going to have to do some more translating,' she shouted in his ear. He could barely hear her over the tumult.

Chapter 18 - Encounters

Danny had lain awake long into the night, his head spinning, though that might have been the effect of the mead. His thoughts were all over the place.

When the shouting had at last died down, there had been questions asked, and some not answered. Kelly had been patient about the translating, or the lack of it, but he couldn't translate and also follow everything. Eventually the hubbub settled. Eventually people started putting things away and tidying up, and drifting off to bed.

The crowd thinned, until only a few stalwarts remained at the top end of the table, sat round it's wrecked planks, with the axe still embedded in it. By now he knew most of their names. Margan, Pinner, Madog, Marrec, and of course Tasgo, but there were others who had come in with the chariots. Jago and Bran Hen were two of them. As they talked reason annealed anger into plans. Some of which made sense to him, others which didn't.

They couldn't know that it was Kuillok who had his men take Moira. There seemed to him little evidence of that, and yet they all assumed it. They assumed it, but they were leaving a way out if they were wrong.

He tried to think it through.

Now that he was here, now that he knew about Moira's time portal, he could believe that a war party from this age had somehow got into his old house. How was another matter, one he set to one side for now. However they had come, that was how they went, taking his parents and much of the house with them.

It made going through the portal seem more hazardous than he liked to think.

Could Kuillok have done that? Did he have control of a time portal? Could a time portal be controlled? Gran had said, 'It just is.'

They were not sure exactly where Kuillok was, but that seemed to be the goal. First find him, then get Moira back, and maybe Freya and Tom too. With or without a battle. From the tone, with seemed to be their preferred route.

He didn't know who or what Kuillok was, but they all seemed to hate him.

His mother used to say, 'Hate is a waste of time.' Or, once, 'Hate is a bad use of good energy.' But he had never understood what that meant.

Dugal was snoring in the big bed next to him, long, slow, soft sounds. Or perhaps it was Gran who was snoring. Or even Kelly. The hut was full of little sounds. People turning over in their beds. The fire crackling. Somebody getting up and moving about before settling again. Even just the sound of so many people breathing, all in the one room. How could anyone fall asleep in that?

He woke with a start, in his own room in his old house, and it was full of smoke. Fire!

But as he jerked up, he saw the open doorway across a wide expanse, with the remnant of a fire in the middle. Someone was moving about quietly, adding wood to the fire, pouring water into a pot and swinging it in to place over new flames. His heart settled down.

It was all true. The blue flame, the round houses, everything. It hadn't been a dream. Here was where he was.

There were sleeping bodies everywhere. He felt achy, as though he had been ill, and yet full of energy. He struggled out from under a weight of skins, and stood. It was smokier higher up, and he needed a pee. He needed fresh air. He remembered what Tasgo had said about always having a weapon at hand, and picked up the broom handle that had slept beside him all night.

He tiptoed through the sleeping bodies. Eles was looking after the fire and pouring something into a pot. She ignored him completely.

A huge mound on one of the trestles proved to be Madog wrapped in a gaudy cloth, and fast asleep.

He ducked under the lintel and out into a grey dawn, and rain.

He hadn't come wearing a coat of course. He was going to get wet. He hurried round to the toilet Kelly had used the night before.

Fortunately it was not already in use, but it was totally open to the sky, and he sat there getting wetter. Also fortunate, it was not as cold as he expected. But not as warm as he would have liked.

The advantage was that he could look around and see what was going on, because there were others about already. Someone was stacking poles into one of the chariots that still stood in the open space near the track. Another was hauling a heavy basket towards them. He could hear horses snickering in the distance, and some talking, far off, the sound softened by the steady patter of rain.

It all had a sleepy unreal feel.

By the time he had finished he was as wet as he could possibly be. His clothes stuck to him, cold and wet. The warmth of the hut was inviting, but he thought it was about time that he took stock of his surroundings. To keep warm, he jogged past the looms, the big hut, past the next, smaller hut, also with smoke rising hazily from the whole roof. There were people moving outside the next one, but they looked at him strangely so he kept going. There were more huts than he expected, tucked in against the rise of the hill so that he hadn't seen them before.

Then there were things he had only seen in open air museums. A couple of ruined kilns, larger than he expected, and a muddy lean-to with tools and pots layered in shelves under the cover. Then the ground darkened around the next building, with walls of stone. It was still round, but the roof was of turf. The sturdy door had been put aside next to the opening, so he went over and looked in.

Heat swelled out, and a swarthy misshapen man swung belligerently towards him. He was short, and broad, but more importantly there was a large hammer in his hands and anger on his face. Danny took a step back. The man stayed where he was. He looked Danny up and down.

'*What d'you want?*' he growled.

'*Nothing,*' said Danny. *'Just to see'*

'Well we don't need your muck.'

Danny stayed where he was, rain running down his face. Then he said, *'That's not very friendly.'* Just to try it out.

A pause, then the hammer lowered.

'Well, you can look. But don't touch.'

'Can I come in?'

'This once.'

And Danny stepped in – to a workshop. It had the feel of his father's basement. Everything had its place, but there was so much of it, it seemed higgledy piggle. There was everything you could need, given no electricity. There were saws and axes, and hammers with straight and bent heads, and a load of other things he couldn't recognise. There were also shaped antlers, and tools made of bronze, and a whole rack of sickles, some with teeth and others without. At the near end were several plain bars of metal.

Its guardian was watching him with suspicion. The hammer was still in his hand. But the room was warm and dry, and Danny could feel the chill seeping out of him.

'What makes it so warm here?' he asked.

The man scowled as if this were some sort of trick.

'The fire,' he offered, cautiously.

'I don't see a fire.'

The man considered this for a long moment. Then decided to answer.

'Outside.' And he jerked his head towards the wall behind him.

Danny stood in the warm and dry. He could go out into the rain and look, but instead he asked *'This warm comes through the wall?'* The man looked at him as if he were an idiot, and nodded slowly. *'It must be a big fire,'* suggested Danny, beginning to feel foolish.

The man nodded, testing the weight of the hammer against his palm ominously. *'Thanks for letting me see,'* said Danny, backing out into the cold of the rain.

Round the back of the workshop was a forge. It was set back from the workshop, and everything about it was black and sooted. The fire bed was raised from the ground on rocks. It was still hot enough that the rain sizzled as it hit the remains of the fire.

Beyond it in a wood fenced field, Marrec was checking the horses, lifting the foot of one to examine it closer. It leaned in on him, its big head glistening with rain over his shoulder. More people were moving about, it was beginning to be a bustle.

It was warm by the forge though. He watched, thinking it would be too wet to go looking for Moira today.

'Are you really Toma's son?'

Tasgo had come up on him from behind. The question was a challenge he didn't think worth answering. Tasgo stood beside him and shrugged. Now Danny knew how bad the shoulder was, he could see that Tasgo was testing it. After a silence Tasgo said, *'Can you fend off a sword with that spear?'*

Good question. He looked at the broom handle. His father had said that it would. Gran had said he should never lie while here. *'I've never tried,'* he said.

'You've never tried,' echoed Tasgo. Was that contempt or challenge in his eyes as he turned to face Danny? Danny looked at him. There was nothing of Grant about Tasgo. Grant was pain and anger. Tasgo was swagger and jokes. As Tasgo opened his mouth to speak Danny said,

'You're hurt. I won't fight you.' Anger flash in the other's eyes. Suddenly that seemed funny. Him and Tasgo having to vie with each other. It may be largely swagger, but Tasgo was coming from way ahead. Tasgo had taken on some huge man with a giant axe. Danny threw his arms wide, with a grin. *'I'm not getting beaten up by you when you're injured. How would that look?'*

That took Tasgo by surprise.

'It'd look like I am so much better than you! As I am.' he proclaimed. But he was grinning too.

And then Cunedag, wet and bedraggled, was rushing through the rain, straight at them.

'Come on, you two!' He warbled, grabbing Danny's sleeve *'they're waiting! Where have you been? Dugal wants you! Now!'*

What now, thought Danny as they ran back towards the main hut, and Cunedag confided, small boy to man, as they ran, *'Kelyn is angry with you! She's very angry.'*

Just as well to be warned thought Danny.

But as he entered the hut she was as much relieved to see him as angry. And she was wearing a woollen tunic over her other clothes. The pale blue suited her he thought, as she turned and railed at him.

'Where have you been! I thought you'd been - taken or something. That you'd gone!'

'Gone for a pee?' he said mildly. No need to tell her the rest.

'You might have said.'

A surly looking youth, maybe a bit older than Danny, but about the same size, was approaching, hands full of cloth. *'I'm to give you this,'* he said, with bad grace, shoving them at Danny. Danny saw that they were a tunic and leggings. Obviously the boy's own.

'Thanks' he said. *'Would you like mine? When they're dry.'*

That changed the boy's expression, He looked down at the t-shirt Danny was wearing, at the jeans. A mixture of emotions were running through his face.

Danny didn't wait to find which one would win, he dragged the wet tee over his head and held it out. The lad grabbed it and pushed his replacement at Danny. It felt soft and warm. He wasn't too sure about the blue and cream check pattern, but it pulled over his head easily and hung rather too loosely round him. A leather strap round it dealt with that. The woollen cloth brought immediate comfort and warmth.

The lad was shaking out the t-shirt, looking at the colours, feeling the cloth. For the moment at least both of them seemed more than satisfied with the swop. Danny was looking around for a suitable place to take off the wet jeans which were clinging to him, when Dugal left off talking to some of the other men and came over. Gran was busy folding some cloth with Eles.

'Good,' said Dugal, looking at the tunic. He smiled. *'You look good in this, a real warrior.'* Behind him the lad whose tunic Danny was wearing was pulling off his leggings, without any regard for privacy. Dugal was going on, *'We'll get you a cloak and a couple of spears of the right length. We leave in mid-day.'*

That caught Danny off guard. He had thought, with the weather, that they would have a day or so. Dugal was already walking away.

'Stop!' Danny called, *'wait!'*

A dozen heads turned towards him in surprise, or was it shock? Dugal turned back, looking a bit surprised himself.

'Are we all going?' Danny demanded.

'All who can fight.'

'No,' said Danny, *'it's a mistake.'*

He could tell at once it was the wrong thing to say. People were staring at him, not in a good way. Dugal wasn't looking too pleased either. Gran put down what she was doing and started towards him.

Danny went on quickly, *'We may have misunderstood. Why the men were there.'* Dugal had come closer, he was listening. *'Two men on the hill. Two men on the hill yesterday, and two men on the hill seven days ago. Perhaps they were there to watch the hill.'*

Dugal cocked his head, thinking. *'It was a trap, bait for a trap, seven days ago.'*

'Or they were holding the ford as a safe retreat,' Danny said. *'When the two men were discovered they pretended to be after the sheep. Really they were watching the hill. When they had to run, then the ford became a trap.'*

He could see that Dugal needed evidence. *'The archers were too far away from the ambush. They weren't meant as an ambush, they were guarding the ford. And when it was over, the men came back here. This time with horses in the wood.'*

'Danny,' said Gran firmly, *'you don't know anything about fighting. Dugal has...'*

'Yes I do!' Danny snapped back. He played a dozen strategy games on the internet. He was always on the leader board. It wasn't the same as being in a battle, but this wasn't a battle, it was strategy.

Dugal said, doubtfully *'Your father taught you to think like this? Toma?'*

No, the computer games taught him this, but they wouldn't understand that.

He said *'Yes.'*

A moment's pause.

'Why?' asked Dougal. *'Why watch the hill?'*

Danny hadn't had time to think it all through. But he knew what the men had done. *'To catch one of us. To find the – the magic place. To take Moira.'*

'Then we need to get after them and get Moira back.'

'Yes. But also, we need to guard the hill.' He sensed resistance. *'We need to guard the hill, because otherwise they can go through to our world. They could attack our world. And you know it is not ready for that.'*

Dugal understood.

He turned and looked at the men, they looked back.

'Aed, Jago, Madog, Cunedag.' He beckoned, they came. Cunedag's eyes were shining to be included. Dugal started with him.

'Cunedag, you will go to Cynmar, and tell them that we are going up the North road to find Kuillok and to free Moira. You tell them politely that we would be honoured if they were to join us. Marrec will take you on his horse. He will leave you there, and when you know how many warriors Gorbed has sent to help, then you will return here, and tell Aed, Tasgo.'

Tasgo startled. *'I go North and west, with you.'*

'Yes, you will. But not until Cunedag comes back. I need to know the numbers. You travel faster than any other. It gives you another day to heal. And you can decide. If Cynmar sends a big force, we will not need Jago and Madog. They can stay here, guard the hill, and Madog can do what he does best. Make more spear tips.'

Tasgo was not happy, but he stayed silent if sullen. Dugal went on, *'Jago, set up a watch on the hill from the Ash grove, Leir can help there. Madog, be ready, but make us more spears if you can.'* Then he turned to Danny. *'You stay here Danny, you and Tasgo will train the youngsters while you wait for Cunedag to get back.'*

Danny didn't think that was such a good idea. For a start he had never been in a real fight, one with weapons and real damage done. And he couldn't see Tasgo working with him. But he guessed it was better to just shut up.

Then everyone was moving, getting things done. And the lad holding Danny's t-shirt was standing bare legged waiting. Danny looked down. The blue and white checked tunic came down over his thighs, so he eased off his trainers, dropped his trousers, stepped out of them and handed them over, and started to pull on the woollen leggings. They caught against his damp skin, so he had to hop about a bit, and the other boy, who was maybe a bit older than him, but no bigger, was having the same problem.

Kelly had turned away to hide a smile, and Gran was giving her orders to help the women with something.

It turned out easier to hold onto one of the posts to put on the trousers, and while doing it Danny learned that this lad was Leir, Marrec's son, and that he was looking forward to some training from Toma's son. The jeans transformed him from ancient to modern. True the tunic would be unusual, but in a shopping centre he would just look stylish. Then he ripped off his tunic and pulled on the t-shirt, still wet. He had muscles. And marks. He saw Danny looking, and explained the white scars on his shoulder as a bite from a difficult horse.

The t-shirt was a little tight on him, but he looked good. Danny told him so, but added that he'd get a bit cold. Leir shrugged, and danced about a bit getting used to the feel of the new clothes, while some of the small kids giggled. He stopped dancing and made some epic poses for their enjoyment, just like some of the showier kids back at school might have, before pulling the tunic back on over the top.

Danny was finding the leggings just a little scratchy, tight in some places and loose in others. They only reached down to his calves. Thankfully he was wearing long socks.

By now all of the men had gone, including Tasgo, and it seemed Kelly had been put on kitchen duties with the other women.

Danny went to the door and looked out. It was still raining. There was a lot of movement out there. He would have liked to get out and see what was going on, but he didn't want to get his new tunic wet. Not straight away.

Suddenly Leir was beside him, with what looked like a horse blanket. He threw it over Danny's shoulders and made a gesture that he should put it over his head. Leir himself now had an impressive looking cloak, striped in lots of soft warm colours.

Danny pulled the blanket over his head, wrapped the rest close round him trying hard not to notice the horsey smell, and stepped out. He was just in time to see Marrec pass by on a prancing pony, spear tucked somehow into the cloth he was sitting on. Bundled in front of him like a parcel, Cunedag was still waving his hands excitedly. Leir waved back as they went out of the compound at a fast trot and off down the track.

Both Chariots were now in place, and a number of horses had been bridled and were lined up along a rail. The spears had been sorted into groups and attached to the insides of the chariots where they would be out of the way, but right to hand.

Shields were stacked upright in a line. Everyone was on the move fetching and carrying, no-one was giving any orders.

Tasgo stood out in his bright orange cloak, thrown back off his head. He went down on one knee to talk to a child, who then went skittering away dodging through what was becoming a crowd. He saw Leir and came over, recognising Danny only as he got close, and then choosing to ignore him. *'Leir,'* he said, *'we'll drill as soon as this lot have gone. It's a big ask for you, but can you choose two leaders for your guard post? They are all young, so you need cool heads, and brave. I'll tell Jago you have it in hand?'*

Leir nodded, speechless with pride and responsibility.

'Drill first, then you can take your leaders up to Jago,' finished Tasgo. Still ignoring Danny, he turned to look through the throng, and then darted away towards Dugal where he stood talking with Margan, and keeping an eye on preparations.

Danny walked away, towards the kilns and workshop. Leir loped along beside him, like a friendly dog. Only when they approached the workshop did he began to put a little space between them, and he seemed relieved when Danny stopped well short of the doorway.

'Who is that man?' asked Danny.

'It's Madog's store.' Of course thought Danny, the blacksmith's work room. But not Madog inside it.

'But who is the man?'

'Brec? He's Madog's.'

'He's Madog's? Madog's what?'

Leir looked puzzled. *'Madog's man. He works iron. Almost as good as Madog. He's strong.'*

'He works for Madog?' said Danny, thinking perhaps he was missing something.

'Bad tempered bastard' Leir agreed happily, and turned away to the flat section of matted grass between the houses and the shore.

'This is where we drill. Sometimes Dugal comes and plays at fighting us.'

'You drill every day?' asked Danny, thinking that was rather hard.

'Most days,' Leir told him. *'Slings one day, spears the next. Toma taught us hand fighting. Your father was good.'* Danny shivered. His father, here. And where was he now? He forced himself to shut down the thought.

'How long do you spend training?'

'Lots,' said Leir striking a pose. *'All day!'* striking another.

'Really?'

Leir tossed his poses aside, *'Not really. We've just had planting, so not so much. Sometimes a whole morning. When Tasgo thinks we aren't taking it serious he can be hard. He jokes, but he takes fighting serious.'*

'That's why he's so good,' Danny said, testing Leir's reaction. Tasgo certainly thought he was.

'I'd rather be a horseman,' said Leir. *'Horses are good for lots of things. Travel and ploughing, as well as fighting. We have a wagon for harvest.'* He was bragging now, thought Danny.

A commotion at the other end of the village caught their attention. *'They're going!'* shouted Leir, and took a few skipping steps towards them then waited to see what Danny would do. Danny took his cue, and they ran back together.

Horses were being backed up to chariots, women were kissing men and men were hefting bags on to their shoulders. A train of women came out from the hut carrying bags, and the smell of hot wheat cakes mixed with the scent of horse and dung. Chickens were squawking, small children were getting under foot. Food parcels were being stuffed into carry bags, everyone was talking at once.

Suddenly Kelly cannoned into him, grabbing his arm in a fierce grip! 'Are you going!' she screamed at him, 'Are you going with them!'

Danny staggered under her attack, 'No!' he yelled back, and she subsided, just like that. And then she apologised. 'I thought you were going with them,' she explained unnecessarily. And when he just looked at her uncomprehending she went on. 'I thought you were leaving me behind with your Gran.'

When that didn't seem to enlighten him either she went on. 'She won't let me go up to the cave. She says it's far too dangerous for me to go back through the flame on my own, and she's been ordering me around like I'm her servant or something. If she tells me what to do one more time...'

A horn blew a wild rhythm and cut her off. A sudden flurry of movement, and Dugal was on a horse, looking around. The horn blew another blast. There was sudden separation between those who were going and those who weren't.

A third blast of the horn, and they were off, horse and chariots together, Dugal in the lead, men and women on foot following, a steady unhurried exodus, down the track that led from the village.

As the last of them left the compound, Tasgo shouted.

'*Any one able to fight, get your spear and come with me.*' He bent towards a lad who only came to his waist and continued, '*You too!*'

There was a laugh at that. No sign of Madog, or Jago either.

Tasgo looked across at Danny. '*Come on,*' he said, '*Dugal says we are to instruct them together. Are you sword or spear? Or bare hands.*'

Danny thought Tasgo already had the answer to that one, but raised his broom handle in response. Leir and Kelly fell in on either side of him as he started to follow.

Kelly said in a worried voice, 'Are you going to fight him Danny? He'll wallop you.' On his other side, Leir was skipping with joy.

Chapter 19 - Training

Danny was surprised at the number of girls who had come down to the practise area. Perhaps, like Kelly they were only there to watch.

By the time they got there two groups had formed. The very young with the old or incapacitated, and the rest, including women. Every one of them held a spear. It soon became apparent that none of them were spectators.

Tasgo was already standing in the centre, between the two groups. Danny walked with Kelly and Leir to the edge of the larger group. He felt uncomfortable. Why had Dugal thought he could teach these people anything? Leir folded his cloak and put it aside on a stone so Danny took the horse blanket off and hung it over a post.

Tasgo was enjoying himself. He held up a hand, and the chatter died away.

'*Our best warriors are gone,*' he said, hardly raising his voice. They had to listen hard to catch his words. '*It's up to us to defend the village. And it may need defending. We will all stay close to home, and keep watch.*

'*You all know how to use a spear. Dannaigh and I will show you effective it can be,*' he beckoned to Danny, and Danny walked out meekly to stand beside him. Standing there, looking at all the faces looking at him, he knew he had been set up, whether by Tasgo, or by Dugal hardly mattered.

Sooner or later it was going to be a fight, between him and Tasgo, and Tasgo would win. Easily. Even with his injured shoulder.

But he wasn't going to play the game. He wasn't going to stand there looking into Tasgo's eyes, each daring the other to do their worst. He could have thrown down his broom handle and walked away, but they would just think him a coward. Besides, he knew he had a lot to learn, and this was obviously going to be where he learned it.

So he stood beside Tasgo, a pace or so away, looking in the same direction as him. He looked out at the empty field where the horses had been, and then down at the ground a few yards away. From there he could see Tasgo, his general shape and the position of his feet. The rain fell steadily, pitting the ground, soaking through his new wool tunic.

Tasgo unfastened his cloak. '*It rains on battles too,*' he said, '*but so close to home, you won't need a cloak. It will tie you up, it will slow you down. If you have no shield, you can use it, so...*' In a quick swirl he had it wrapped round his left arm which he held across him as he would a shield.

He must have loosened the tie on his sword earlier, and now he plucked it from its cords. In his hand it looked shorter than Danny had expected.

Tasgo held it nonchalantly, explaining how it was not just for stabbing but for cutting or slashing. And as he said it he swung it negligently toward Danny's chest.

The broom handle caught it near the hilt, Danny felt the jar as it hit. The sword bounced off, and he felt rather than saw a shift in Tasgo's stance. But Tasgo's voice did not waver.

He went on explaining that the spear would stop a blade, but to lessen the chance of it weakening the spear too much it was best to meet it at an angle, so that the cut was less deep and the blade would bounce along the spear to a new spot.

This time there was power behind the blow, but again Danny caught it, felt the wood shiver under the blow, felt the sword bounce and strike again, lightly. When he had practised with his father it was always just with staves. He had never warded a sharp blade. Of course not, that would be stupid, and dangerous. It was different, it felt different. He remembered to hold the broom handle firmly but lightly, his hands ready to slide along the shaft.

Tasgo had turned a little towards him as he continued his comments, but Danny stood where he was, head bowed, every nerve now focussed on Tasgo, his hands, his feet, the tension in his body. Each slash cut into the broom handle, leaving a mark. Once the bouncing blade nearly caught his hand. He was beginning to get a feel for how the sword would react, how the swordsman would have to move. Rain made the wood slick, and he tightened his hold a little.

But each blow was getting heavier, and now it was not enough to just swirl the pole to catch the blows, he had to take the weight, withstand the pressure. These things he already knew. It was the speed he had not been expecting. Blow on blow. Tasgo had given up speaking. The blows rained down, and sometime up, from all angles, time and again, relentlessly.

And then Tasgo turned as he slashed, and his sword leapt as if of its own will from right hand to left and was coming down again, swift and sharp.

Danny leapt back, dropping the handle.

Tasgo stopped dead, his face full of astonishment. '*What sort of move is that?*' he snapped.

'*Don't use your left hand,*' said Danny, and added a polite, '*Please*' though that wasn't going to help.

'*You can't defend against the left hand!*' Tasgo was contemptuous.

'*No,*' said Danny as calmly as he could, '*Gamma will have my hide if you open your wound again.*'

A shock of laughter from the crowd. For a moment Danny thought Tasgo was going to take it badly, the sword was rock steady. But then Tasgo eased back and came out of attack mode. He tossed the blade to his right hand and swirled the sword with his wrist. '*Well*', he said mockingly, '*if it will save you from Gamma... But not a move to make in front of the enemy.*'

They laughed again, and Danny was aware of the tension that had been in the crowd.

Tasgo was turning now, taking in every face. '*This is all defensive*' he said. '*For these few days that is what we need.*' In an aside to Danny he added, '*Pick up your spear.*' Then went on addressing the others. '*But even so, defensive is never all you need.*'

He had not checked that Danny was ready, but with his next words, '*When an enemy attacks,*' he whirled, his arm out wide to the side ready to slash. Danny saw how wide he was making it, took a side step out of the way, and brought the end of the broom round under the arm with such speed that he hardly managed to stop it as it just touched Tasgo's ribs. Tasgo had seen it coming, and not tried to avoid it, and now his eyes met Danny's with a smile. He had frozen in position, so Danny did too.

Tasgo was saying, *'See how the staff is in position to defend against the blade if he missed me.'*

Then turning again to face them, *'We have only three swords here, so most of you will fight spear against spear. One of you will attack only, and the other will defend. Try not to break any heads. Or spears. Then swop over.*

'Leir, use a sword. Attack with the back edge only, and not Kelyn.' Leir gave a little leap, and thrusting his spear for Kelly to hold, he dashed across to a bench, where the two other swords were. One of the men with the children and old folk was picking up the other.

As the crowd expanded to fill the space and spears began to be brandished, Tasgo turned to Danny. *'Your Staff has no point,'* he said, *and it's too thick and heavy. You couldn't throw it far.'*

'But if I did, then I wouldn't have it any more,' countered Danny. Running his hands down the shaft he could feel how badly it had been cut.

'I'll get you a proper spear.' Tasgo went on as if he hadn't spoken. *'You need to change your fighting style or you'll lose a hand. Meanwhile, can you make sure the little ones know how well placed they are for groins, shins and feet.'*

He gestured over to where the man with the sword was trying to marshal the youngsters, and one exuberant child was lashing about with his stick, hitting any and everything within reach. Danny was relieved to see that only the old folk had real spears, and most of the children had nothing more than thin sticks.

He moved towards them dutifully, wondering how you tell young kids where hitting you will really hurt, without getting really hurt.

It helped that they all looked up in something like awe when he moved over to them. Considering he had never been in a real fight, and his only knowledge of sword play had been in the last fifteen minutes, he thought awe was a little misplaced.

He used the man with the sword as an example when pointing out areas of vulnerability, and then took charge of the lad who just wanted to hit everything.

He couldn't have been more than five years old, but he could thwack hard. Danny's only way of getting him under control was to put him on the defensive.

Slow and obvious attacks were no help. Inevitably he ended up hitting the poor kid quite hard, knocking him over. There were no squalls or tears, Danny was afraid he had done some real harm. Alarmed he went to see what damage had been done and what comfort was needed.

He found the boy was a quick learner on points of vulnerability.

He was glad when it was all over, and not much later either. His shoulders were already aching when Tasgo called a halt.

'Remember,' Tasgo proclaimed loudly, *'when the enemy runs at you screaming, face hard with hate, that is when you gauge how he is going to attack, high or low. Stand firm. Decide whether to defend or thrust. His next scream may be his last.*

'Keep a weapon by you at all times,' was his last command, and the meeting broke up. Some of the youngsters stayed on practising strokes, but it seemed everyone else had something to do, somewhere to be.

Kelly sauntered over to Danny, spear in hand looking very much the warrior maid. 'When did you have time to practise that?' she asked

'What?'

'That fight with Tasgo. It was hilarious.'

Hilarious? Danny looked at her, she didn't look as if she was joking.

'He made you look, like, what -? A Ninja warrior, standing there all calm and distant and fending off all his moves without breaking a sweat, hardly moving.'

Hot sweat was still trickling down his back, rain was a cooling freshness on his face. Kelly didn't seem to notice any of this. 'Where did you learn to do all that?' she was asking blithely.

He went over to get the horse blanket and wrap it round him before he started to get cold.

Leir bounded over to them, full of himself. *'You hold a spear well now,'* he told Kelly, and Danny translated. Kelly laughed. 'Tasgo's a good teacher, but I wouldn't say 'well'. At least I don't drop it when he hits it now.'

And then she smiled over Danny's shoulder, and there was Tasgo coming towards them. That was all Danny needed. He drew the blanket round him, feeling suddenly cold.

Kelly turned back to him starting to say something, but then she stopped, and her face changed,

'Danny,' she said, 'are you all right? There's blood on your – cloak.'

Danny looked down. There was a smear of blood across one side of the cloak. He pulled it up to see better, and there was another smear where his hand had been, and another where he had just been holding it.

And on the broom stick. Rain was running red down the wood. He turned his free hand over and the palm and fingers were bright with blood. He dropped the stick and looked at the other palm. Crimson.

Kelly's little cry of alarm brought Tasgo quickly to their side. He saw Kelly's alarmed face, and then Danny's red hands. He looked down quickly at the broomstick, where it was staining the ground red. Nonplussed, he looked into Danny's face, finding mostly surprise there.

There was a stillness about him, and then he asked cautiously *'Is this a problem?'* glancing down at the stick as if that might be where the problem lay.

The blood was so thick on Danny's hands that it was impossible to see where it was coming from. There were no deep cuts that he could see, and his hands still had a sort of numb tingling from the vibration of the wood during the fighting.

Where the raindrops hit, they left circles of ordinary skin, before the blood flowed back in. *'It's only a bit of blood'* said Danny, but he felt strange.

Tasgo took command. Danny was not surprised. *'Come,'* said Tasgo to Danny and then *'Bring the spear,'* to Kelly and Leir, as if it were beneath him to pick it up. Grabbing Danny by the arm he hurried him down towards the edge of the grass, where it made a mini cliff of a few feet down to the boulders below. Behind them Leir looked reluctantly at the bloody stick and made no move to pick it up. Kelly had seen the gesture though, and grabbed it and followed, with Leir trailing her.

Danny was getting a little tired of being given orders. He remembered what Kelly had said only a few hours earlier, about his Gran. But Tasgo seemed to be taking the blood on his hands seriously, so he went without protest.

Below the grass, big boulders edged a pebble beach, but to their left some rougher rocks pointed out into the water, and Tasgo was heading for these, throwing the trailing edges of his cloak over his shoulders, to make sure they stayed out of the puddles. He kept a firm hand on Danny's arm as they reached the rocks, and clambered to a rock pool out of reach of the waves.

There they stopped. *'Wash your hands in the blessed sea,'* he commanded, pointing at the pool. The blessed sea, noted Danny, but he knelt and dipped his cold hands in the colder water. The pool turned pink as he washed his hands, and the salt stung.

But as he took his hands out of the water, things became obvious. Apart from two burst blisters, there were dozens of tiny cuts filling up again with blood. Now that he knew they were cut, his hands hurt! But that might just have been the salt in the water.

Tasgo looked at Danny's hands suspiciously, then told Kelly, who had come up behind them, to throw the stick into the water.

Danny didn't bother to explain, but took it from her and tossed it into the pool, where it floated in its own deeper pink cloud. And since wood swells when wet, he put his hands back in and wiped the blood off it, feeling every nick and sharp sliver in it, and took it out again.

'Does it still bleed?' demanded Tasgo.

Danny looked at him. He was serious.

'It's a stick,' said Danny. *'Just a stick. With a lot of sharp edges on it.'* It was more sharp edges than solid. It no longer resembled a broom handle. And he had been running his hands up and down it with speed, for some time. There were splinters in his palms as well as cuts.

Tasgo looked at the hands, and then looked at Danny with a strange expression on his face. Danny recognised it at once. He had been wearing that expression for the last week, ever since the world shook itself out and showed it to be something different from what he had always thought it was.

'Your hands are as soft as a new-born child's,' said Tasgo, looking into Danny's eyes as if searching for something. Then tentatively, as if stretching the boundaries of possibility, he said, *'That really was the first time you have fended a sword, wasn't it?'*

Danny nodded, noting with interest that it was possible to see the blood drain from someone's face. Whatever Tasgo was thinking, it was life changing.

But Tasgo took it well, he glanced at Kelly and at Leir, who were watching. Kelly had obviously realised that something serious was going on, and was somehow managing not to ask for translations. When Tasgo said, *'We'll go back to Gamma, she'll have something for the cuts,'* his voice was very close to normal. He didn't help Danny clamber back over the rocks. Kelly took the stick from Danny and carried it, carefully, as they started to walk back.

Kelly whispered, 'What did he say?'

'Gamma will do something for the cuts.'

'Before that.' She hissed.

'He hadn't realised I hadn't defended against a blade before.'

She stopped. 'Don't you lie to me Danny Sharp!'

But Danny was too tired to argue, and just kept walking. So she caught up, obviously angry again, and strode beside him, not talking too.

As they crossed the practise ground, where some of the older children were still practising, Tasgo turned to Danny.

'You are your father's son,' he said. It sounded like an apology.

Danny had no idea what that meant.

Chapter 20 - Early Morning

He had slept like a log, and woke in velvet darkness that smelt of smoke and animal skins and people. It felt normal.

His second night in an impossible past. He lay there re-assessing 'impossible'. All that he had to do to change impossible to possible, was to believe in a time portal. Since he had passed through one, it seemed logical to believe in it. If true, all he had to do was learn to accept life in prehistory. His hands felt stiff from all of the little cuts. His shoulders ached from exercise, but it was a pleasant ache.

The alternatives to a time portal were not promising, but he put some time into sorting them out.

Firstly, he might have taken a bang on the head when the house exploded, and could be lying in a hospital bed in a coma, dreaming all this. He flexed his hands and felt the tiny scars cracking. He had a good imagination, but surely not this good.

Or, the house had not in fact exploded, but he had had some catastrophic brain episode, and was imagining all this. In which case also, his imagination would have to be epic. But if it were true, then he would be lying on a hospital bed with his mother and his father on either side, willing him to wake up. He spent a little while imagining this and trying desperately to wake up. It obviously wasn't going to happen.

Or the house had exploded, and he and Kelly had found the hidden cave and the blue fire, but when it had dragged him into it... Well, if he were dead, it didn't matter what was happening here, he was already dead, and he might as well get on with things as if he weren't. And if he wasn't, well the same was true.

He had no idea what time it was.

He lay for a while thinking, and then sat up.

The only light was from the remains of the fire, a dull glow.

Tonight the only snoring came from the distant reaches of the hut. He thought of Tasgo, with that wound to his shoulder, rushing around organising things. Tasgo slashing at him with that sword, the power behind it.

Then, while Danny had been sitting in the hut being scolded by his Gran and having his hands rubbed with a ghastly smelling ointment to help them mend fast, Tasgo had taken Leir up to the Ash wood, where-ever that was, and Kelly had gone with them.

She reported that Jago had set up a sort of hide on the edge of the wood, with a view of the whole of the other side of the hill. There were some other spots nearby where the teams could hang out, within shouting or running distance from the hide.

She seemed surprised at how seriously the youngsters were taking it. Danny's shins were still smarting from how seriously they had taken it at practise, but he said nothing.

The words that kept coming back to haunt him were, 'You are your father's son.'

He pulled on his shoes and got up. The door was obviously still in place, either that or it was still inky dark outside. There were fewer people in the hut now, with so many of the men, and some of the women, gone. Many of those that remained were sleeping in other huts. He made his way slowly to the fire, trying not to trip over or knock anything.

The embers were still hot, but there were only two blackened bits of wood left, glowing gently when the air stirred them. He nudged them closer together, and found a few more remnants near the edge of the pit and pushed them into the centre. Everyone was asleep but him. The fire wakened a few flames for him.

What he needed, he thought, was to be on his own for a bit. To test what was real. He got up from the fire and made his way towards where he thought the door would be. When at last he reached it, the door itself was so much in darkness that he had to feel to find how it was held in place.

There were two bars of wood across it, and he had to slide them carefully across, only too aware of the rasping sound. And then the door itself was heavier than he expected, and he knocked something in trying to move it.

A voice from somewhere near him suddenly called out '*Who?*'

'Only me. Dannaigh,' he whispered.

'What're you doing?' was the gist of the reply.

'Going for a pee?' suggested Danny.

'You can piss in here.'

'Didn't want to piss ON someone,' said Danny.

There was a grunt, then, *'Shut the door after you.'*

Which he did, leaning it in place where before it had been barred.

Outside it was lighter than he had expected. The rain had stopped, which was just as well since he had neglected to bring the horse blanket. It was probably still damp anyway, unlike his tunic which had dried in the warmth of his bed.

Clouds drifted slowly across a sky brilliant with stars. Though shadowy and monochrome there was enough light to see where he was going, so long as he stayed out in the open. He walked down past the huts to the exercise ground, and then on down to the sea.

The tide had come in, and the place where he had washed his hands was being washed by the sea. Was that what was meant by 'blessed sea', that it washed all things clean? Had Tasgo really thought that his stick was bleeding? He stood listening to the lap of the waves, feeling the breeze on his face, cool not cold. Out over the sea the sky was beginning to lighten.

If he tried hard he could work out where the sea wall would be built, where the quay would be. One day, in a couple of thousand years from now.

Looking back the whole village was a dark shadow against the trees. Nothing more. He felt very alone. And free. Alive. More alive than any other time – except for when he had been running, and had turned, and seen that his mother was not there, and then everything had exploded.

What he ought to do, he decided with sudden urgent resolve, was to go and find the hide from which they were watching the hill, to see for himself what they had arranged. If only he knew where the Ash Grove was.

The thing to do would be to walk along the edge of the wood, keeping close to the trees, so he would not alarm anyone.

As he passed like a shadow through the village, one of the women was up, and walking down towards the stream with a bucket. He didn't think she noticed him as he slipped into the darkness of the trees.

A small track, hard to make out in the gloom, took him up and through the trees to open land. Light was stronger now, the long lines of new green growth showing how the field had been planted.

At the edge of the wood trees leaned out into the open air, and there was space for him to walk in their shadow. Birds were beginning to sing as the light increased. He felt as if he were alone in the world, and for once that felt good.

The trees filled the valley, but beyond the fields above them the hill was open and wild, and as he walked along the edge of the sown, more and more of the back of the hill became exposed. He was trying to remember what Ash trees looked like, because this was beginning to look like a good spot to watch from.

The hide turned out to be simple thing, a few branches laid against a fallen tree, enough to make a covered hollow. Inside, Leir had propped himself against the tree where he could see the whole hill, and, wrapped in a warm blanket, was now fast asleep.

Danny stood for a while, wondering whether to wake him, then moved off to sit on a log amongst a group of saplings, hoping that the young leaves might disguise his blue and cream tunic as dappled light.

The wood was full of life. It smelt damp after the rain, and of rotting leaves and soft wood smells. Small birds flitted through the trees, the earth was bursting with new growth. It was spring, he realised. Two days ago it had been early October in a town, and now it was spring in the countryside. Life was full of surprises.

He sat and kept watch for Leir, not just of the hill, but also of the wood. Someone was bound to turn up sooner or later to relieve Leir, and they wouldn't be pleased to find him asleep.

Time passed. Birds accepted him as part of the forest and flew close by. Something small snuffled through the leaves and darted for cover when he moved to see what it was. He felt strangely whole.

Then a twig cracked, and he saw a movement through the trees, someone coming up through the wood, walking quietly, appearing and disappearing behind the trees as he came. Danny kept very still, until

Jago was walking into full view. He hadn't noticed Danny, at a wide angle to his approach to the hide. The young leaves and Danny's stillness seemed to work.

He waited until Jago was almost at the hide and then said quietly, *'Don't wake him.'*

Jago whirled, *'Who?'* on his lips, the sword half way out of its sheath.

Danny was surprised at the sheath. *'Only me'*, he said standing up, *'Dannaigh. I took over from Leir.'*

Jago slipped the sword back in its sheath, but he was looking around suspiciously, making sure that all was well.

'How long have you been there?' he asked.

'A while. I see you have a…' he had no word for scabbard or sheath, so went with, *'thing to carry your sword.'*

Jago kept his hand on the hilt. For a moment he was thinking, still a bit uncertain of Danny, who was stepping out from the soft shadows of the saplings. He made his mind up and came over in a friendly fashion to Danny,

'We are Parisi,' he said proudly, *'Not Brigante. A scabbard is a good way to carry a sharp blade.'* He turned so that Danny could see it better, lifting it a little.

It was no plain covering. It seemed to be made from thick leather wrapped in a network of metal. Animals twisted, patterns swirled. Some red and pink stone had been laid into it near the top. It was a beautiful thing, and Danny said so. Jago was proud of it. Then Jago said,

'Aed says you did well yesterday. He slashed your spear to shreds, but couldn't get near you.'

That was a surprise. Danny hurried to say, *'I wouldn't have liked him any nearer than he did.'*

Jago laughed. Behind him Danny saw Leir stick his head out of the hide, woken by their voices. Guilt was written all over his face. Danny liked Leir. He acted young, but he was so full of life. So before he could make some cringing apology for having been asleep on watch, Danny said,

'Leir was tired last night, so I took over from him. He deserves some sleep.'

'That's good of you,' said Jago, while behind him Leir just looked a bit surprised and puzzled. *'He's a good lad, but he's got a lot to learn.'*

Danny nodded towards Leir, and Jago turned and saw him. *'You'll be all right for the morning watch then,'* he told him.

So much for trying to do good turns.

Leir started to protest, but Jago just said, *'The hill's behind you.'* And Leir gave up, and turned sullenly to look out on the moor. From inside the makeshift hide another head appeared, tousled from sleep, one of the younger children, about Cunedag's age. They took one look at Danny and Jago and tucked back in out of sight.

'You'll be wanting food,' said Jago to Danny, and Leir sent an angry glance at them. *'And that lass of yours will be looking for you. I'll walk you down,'* he went on. He had taken down the bag that hung over his shoulder, and was feeling inside it. Danny could smell wheat cake, and sweetness.

Jago strode across to Leir, and put the cakes into his hands. *'You've earned it,'* he said, and Leir was at once smiles again.

Jago and Danny started back through the wood while Leir and his helper tucked noisily into the cakes. Danny hoped they'd settle down quickly, there was no chance of not being seen or heard for now.

Beams of light lay across the trunks of trees, banishing shadows and making the woods seem magical.

Once they were out of earshot Jago confessed that the boys would be relieved from watch very soon. As soon as others had eaten, they would be sent up to replace them.

'Why didn't you tell them that?'

'Because they have to learn. They have to be serious about it, or they will die young.'

'You give them a lot of responsibility.'

Jago looked at him seriously. *'How else could it be?'*

Danny thought about it as they descended, and the smell of smoke from the village began to taint the air. He thought Jago had taken a decision back there. He had decided to trust Danny. That felt good. It felt as though he could ask Jago anything, and get a straight answer.

'Dugal sent Cunedag to Cynmar to ask for help. He's really young for that job. A child,' he said at last.

Jago laughed. *'Marrec will see the message is properly put. It is practise for young Cun. But the real purpose is to put Cunedag in Gorbed's eye.'* He looked sideways at Danny to see if he understood, and then explained. *'He is telling Gorbed that Cunedag is our boy, of whom we have high hopes. Take note of him. Look after him. They will probably send him back with a horseman, like a real ambassador.'*

So, much more complex than it had appeared, thought Danny as they came out into the open. After the bustle of yesterday, the village seemed quiet.

As they passed the forge Madog's man was spreading charcoal onto a smoky fire. As he saw them he picked up the large hammer and rested it against his shoulder as he watched them pass, eyes on them all the way.

When they were well past Jago said *'Don't pay any attention to Brec. His brain is addled. He understands only fire and metal.'* He raised his hand in greeting then as Tasgo came towards them, along with a young man Danny had noticed at the practice session. He had been with the children and the ancients, and wore a scowl and a limp. The two may have been connected.

Jago opened with *'Dannaigh has been taking a turn at watching the hill. I've fed the boys.'*

Tasgo seemed surprised. *'When did you go up there?'* he asked.

Danny had no idea what time it had been. But then of course, no-one here had a watch or counted the hours. *'Before dawn'* he said.

'The boys were asleep?' suggested Tasgo, which Danny thought was a bit rich since he was pretty sure Tasgo had been, when he was supposed to be guarding the hilltop.

'When do you think Cunedag will get back?' he asked in response.

'When it suits him,' Tasgo replied bitterly. *'When Gorbed gets around to taking men North to help us. Tomorrow, the next day, whenever.'* He seemed in a bad mood.

Jago was more forthcoming. *'It will take a day to get his men together, and then a day for Cunedag to get back here. Tomorrow night. Maybe the next.'*

'If Gorbed sends anyone,' added Tasgo.

'He will,' Jago assured him.

'I'll sort the watches on the hill,' said Tasgo, and then over his shoulder as he walked away, *'Gamma wants to know where you are Dannaigh. Maybe the girl is a chieftain's daughter.'*

Danny hid a smile. Maybe Tasgo had good reason for his bad mood.

He wasn't the only one, as Danny found out inside the main Hut

Chapter 21 – Lies and betrayal

Kelly slapped a bowl of porridge into his hands saying, 'I managed to save you some breakfast,' which could have been nice, but she made it sound like a curse. The porridge was a thin gruel, and there was no other way to eat it than to tip it up and slurp it from the bowl.

'The only person I can talk with is your Gran, and she only gives me orders,' Kelly told him angrily.

Danny licked out the bowl. He hadn't realised how hungry he was.

'Where have you been!' she demanded.

He started to explain about the hide, and the watch on the hill. Then his Gran called across the hall, 'Kelyn, there's washing to do!'

'Take no notice,' said Danny, 'if you weren't here someone else would do it.'

'I want to go back!' said Kelly urgently. 'It's been two days. My Mum will be so worried.'

Not yet two whole days thought Danny but said, 'We have to find Moira.'

'They can look for your Aunt. We have to go home.'

'It's not just a matter of looking, Kelly. Moira's been kidnapped. They knocked her out and threw her on a horse. She's been taken! We have to get her back.'

Kelly's mouth went into a taut line. He could almost hear the cogs turning as she thought. Across the room Gran was straightening her back and brushing off her hands. She was watching them and Danny guessed she would be here very soon.

Kelly said, 'Then have you got time to go back with me, and then come straight back here?' Her tongue darted along her lips. She confessed, 'I don't think I can go into that cave on my own.'

His left arm prickled with the memory of being in the flame. The pain. If he were honest he'd confess to her how little he wanted to go into that fire again. But that was the least of the problems.

'What about D. I. Raynes,' he said. 'What would you tell the police? Where have you been all this time? What's happened to me, and

Moira, and…' words stopped in his mouth. The day that had started so well was falling apart, just like that. And Gran was on her way, picking her way round the fire, speaking to some of the other women as she came.

'I won't tell them anything,' Kelly said, crossly. 'If your 'family secret' is so precious, keep it. I just won't say.'

Danny didn't think D. I. Raynes was going to accept that. Kelly hadn't seen him at work, not properly. He was fairly sure he'd find a way to wheedle it out of her.

'There's work to be done Kelly.' Gran had reached them.

Kelly was nettled enough to say, 'I'm not your servant.'

Gran took it well, 'But you do have to pull your weight,' she said evenly. 'We all do.'

'I don't. I'm going back.'

'Remember what I said that first afternoon?' Said Gran, kindly. 'It's not the whole truth. You can't go back, not just yet.'

'Why not?'

Yes, thought Danny, why not?

'It's not the way it works. Sit down, please sit down and I'll explain.'

Kelly didn't want to sit down. From where she was standing she could see the door, and Danny knew she could outrun Gran as easy as you like.

'Another few minutes won't hurt,' said Gran softly, and Danny remembered that was what she had said that first day, and here they were, two nights on.

But Kelly was sitting down on a little bench, and Gran was sitting on a stool.

'Moira would be a lot better at explaining it than me,' said Gran. 'When she gets here, she can tell you all the ins and outs. It's sort of a power thing. When you come through, you use up the power, and it has to recharge. It takes a certain amount of time.'

Danny felt suddenly hollow. He could hardly believe his Gran was saying this.

'How long?' demanded Kelly.

'For the two of you? It's hard to say. Moira would do an experiment I should think. A few more days.'

Over Gran's shoulder Danny could see one of the women Gran had spoken to talking to Jago, and now Jago was looking at them.

'You don't really know,' concluded Kelly.

'I do know you don't want to try. You could end up anywhere. Wars of the Roses, Black Death, any place in the time line.' Gran smiled. She had a nice smile, a kind smile. 'When Moira gets back, she'll know. She's a clever lass, like you. She'll be back in no time.'

'If we're lucky,' said Danny. He felt torn in two. There must be a good reason for his Gran to be lying like this, but he didn't want to be part of it. All his life they had been lying to him, keeping secrets, leaving him in the dark. And now this, this hurtful pack of lies. Why?

And Now Jago was coming towards them, smiling, excusing himself for interrupting. '*You need spears*,' he said. '*Shall we get them now?*'

That would be a Gran ploy. Keep them busy. He had to decide which way he was going to jump. But really, there was no question. He turned to Kelly. He looked her in the eye.

'If you go with Jago, he'll get you a spear. You'll need one. I'll be along in a minute.' Then he told Jago that he just had to speak with Gamma for a moment, and then he would come. '*To the forge?*' 'he confirmed.

Kelly looked at him for a long second, then Danny turned to his Grandmother. 'I'll go with Tasgo, to get Moira,' he said, 'the sooner the better,' while behind him Kelly got to her feet, a hard look on her face. As soon as they were gone he was swallowing his anger to say 'You were lying! Why? You used to come back just for the day, for a few hours! You said so.'

'I was exaggerating,' she smiled at him, 'You know how I like a good story.'

'There is no power-up delay! That's just an excuse. She's not stupid. She'll know as well as I do that you've...'

'She can't go back,' interrupted Gran, implacably.

'What! Ever?'

'I don't know, it depends how sensible she is.'

'Why?'

'It would be the end of the world,' said his Gran as though that were a normal thing to say. And it wasn't true.

'What, like it was when you went back?' he snapped.

'That was different.'

'Because it was you?'

'No! Because no-one would have believed me. There had been no big explosion, no people missing.'

All right, but... 'She won't tell.' But then there was Raynes, who wouldn't give up.

'You think she'll stand against the might of the authorities? And she knows where the flame is, thanks to you!'

That one struck home.

'It wouldn't be the end of the world,' he said doggedly. 'That's just silly.'

'OH!' snorted Gran. 'Like Nuclear fission wouldn't put the entire planet under the threat of destruction? You want to be responsible for time wars that destroy the past and thereby the future?' She looked at him with scorn. 'You haven't thought it through boy!'

He looked round, Eles was staring at them. So was Drustan. He didn't care. From the moment they had got here Gamma had been lying to them to keep them from going back.

'You think we're going to stay here for the rest of our lives?'

She smiled, knowing she had won. 'Just till we think up a good cover story, is all.'

'Another set of lies?' He had had enough. More than enough. He turned and walked away.

His Gran called after him, 'Stay away from the hill, both of you.' He ducked under the lintel, and she was out of hearing.

He strode towards the forge, anger swelling inside him.

She lied.

She lied, she lied, she lied!

This was his grandmother, his Gran. Whenever she came home she would open her arms, and he would run into them.

This was his Gran, who when he was small would tell him he was a brave boy, that there was nothing he could not achieve. She brought him presents from exotic lands, and told wonderful stories.

'Tell me a story,' he would say, and she would say, 'What about?' and he would say, and she would tell him something wonderful and strange.

Lies! Nothing but lies!

When he had come home from school after everyone had laughed at him and called him a liar, she had taken him in her arms, with warmth and love, and told him of the re-enactors and how they had been playing games with him. How Dugal was not Dugal. How stupid he must have seemed!

She had never met Kelly's Mum, but she could dismiss Kelly's fears in a heartbeat. Self-centred, self-serving, Lies!

His heart was beating so hard in his chest he thought he might explode.

He stopped suddenly. He wanted to rage, and scream and shout, but that would not do any good. He had to find Kelly, and let her know that she was not alone. That she did not have to face this alone.

He strode on.

There they were by the forge, Kelly and Jago and Madog. And on the far side of the forge, Brec, with his hammer across his chest as if it were a shield. Kelly was standing still as a statue, while Madog held a spear up beside her, to check it against her height.

Jago turned towards him with a smile, and it dropped off him like ice.

'*What happened?*' he demanded. The others turned. They looked, they saw Danny's face, and then they looked beyond him for the destruction which must surely be following.

He ignored them. 'I'll get you home Kelly,' he vowed, coming to a stop in front of her. 'I'll get you safe home!'

She put a hand on his sleeve, her face full of concern. 'What happened?'

'She lies,' he said. His breath was coming back now, now that he had said the important words.

Jago was gone. He was running full pelt back towards Gamma. Perhaps he thought Danny had killed her. He felt like it. No doubt she'd have a fine tale to give him.

Madog stood and waited, alert. Then he asked, as Jago had done, as Kelly had done, '*What happened?*'

Danny took a deep breath. His head was clearing.

'*Family,*' he said shortly. '*She is my Grandmother.*'

Now, just to make everything as bad as it could possibly be, Tasgo was walking out of the wood towards them. Walking towards them and taking in the stances, the hand on the sleeve, the way Madog stood, easy, and ready, ready for the worst, ready for action. And Danny, still getting his breath back, still furious, but fighting for control.

Tasgo stopped well short of the group, standing totally at ease, alert, ready. All he said was '*What?*'

Suddenly Danny knew that if there was any hope of an ally here, unlikely as it might seem, this was it. He spoke clearly, with intent. '*I am coming with you to get Moira. Then I will take her and Kelly back, to where we came from.*'

Tasgo glanced at Kelly, at her hand still resting on Danny's sleeve. He said, '*And the problem?*'

'*No problem. That is what I am going to do.*' The fury was evaporating. What he had now was purpose.

Tasgo thought. Then he said, '*Freya*?'

His Mother? Was that possible? '*Freya. Yes. If it's possible.*'

Tasgo nodded. '*If it is possible. If it is possible, we will do it,*' he agreed. And then, because he couldn't resist it '*Though why a man of your age needs three women, I don't know.*'

Just like that, thought Danny, relief flooding through him.

Chapter 22 – An Uncertain Start

Tasgo was turning to Madog, *'He needs a spear,'* he said. On the far side of the forge Brec muttered something guttural, words Danny did not know. Madog turned his head and spoke with surprising gentleness. He said, *'I will do it. And anything touched but not taken, I will destroy.'*

Tasgo looked angry, but Madog was beckoning Danny over towards the stack of spears against the wall of the workshop, including Kelly in the gesture.

'Your old stick was thicker than these. You fight rather than throw?' asked Madog. Danny nodded, translating the whole to Kelly with just, 'Talking spears.'

At the forge Brec had turned away and was beginning to hammer out another piece, the blows at first hesitant, but growing stronger. Tasgo, who surely had better things to do, stood and watched.

'But Kelyn,' Madog's tone softened again for Kelyn, *'she will throw I think.'*

When Danny translated she just shrugged. 'So far I've just learned how to hold one.'

Tasgo butted in with, *'Flexible, and not too long. Defensive.'* Madog worked his way through the spears testing weight, straightness and length, judging heights, but not offering any to be tried. Eventually he showed one to Tasgo, and with his approval gave it to Kelly. The hammer blows at the forge were getting heavier and faster, an incessant angry sound.

Danny was offered a thicker spear, still with its reddish bark. It felt good. He hefted it, and it felt better.

Danny took a stance, having an end capped with a sharp metal head changed everything. Holding it felt different. What he should do with it was different.

Sparks were flying under Brec's hammer. He was a short, twisted figure, drawn in tight on himself, an embodiment of anger and violence. The hammer rose and fell in a fury. Finally Madog turned and strode to him. But the hand he put on Brec's shoulder was not heavy, and his voice was light.

'It's not bloom, Brec. You'll have all the hardness out of it.' The hammer stilled. Brec shoulders lowered. Like a child he picked up the spear head and touched its edges. It went back against the anvil and the hammer tapped it lightly. But the glance he gave across hot charcoal to Danny was acid.

Tasgo said, as if nothing had happened, turning towards the practise area. *'You should try them. Have you thrown a spear, Dannaigh?'*

'No.'

Tasgo's jaw tightened. *'That good, eh?'* he muttered as he strode ahead, taking a spare spear with him.

It soon became apparent that Danny was never going to be without a spear. To throw it was to waste it. Kelly on the other hand was doing quite well, though that might have been down to the amount of tuition she got from Tasgo.

He stood behind her and positioned her arms, his face brushed by her hair. He made her test the weight of the spear, helped with the flow of the arm in slow motion. Danny watched; it didn't help him. Perhaps because holding the spear woke all the little cuts he had suffered the day before. Some of them wept, and stained the red bark of the spear as though they were bleeding again. If Tasgo noticed. he didn't show it.

Kelly could get her spear more or less into the heap of straw at the far end. There was no telling where Danny's would land. At least that seemed to make Tasgo feel better.

Suddenly there was a sound of shouting up near the main hut, a shout which echoed down towards them in different voices.

When it had become clear, Tasgo bellowed *'Horses!'* too, sending the word further, and he was off at the run, while Danny was still translating. They all ran. Everyone was running, and they all had spears.

It was a surprise to see Cunedag, Jago had thought it would be days before he got back. The lad was well pleased with his reception.

He was sat atop his own horse, but the reins were held by the fellow on the other one.

The newcomer was a sight to see. The left side of his face had been painted blue. Danny recognised that blue with a body shock that ran through him. His hair was in stiff spikes of white mud. His shield hung over his back, like the carapace of a beetle, and the spear jutted by his right hand.

He was looking round at faces, and had found Jago, standing beside Danny's Gran.

As Tasgo, Danny and Kelly arrived the newcomer was saying, '*We were ready enough. And now I must go. Who comes with me?*'

Tasgo turned his head and spat. '*Gorbeduc's half-brother,*' he muttered to Danny. '*NOT a chief's son.*' He shifted the shoulder that had been painted so painfully when he last met Gorbeduc. '*They call him Menki, the stone wolf,*' and made his way towards Cunedag.

'*How many has Gorbed taken with him?*' Jago was demanding.

'*He sent Braighden, with a chariot, ten horses.*'

Tasgo had moved round behind the horses and was whispering in Cunedag's ear as he swept him off his horse. Cunedag was whispering back as Madog joined Jago.

'*On foot?*' Asked Madog.

Menki shrugged, negligently. '*I didn't count.*'

Cunedag was flashing fingers at Tasgo, who straightened up.

'*About ten*', he said with as much certainty as if he had been there. '*Madog, stay, you can make as many spearheads as you like.*' Then he looked at Jago.

Danny's Gran, Gamma, said '*Jago stays too. You have enough to do the job.*'

Danny looked at her, seeing her in new light. This was her own daughter she was talking about. Kidnapped, dragged away by strangers, but she was looking after her own interests. Keeping protection at home instead of out there, finding her daughter. The transformation of his image of his grandmother was complete.

Tasgo looked up at the horseman. '*Can we use the other horse?*'

Again the shrug. '*It is Cunedag's horse,*' said the rider, to a rustle of surprised comment.

Cunedag said loftily, *'Take it,'* then spoiled it by adding, *'but it is mine and you will bring it back won't you?'* to a ripple of laughter.

Tasgo said, *'Dannaigh will ride, I'll run.'*

'I haven't,' said Danny, in alarm, *'not ever, been on a horse.'*

'You'll be fine' Tasgo told him, and to Menki, *'You need food?'*

'I need to travel.'

'I'll show you the best way, wait.' Tasgo darted into the hut. Jago moved up to the rider, and they spoke together quietly, while Danny explained what was going on to Kelly. He finished with 'I can't ride.'

'It's easy, she said. 'You sit on its back and hold on with your knees. And guide with the rein.' Danny looked at the horse, the horse seemed to be eying him with disdain. Kelly added, 'Even Cunedag can do it,' as if that settled it.

Tasgo re-emerged, a shield slung over his back, another in his hands. *'Jago, may he?'* he asked and Jago glanced from the shield to Danny, and nodded.

It took a moment for Tasgo sling the shield on a strap and adjust it on Danny's back. It felt heavy and cumbersome. Danny was looking at the horse. Its back was up there and he was down here. There was no stirrup or saddle, just a blanket on its back. He had no idea how to get on.

The rider, Menki, had been watching Tasgo put the shield on Danny's back, was watching the way he eyed the horse. With no apparent command the two horses were suddenly moving, and Danny's mount was now standing by a large stone. Everyone was watching. Danny moved over, stood on the stone, and with a little jump, had his hands on its back, was struggling to get a leg over it. The horse shied, the stone was gone and Danny was dangling. But Kelly was suddenly standing by the horse's head, holding the reins and speaking softly to it, and it stopped. Suddenly Danny was aboard and seated. It felt precarious, distinctly unsafe.

Kelly had taken the reins, and now handed them up to him. His horse blanket cloak was tangled round him uncomfortably. He didn't feel in control.

At once, they were off, Tasgo walking on one side of the stranger, Danny riding on the other, with Kelly walking along beside him.

'We shouldn't be long,' he told her. 'A few days maybe.' Behind them he could hear his Grandmother calling her name imperiously. Menki broke into a trot, so did Danny's horse and Tasgo started to run. So did Kelly. 'You'd better go,' he told her.

'I'm coming with you.'

He hadn't expected that. 'It's not a journey!' He snapped. 'There'll be fighting. It's dangerous!'

'I'm not staying here with her!' answered Kelly.

They were out of the compound now, and picking up speed. Kelly was keeping up easily.

'Kelly! Go back. You have to go back! It's not safe,' shouted Danny, as if being loud would make her change her mind. He didn't know how to stop the horse. He saw Tasgo look round the horses to Kelly, then say something to Menki. Menki leaned forward on his horse, and spoke. Thinking about it later Danny realised it was simply the all-purpose 'Ha!'

Suddenly the muscles under Danny changed rhythm, and the quick clop of the hooves turned to something more fluid. There was nothing to hold onto, and they were flying over the ground to the thunder of hooves.

Kelly was running too, and Tasgo, but they couldn't keep up the pace. Without any instruction from him, Danny's horse was keeping up with the other, the track flashing past beneath them, the road ahead a blur beyond the ears of the horse.

The road ahead dropped and turned around the hill.

He came off at the bend.

He landed shield first and rolled, down a fortunately soft and springy slope. The horses dashed on.

He got clumsily to his feet. The shield got in the way, so everything seemed awkward. Nothing broken, not even his spear. Behind them no sign of Kelly and Tasgo. Ahead the horses had come to a stop, and the rider had gathered up the reins without getting off his horse. He was bringing them both back.

Danny looked down at the definitely hard and unyielding rock that he had just missed.

Getting on that horse again would be madness.

Then the sound of a voice reached him. Kelly came round the bend head down, feet pounding. She looked up and Danny knew that expression on her face. She didn't slow.

Tasgo appeared behind her, rounding the bend. There was nothing of her unfettered determination about him. He ran easily, steadily. No short term race to win, this was long haul, mile-eating running.

Kelly came up to Danny and stopped, breathing hard, but not breathless, taking in the mud on his clothes. 'Fell off?' she asked, as if it was the most natural thing for him to do.

He said, 'Go back. You could get killed.'

'So could you.'

'I can use the spear. I can fight,' he told her. 'You...'

'Lots of women went. Girls younger than me.' He didn't think so, but that wasn't the point.

'Kelly, you'd be a liability, we'd have to look after you.'

'Just you try!'

The rider had stopped the horses just behind him.

Tasgo stopped just short of Kelly, '*Go back,*' he told her.

'He agrees with me,' said Danny

Menki said to Tasgo, *'They are both useless. Get on the horse and leave them.'*

Tasgo swung his shield over his head, and then held it in his left hand. The sword was still hanging from its tie. He said in a tired voice, '*Dannaigh comes with me. It is an honour bond. Kelyn, there is no place for you here. Go back.*'

'You have to go back,' Danny told her.

She looked him in the eye. 'The only person who can speak with me is your Gran, that...'

'Nice little old lady?' filled in Danny quickly. She was still his Gran, and besides, Kelly knew what he meant. She grinned.

'Bossy lying termagant,' corrected Kelly. He would have to look that up later. 'I would NOT be safe there.'

That was a jarring thought. Was his Gran capable of ...

Tasgo took a step forward. '*Go back,*' he said gently, and pushed her with his shield.

She stepped back and he pushed again, harder, leaning into the shield. '*Go back, the battle ground is no place for you.*' He sounded sad, and sorry.

Danny felt the same. 'It will come to a fight, and then there's nothing you can do but get in the way. '

He saw her shoulders droop. She took a step back, she looked from one to the other of them. Then she stepped aside, off the track, angling away towards the sea. She looked at Danny with the sadness of goodbye on her face, and a sudden gleam in her eye.

'I can ride though,' she said, and with a sudden spurt she tossed him her spear, and was past them both, and vaulting onto the back of the horse like a circus performer.

Where had she learned to do that? Even the horse looked surprised.

She snatched up the reins. Now the horse was sidling towards them.

'Danny Sharp,' she commanded, 'give me your shield. You'll run a lot faster without it.' The other rider pressed his horse forward to grab her reins, but Kelly was too quick, turning the horse away. The horse had a sudden sprightly air, as if this were a new adventure it was glad to be in on. They were a team.

Danny couldn't help but smile. He said to Tasgo, '*She says we'll run faster if she carries our shields*.'

Menki said, with grudging approval, '*At least she can ride*.'

Tasgo looked at her, as much angry as anything.

'*This is stupid,*' he said.

'*Like me trying to ride?*' agreed Danny, taking off his shield and passing it up to her. She slipped the strap over her head and eased the shield onto her back.

The horse sidled closer to Tasgo. 'Tasgo?' she asked.

'*This is not right,*' said Tasgo angrily.

'*You'd have trouble getting her off that horse,*' Danny told him, '*and we're in a hurry.*'

'*Is she always like this,*' growled Tasgo, but he took off his shield and passed it up to her.

'*You set the pace,*' she said happily, moving the horse out of their way, '*we'll keep up with you.*'

Chapter 23 – A Jaunt in the Country

And so they went, a quarter mile running, a quarter walking, with the horses following.

Clouds gathered, and Tasgo took them across a flat hillside and up a steep slope to a rather better track, and they went North. They waded across a ford, and the road turned west. The miles passed.

Danny wished he had asked the obvious question. How far were they going? His legs ached, the pace was unrelenting. They had not stopped once for a rest. He had started off counting the cycles of running and walking, but had long since given up.

Tasgo, with a shoulder full of pain, looked unstoppable. Danny was beginning to find it hard to keep up with him. There was no way he was going to ask for respite if Tasgo wasn't. He wondered if Tasgo was thinking the same.

They ran on.

The clouds blew away.

The sky began to tinge with purple and pink.

Tasgo began to pull ahead of him. There was nothing he could do to stop it.

'How far do we go?' Kelly called to Danny. 'Do we ride through the night?'

The thought alone nearly felled him. If his legs had ached before, they were hurting now. He felt ready to drop.

When he put the question, breathlessly, to Tasgo, running ahead of him, Tasgo sounded tired too. But then, his shoulder was still one big bruise.

'Choices. There is a farmstead,' he waved one hand vaguely, to the left *'or the village. Not much further.'*

'How much, not much?' asked Danny. While Tasgo was finding an answer, Danny called back to Kelly, 'Will that horse take two?'

'Are you tired?'

Silly question, he was knackered. He didn't have the breath to shout back. He thought Tasgo would just keep running till he dropped.

Then Menki gave a low cry, and moved his horse up quickly beside Tasgo. '*Company,*' he said in a warning tone.

There they were, ahead, three horsemen, coming towards them. As they were sighted in their turn, two of them urged forward at speed.

Danny stopped running, and readied his spear. Without the endless rhythm of the run, his legs felt like jelly. He fought to say upright. Then Tasgo, twenty yards ahead called out '*Friends!*' He sounded relieved. '*Marrec,*' he said.

But neither of the two horsemen galloping towards them was Marrec. They were younger, and brightly dressed, and one was yelling something. Danny grounded his spear behind him, leaning his weight on it, partly just to keep himself upright.

The horses separated to go past either side, and between them he could see Marrec further off, cantering towards them, unalarmed.

One of the riders reined in at the last moment and greeted Menki with whoops and a heavy clasping of arms. The other dashed on past, turned swiftly and barged his horse between Kelly's and Menki's. His target was Kelly.

'*Hello beautiful!*' he exclaimed with a wide smile of delight. He was not much older than her, strong and confident. '*What are you doing, riding with this fool. You should be with me!*'

He reached out for her, but she was sidling her horse away. She didn't understand the words, but she had the message well enough.

He laughed, and turned to Menki. '*Is she playing hard to get, or is she yours already?*' They exchanged hand clasps like old friends, slapping each other on the shoulders.

Danny was relieved to see that they were more interested in renewing old friendship than in Kelly.

Behind him Marrec had slid off his horse, and was giving Tasgo a bunk up onto it. Tasgo was pale, he saw, and drawn. But he had somehow managed to keep going all this way. Now he sat astride the horse, looking collected. He looked towards Danny and said something to Marrec.

Marrec came over. '*You look like death,*' was his greeting.

'Feel it too,' Danny confessed. It was no time to pretend strength he did not have.

'You may be good looking,' said Marrec sympathetically, *'and tough,'* he added, as a concession, *'but you lack stamina.'*

That was a bit much, thought Danny resentfully. He had been walking and running for hours. For miles. So many miles.

But Marrec had turned to the three young men on their horses. They were catching up, exchanging thoughts, laughing.

'Hey,' he said, *'which of you is going to run?'*

'For you?' asked one of the young bloods, with disdain. But Menki looked direct at Danny, and spoke to the older of the two new-comers. His horse moved restively.

Then Tasgo trotted up to them. Somehow he looked refreshed, collected. He said clearly, *'We have an early start in the morning. Menki, he needs a horse.'* Again the horse shifted as if aware of its rider's tensions. The younger one who had approached Kelly said,

'The horse would spook.'

'Like hers?' asked Tasgo with a nod to where Kelly had ridden off to one side.

The younger rider looked at her, and then he grinned.

Suddenly he drove his horse forward to Danny.

'We can take two,' he said, and leant down, grabbed Danny under the shoulder and hefted him up.

Danny struggled to get himself onto the horse, the spear got in the way. He knew he was making a fool of himself, not showing up in a good light, but he was too whacked to care. It was relief to take the weight off his legs. It would be relief to actually get on the horse rather than dangle.

But hardly had he got himself seated behind the rider before they took off as if it were a race.

At least this time there was something to hold onto. Not that a loose cloak and a rough tunic were the best of holds.

They were thundering along the track. The rider looked back and laughed, urging his horse on even faster. Danny leant against the back in front of him and looked back himself.

Kelly was low over her horse's neck as it raced after them. The others were already a long way behind them. That was stupid. That was just what this young blood wanted. Danny closed his eyes, willing her to give up the race, to wait for Marrec and Tasgo, people they knew were friendly.

But when he opened his eyes there she was, gaining on them, and the others almost out of sight.

'She is yours, isn't she?' demanded his rider triumphantly over his shoulder.

He could have just let go and let himself slide over the side of the horse. At this speed he didn't fancy his chances when he hit the ground, even if he managed to avoid the flying hooves.

He could have explained that Kelly was no-one's, and never would be. She would always be her own self. He doubted that would cut it either.

He could have taken a tight hold and thrown himself sideways, taking them both to the ground, but that would be opening hostilities which he was in no state to deal with.

So he hung on and watched Kelly getting steadily closer.

As she got closer she called out, 'Danny, tell him to slow down!'

Danny rather thought that would have the opposite effect.

'We'll wear out the horses,' she shouted over the thunder of the hooves.

So Danny turned his head toward the ear so close before him. He borrowed Tasgo's words. *'The princess asks you to slow down and spare the horses.'*

It was met by a gust of laughter, but to Danny's surprise, the horse slowed to a trot.

Kelly's mare slowed too as she came alongside. Danny warned her to keep her distance, but the rider in front of him was still laughing.

'She must love you,' he said turning to share his enjoyment, *'She really loves you! To spare the horses!'* He was shaking his head. It was a great joke.

Danny didn't translate.

Chapter 24 – A Need for Speed

It was twilight as they entered the village, with its low walls and huddled huts. The smell of roasting meat met them as they rode into the village. Dugal and the rest had passed through the night before and warned that others would follow. Everyone seemed to know Tasgo and Menki. The chief, with his thick moustache, welcomed them warmly into the main hut, ignoring Danny and Kelly entirely.

Menki in particular seemed to be well known and liked, especially by the young folk. He sat in the centre of a gaggle of them at one side of the fire, young men and woman only a year or two older than Kelly and Danny, if that.

All of them had eyes for Kelly, like she was some sort of celebrity. No wonder, she stood out, with her dark hair and milky skin. She looked polished and perfect by comparison.

Tasgo was going from group to group, talking mostly to the old men. People the age of Danny's parents. He didn't seem to be the least tired by an afternoon of running. He seemed to thrive on it.

Danny parked himself on a low bench by the fire. He wished he could throw himself down on a bed and just sleep. Kelly looked around. The young rider who had tried to chat her up, made room for her to come and join him, but she came over and sat by Danny on the rickety bench and said,

'Teach me some words.'

The words she wanted were 'thank you' which was quick and easy enough, and then 'I'm sorry, I don't understand you' which Danny shortened to the more brusque but universal 'I don't understand.' And finally she wanted 'Go away and leave me alone.' Danny pointed out that it would sound very different depending on who she was saying it to. She gave a wry smile.

'Try, 'Go away and leave me alone you stupid little randy twit.''

Danny looked at her in surprise. 'Is that what you say to boys at school?'

She looked right back. 'This isn't school.'

The words Danny taught her to say were, *'I'm promised.'*

The beaker of ale that he had been greeted with, was being refilled whenever it was empty. The roasted pig that had been on a spit in front of a fine fire out in the open was tasty and tender, but his body was exhausted. He should have been hungry, but he wasn't. He was just exhausted. And then they started on the mead.

He dozed through the chatter. If there were speeches, he didn't hear them. It was a blessed relief when Tasgo came and showed them where they were going to sleep. They lay down together fully clothed, with Kelly against the wall of the hut, Danny in the middle and Tasgo on the other edge of a makeshift bed of straw and skins

The sound of laughter and talk faded and died. Sleep folded over Danny the instant the furs covered him, as he had known it would.

He woke in warm darkness, in the quiet of night. But not silence. Not far away people were talking in the low voices of an evening passed late into night.

'-he's totally useless. Can't even stay on a horse,' a voice was saying.

With a soft laugh another answered, *'I noticed that too.'* Danny recognised the laugh. It was the lad who had taken him onto his horse. *'She's a looker though isn't she?'*

'They're soft. Even Tasgo could outrun him,' Danny thought that was Menki.

'Tasgo's tough,' countered someone else.

'Don't let them fool you, Brad. Gorbeduc bested him.'

'I heard he had help.'

'I heard it was easy,' growled Menki. There was a slight pause, then he went on, more urgently, *'He is mine!'*

Danny's heart leapt with alarm. But Menki was going on, *'If we catch up with him, leave him for me. I want the waesuck little bastard to know it's me doing him.'* Danny didn't know the adjective, but he committed it to memory. His parents had neglected a whole area of language that was going to be essential.

The younger one laughed quietly, *'I'm glad my half-brother isn't a half-wit.'*

'Oh, he's got brains,' muttered Menki, *'He's just given them to Kuillok.'* Then some-one, possibly Brad said, *'We ride early. Better sleep.'*

And the younger one said, *'Just so long as I don't have to carry dead weight tomorrow too.'*

The voices were moving away as Menki said, *'I hear he'll have a different sort of a ride.'*

Danny lay for a while taking that in. He was debating what he should say to Tasgo, if anything, but weariness was a stronger power.

Kelly kicked him awake. She was learning old ways far too easily, Danny thought. There was a bustle of movement. Tasgo was already gone. Danny found out how stiff he was when he rolled over and got out of Kelly's way.

Porridge was a help yourself affair from a pot over the fire, bring your own bowl. Fortunately the visitors were provided for. There were no explanations, no helpful comments from those around them.

Outside was a sort of chaos, lots of people getting in the way, few people getting things done. Danny was looking round for Tasgo or Marrec, and then found that Kelly too had gone.

Failing friends, he went to find somewhere to pee, or perhaps wash his face. His tongue felt furry, and the low dawn light seemed blinding. When he finally located the midden, mostly by the smell. Kelly was just coming away from it. She made a face. He could already smell why. It was nowhere near as civilised as the one they had left yesterday.

She stood around with her back to the place, until Danny came back.

'I could do,' she said, 'with a change of underwear, a bathtub full of hot soapy water, and just a little bit of privacy.'

He felt his face redden. Too much information. 'When the battle is over,' he suggested, as if he were used to this sort of conversation. Then, as they walked back to the main building, where all the action seemed to be, he told of the conversation he had overheard.

She wasn't sympathetic. 'Boys! It's just boys, for heaven's sake, just ignore them.' If only it were that easy.

Outside the hut a chariot had been brought out, and the two young bloods who had met them were there with Menki. The younger one had even found the time to chalk his hair up in spikes like his hero. He swaggered over to Kelly, *'Hello beautiful,'* he called, *'will you wait for me? I ride into danger with your name on my lips!'*

Kelly didn't even look to Danny for a translation. She blanked him out completely. Danny realised with a thump that Kelly was not expected to come with them.

Here she would not have the protection of being Dugal's guest, nor have Gamma to translate or to answer her questions. Leaving her here was entirely out of the question. He looked around for someone he knew.

There was the local Chieftain, with his spectacular bushy moustache, but also his total lack of interest in Danny or Kelly. He had virtually ignored them when they arrived, greeting Tasgo with courtesy and pride, but not even acknowledging Danny or Kelly.

Fortunately Marrec was coming towards them, his horse following at his shoulder. Kelly smiled at Marrec, and greeted the horse with soft words. It nuzzled her cupped hand.

Marrec, asked, with little expectation in his tone, if Danny had ever driven a chariot. He would have been surprised if he had.

'You ride with me then,' he said.

'Where's Kelyn's horse?' Danny wanted to know. It had been taken from them when they arrived, and Danny had been too tired to ask.

'Cunedag's horse,' corrected Marrec, turning to Menki's young friend, still loitering in the hope of being spoken to by Kelly. *'Brice isn't it? Will you help set up the chariot?'* Danny could see the boy wavering between a swaggering rejection or a chance to stay close. He chose the hopeful option and he and Marrec set about backing two rough looking ponies into the shafts.

'That's going to be slow,' said Kelly. *'We won't catch them up with that.'*

Danny looked at the chariot. The carrier part was bigger than he had expected. It would take him and a driver easily. Maybe Kelly as well. His legs were stiff rather than aching now. A ride in that would be good.

'How much slower?' he asked.

'Lots,' said Kelly, 'and we're way behind.'

Dugal had taken chariots though. Why had he taken chariots? He asked Marrec.

Marrec was surprised at the question. *'If Kuillok is with them, without chariots we are dead,'* he said. Brice looked at him with sudden surprise, or was that fear?

'If we get to them before they reach Kuillok, we won't be,' countered Danny.

'Then we will need Chariots to bring back Moira, and the wounded.'

Brice gave a snort of contemptuous laughter. *'Wounded? Four of them? Against all of us?'*

'There were twenty at the ford,' Danny told him as evenly as he could. *'Maybe fourteen of those can still fight.'*

Brice laughed outright. *'Don't worry yourself, this time we will be with you. There will be no need to run away.'*

Danny wanted to knock the smile off his face. Marrec was no fool. His warning should carry some weight. As to the rest – Kelly was right. They needed to be fast.

'The chariot can follow,' he told Marrec, *'We need horses.'*

It was Marrec's turn to smile. *'You?'* he said, *'on a horse?'*

Why not, thought Danny. Even Cunedag can ride a horse. *'Where is Cunedag's horse?'* he asked for the second time.

Marrec carried on fastening straps. He didn't look at Danny. *'It's the chariot,'* he said, *'we get the horse back later. It's a swop for the chariot.'*

One horse for two horses and a chariot. It was a generous swop. Or it would be if what they needed was a chariot rather than speed.

Danny jumped up onto a log and looked around. There was Tasgo, talking to one of the older women who seemed to be in charge. He ran over, interrupting what was being said.

'We need horses, Tasgo, not chariots.'

'Please excuse my rude young friend, Kennis,' Tasgo said to the woman, *'he is a stranger. This is Dannaigh, Toma's son, Gamma's grandson. Dannaigh, this is Kennis, wise and beautiful.'* Wise she may

have been, beautiful she was not. *'She runs this village, and gave you your food last night.'*

This was no time for polite niceness, but he managed, *'Thank you, Kennis, very generous,'* before turning back to Tasgo, *'We need to move fast! We need horses.'* Already the twilight of dawn had brightened to day.

'You can't ride,' began Tasgo.

'Then I'll have to learn.'

'You don't like my chariot?' asked Kennis mildly. She was old, but not as old as Gamma, and she seemed as much amused as insulted.

'It's beautiful,' Danny told her, he had looked at it. It was a lovely bit of craftsmanship, and brilliantly painted, *'But what we need is speed. We have to find my Aunt before they get her to Kuillok.'*

Again that name cast a dark shadow on her expression.

'You want Speed?' she asked.

'Yes,' if she ran the village as Tasgo said, she was the one to ask. *'Please.'*

She turned to a woman behind and gave a few quick orders. One of which strangely enough was to prepare 'speed'. To Tasgo she said, *'He gets to the point. I like him. There, you both have food and horses.'*

Tasgo grabbed Danny and, with profuse thanks to Kennis, pulled him away. As they left Danny heard her saying to another of the woman, *'He reminds me of his uncle Aod, so good looking, especially the girl.'*

'You were lucky to get away with that.' Tasgo growled as they moved away. *'She's the real force here. You don't want to get on the wrong side of her.'*

'But Kelly needs a horse too!'

'She isn't coming.'

Danny stepped in front of him, barring his way. He was sick of being passed over, having no say in things. *'Kelly comes with us. She can't stay here.'*

'She'll be safe…'

'She comes!'

Heads were turning towards them.

Tasgo was angry, but he took a step back. He explained, as to a child, *'She isn't trained to fight.'*

'She won't fight.'

'Then why come.'

'Because I can't leave her here.'

It meant nothing to Tasgo. To him it was unreasonable, stupid, nonsense.

Danny said urgently, *'She doesn't belong here. She doesn't know your ways. She doesn't understand what is said to her.'* They were wasting valuable time. *'She comes with me!'*

Tasgo, head to one side, found something that made some sense to him.

'It is an honour pledge?' he suggested.

That would do. *'Yes.'*

Tasgo sighed. *'Then you will have to run.'*

Danny's heart fell. His legs felt weak. To do that again was impossible. Tasgo pushed past him towards Kelly, and Marrec's mount. As he went he said, *'We'll take turns.'*

Which part would be worst as the day progressed, the running or the riding?

Reality was hitting him again. This was a task which he could not perform. It was beyond him. It had been stupid to suggest he might. Worse to bring Kelly along in his fantasy.

His only hope would be if Dugal and the others had succeeded where he would fail. They were a whole day ahead. Perhaps they had already caught up with Moira, and saved her. Perhaps they would meet them coming back victorious. Or at least, with Moira.

Perhaps he was still just clutching at wild dreams and impossible hopes.

The chariot was ready, and Marrec was standing impatient in it. Kelly had mounted Marrec's horse, while Brice stood beside her, talking to her, no doubt telling her how great he was, or at least demanding some recognition. And through the crowd came another horse, led by a young woman.

It seemed a nondescript animal to Danny, but Kelly looked impressed. Kennis was also coming towards them from the hut, looking pleased with herself. She patted the horse's neck, and it shook its head and pricked its ears. Turning to Danny she said, *'He can run but needs resting. Pace him well, and Speed will take you far and fast.'*

Danny looked at the horse, and Speed twitched his ears and snorted at him, as if he knew what an unworthy rider this was going to be.

Danny gathered his wits. *'Thank you kind Kennis, this fine horse deserves the best rider, and Tasgo is better than me in all things.'* He took a steadying breath. *'I will ride in the chariot.'* That could be sorted later.

Kennis laughed. *'At least he knows his betters,'* she told Tasgo. Then she told Danny, *'No, you asked for Speed, and you have him for your mission. I want him back in fine form. The girl can ride in the chariot.'*

Chapter 25 – Riding Lesson

Everyone was gathering round, there would be an audience for his humiliation, and maybe Kennis would take her fine horse back. To cover his confusion, he turned and translated for Kelly. She looked round at the elements of the forthcoming disaster.

'The horse is for you. Personally?' she asked. He nodded miserably. He expected her to protest.

She slung one leg back over her horse and jumped down beside him, and began talking quietly and steadily as she moved him toward the Speed that he had unwittingly asked for.

'Take time to get your balance right and settle yourself. Let your legs dangle. Grip with your knees.' She was expecting him to get on and ride! 'To move forward, lean forward and press with your heels, kick only if you have to. To slow down lean slightly back and don't pull on the reins, this horse has a tender mouth, I can tell by the way he chews the bit. Be gentle with the reins, leave them slack unless you want to tell him to slow or to turn.'

The flow of words went on and on. Danny's mind was stuck on; how do I get up there?

Tasgo could see disaster coming, Danny could see him trying to find a way out the humiliation that would reflect onto him and the whole group of them. As if in answer Tasgo stepped over to Marrec's horse, turning his back on them. Maybe a quick exit would be best.

Kelly punched Danny lightly in the ribs to get his full attention. 'I am going to make a stirrup of my hands. Face the horse, look to his head, put your foot in my hands and step up. Throw your other foot out and over the horse and come down gently on his back. Get yourself comfortable.'

Comfortable was the very last thing he would feel.

'Smile,' said Kelly. He made a grimace. She stood at the horse's shoulder and linked her hands into a stirrup. He had doubts about whether she could hold his weight, but she seemed confident.

He got on the horse.

It wasn't elegant, but he was there. The horse moved uneasily under him. Kelly's voice floated up to him quiet and soft.

'Relax, let your legs dangle, get comfortable, find your balance. She was moving out of the way because Tasgo was riding Marrec's horse up beside Danny.

'Thanks, Kennis, for all your help,' said Tasgo.

'Grip with your knees, lean slightly back, just a little, for slow, and forward for go. Stop when this place is out of sight.' Kelly's voice droned on as she moved away towards the chariot. 'Keep the reins loose, but so that the horse knows you have control.'

'Good hunting!' exclaimed Kennis.

Danny remembered to thank her too, but Tasgo was moving forward and Speed was standing still, so he leant forward and squeezed with his heels, and sure enough, they were away.

Next to Marrec in the chariot, Kelly called out, *'Thank you,'* waving to Kennis, and gaily, to the crowd in general, and even to Menki and his two young friends, who were also mounted and coming forward.

There they were, a small procession, moving out of the village into open country.

Only, Speed was living up to his name. Even at a walk he was outpacing Marrec's nag, and he felt eager to go.

Tasgo looked sideways at Danny. *'So this is your second time on a horse?'* he growled, *'Or were you just playing with us?'*

'No play.'

Then Menki and his two friends trotted up on either side of them. Young Brice was calling out, *'I thought we were supposed to be in a hurry,'* as they overtook.

Speed pranced a little, and Danny had to grip hard with his knees. The horse felt the added pressure, and bounded eagerly forward, almost jerking Danny from his seat. His weight may have shifted backwards, but Speed seemed more ready to accept 'forward' than back. The movement seemed slow and rocking, but already they were past the others. The landscape rushed towards them at an alarming rate.

He was still on the horse. Which is how he would like it to remain. Hitting the ground at this speed would not be fun. Behind him he could hear the thunder of hooves, but the sound was fading and the rush of passing air was taking over. Everything seemed to blur but the horse, the rhythm of its head, the powerful movement of its shoulders.

Kelly had said, 'lean back for slow', so he leaned back. If it made any difference, he couldn't feel it. He leant back further until it began to feel unsafe, and when he sat upright there was no change in speed.

What else had Kelly said?

Keep the reins slack? Had she said that? But surely, weren't reins for reining in?

Ahead the track curved slowly into a valley, and into deep woods. Not a sharp bend, but a bend.

He tightened his grip on the reins, pulling them toward him until he could feel the motion of the horse's head. Gently he pulled a little more, leaning slightly back.

Amazing, they were slowing. The horse's gait was changing to the jerking motion of a trot, everything came back into focus. He took the curve easily, staying upright, the reins slightly slacker. When he dared to glance over his shoulder to the brow of the hill there was no-one else in sight.

He took the chance to experiment further, and brought Speed to a successful halt. By that time he could hear the others approaching. Young Brice in the lead, as though it were a race.

Speed could hear them too and began to move restively. Danny took the opportunity to try moving him forward and turn to face the oncoming arrivals, finally managing it as Brice arrived in a flurry of small stones in what a driving instructor could only have described as an emergency stop.

'*Yesterday you couldn't ride,*' he said accusingly.

'*Still learning,*' said Danny. The horse was moving impatiently under him and he could see Menki and the others approaching fast. If they didn't stop, Speed would probably whirl and go with them. Whirl, he thought. Perhaps facing this way was not such a good idea.

Behind them Tasgo appeared at an unhurried canter. At least there would be someone to pick up the pieces.

But Menki and his friend slowed to a walk. '*Why are we stopping?*' he demanded as they came up.

'For Kelyn.'

'We have horses and we go at the speed of a chariot?' Menki said contemptuously.

Danny waited for Tasgo to arrive. Then he said, *'There are six of us, with Kelyn, and five horses. If we share doubling up, we can go just as fast.'*

Menki cut across him. *'She does not ride on my horse.'* But Brice's face had lightened.

'My horse is strong, she can come with me the whole way!' His eyes were bright at the thought of having her in his arms.

Before anyone else could speak Danny said firmly, *'Kelyn will ride Speed to start with, and I will go with Tasgo. We'll change later.'* He looked to Tasgo, hoping he was going to back him up.

Menki spoke first, *'She can travel in the chariot. If there is a fight, she can hand out spears. Safer for her.'*

He had a point, she might be safer in the chariot. But the chances of them getting separated was too great. On her own, not speaking the language, ignorant of the customs, she would vanish without trace.

'There is no choice,' said Tasgo moving his horse between Menki and Danny, *'The girl goes where Dannaigh goes. He comes with me.'*

Brice laughed. *'You can all ride safe in the cart, then. We'll protect you.'*

Tasgo transferred all his attention to Brice and suddenly the air was electric. *'And who will protect you from me?'* asked Tasgo mildly.

Mirth fell from Brice's face. His eyes turned to Menki, expecting to be backed up.

Menki said *'Don't be a fool,'* and his horse burst into a trot, moving out of the way. The other rider followed suit.

'Well?' Asked Tasgo.

'It was just a joke,' muttered Brice.

'Spears have been broken for less.'

Brice's horse moved back, but Brice wasn't taking his eyes of Tasgo. The other two were trotting away.

'Well?' asked Tasgo again.

Brice's shoulders dropped. *'It was a bad joke,'* he said, lowering his gaze. *'I'm sorry.'*

'No offence taken,' smiled Tasgo, *'this once.'*

And fortunately at that point the chariot came over the hill.

With a cheerful cry of, *'Here comes Kelyn,'* Danny turned away from total humiliation to watch the chariot rumble towards them. He was frantically searching for something to say that would wipe out the last two minutes. Or at least something that would not make matters worse.

The three of them waited in silence as the chariot came up. Kelly looked excited. The wind had blown her hair, and put colour in her face. Marrec looked quite pleased with the world too. Neither of them noticed the tension in the air.

Danny said, 'You're going to ride Speed. Tell me the best way to get off him.'

'I'll hold him,' she said, jumping down from the back of the chariot.

'Ask the guy with the white hair to do that,' he suggested. She picked up on his tone and started to turn her head to see what was going on. 'Just smile and ask,' he said.

She looked up at him, and pulled a face. Then she smiled and turned to Brice, sulking on his horse. 'Brice,' she said, 'you don't understand a word I'm saying, do you?

Danny translated, *'She would like you to hold Speed's reins for me.'*

'Have you boys been clashing antlers?' She asked.

'How should I get down? And then I have to bunk up with Tasgo, and you have to get on this one.

'Easy peasy,' she said, she was in very good humour. It was amazing what half an hour of easy travel could do for you.

Chapter 26 - Battle.

They had eaten in the saddle, Tasgo passing out the food that Kennis had prepared while the horses ambled. Tasgo had been coaching Danny all the way on how to ride, and now thought he was ready for the next stage on his own. Danny was not so sure.

Tasgo moved them closer to Brice.

'*No hard feelings,*' said Tasgo with a smile, handing over another wheat cake. '*As you said, your horse is strong, you'll take me for the next while?*'

Brice took the cake. '*You're not as light as Kelyn,*' he said, with a wishful glance in her direction, '*but, well, if you like.*' He was not yet back to banter, but he wasn't going to bear a grudge.

When the wheat cake was eaten, Tasgo handed the reins over his shoulder to Danny, and transferred direct to Brice's horse, horseback to horseback. If Danny hadn't got a horse to handle he would have been impressed.

Then they rode on.

Riding a horse used an entirely different set of muscles to running, Danny was finding. Now every single part of him was aching. He wondered whether he would be able to stand once he got off. He thought the horse was probably tired too. It was certainly more docile than Speed, though with Kelly riding, Speed seemed quiet enough now.

Even Speed was happy to settle for a period of trotting. Kelly hung back to get beside Danny and confided. 'Are they never going to stop? I'm exhausted. The horses need a rest too.'

It didn't seem like it. They all had a look of dogged determination. Part of it, Danny guessed, being that no-one wanted to be the one who gave up first.

'I think they're just, generally, tougher than us,' he told her. 'I think they're used to this.'

What they were, he thought, was focused.

The young bloods were ahead of them, even Brice, with Tasgo up too, was ahead of them. Suddenly, at the top of the next rise, they had stopped, and were getting their shields from their backs. Brice trotted up to them, and Tasgo slipped down to the ground.

'Something's up,' said Danny unnecessarily, and they urged their horses faster. Tasgo was still wearing his shield beetle wise on his back, and as they caught up he was walking forward ahead of the group.

Coming up the hill from the other side was a chariot with two people in it. Confronted by the strangers on the hill, it had come to a stop. Then Tasgo hailed it loudly, and it came on, with one of the occupants waving. Danny recognised him as one of what he now thought of as 'their' villagers.

'*We were coming for you,*' called Molven. '*We have found them! We cut them off. They had to turn back.*'

Danny's attention was on the other man in the chariot. He must have been from Gorbed's group, Danny didn't know him. He was propped up against the side of the chariot, and there was no sign of anything wrong with him except he was not taking any notice of anything. Spittle was running down his chin, and his eyes were vacant. It seemed no-one else took any notice of him at all.

There followed some excited description of the terrain, and where the enemy might now be. The bad news was, the hunted party was now more than twenty strong. Finally, Danny got a word in.

'Moira?'

'*Alive,*' was the answer which didn't give information as well as Danny liked. But knowing more would not help.

There was too much talk. He turned to Tasgo. '*If we know where we are going, why are we still here?*'

In answer Tasgo looked up at Brice and said something. With a more serious air than Danny had yet seen, the boy hefted Tasgo up behind him. With a kick of his heels they were on their way.

Danny nodded to Kelly, making sure she was going to come too, and leaning forward, for the first time kicked a horse into action.

They were away from the questions and the talk, following Brice and Tasgo. Within seconds Kelly was at his side. She looked sideways at his expression, and didn't ask any of the questions she might have.

They rode.

Some shouts followed them, and then the sound of hoof beats in pursuit by those they had left behind.

It seemed that Tasgo knew this landscape. After a while they left the track and followed the line of a ridge. The sun was well past noon, and lowering in the sky when they sighted Cadryn, perched in a tree on the crest of a hill. He glanced in their direction, then continued looking back the other way. When they stopped beneath the tree, he didn't look down at them. His left arm was cradled in a sling and his face was a mass of congealed blood. A horn was strung round his neck.

From here he had a clear view of the moor ahead, and of another distant figure sat atop a lone Howe. Beyond that the land fell away.

'Bran has the ford in sight,' he said with a nod to the distant figure, but without looking down. *'We'll see anyone who crosses this line. They're somewhere to the right, between here and the river. They saw us and ran.'*

'What happened to you?' Tasgo demanded.

'Horse fell.' His voice wavered, and he looked away. Danny wondered where the horse was, and if it could be ridden. Tasgo was looking across the moor ahead.

'Where were they when you saw them?'

Cadryn pointed to the tree tops that poked above the hill line ahead. *'Heading out of the woods toward the river. They saw we would reach them before they could cross, and they doubled back. Twenty strong. More.'*

Menki and his friend had arrived now.

Tasgo said, *'Dugal made a charge at the ford?'*

'He cut them off from it,' agreed Cadryn

'He'll harry them through the wood,' Tasgo was thinking out loud. *'Did they have archers?'*

'Dunno, they ran.'

'What are we waiting for,' demanded Menki, *'it will be finished before we arrive.'*

'They'll rear guard and run,' decided Tasgo, pointing almost back the way they had come, but at an oblique angle, going down the slope of the hill, towards the woods. *'We go this way.'*

Menki pointed angrily to the woods ahead, beyond the moor. *'The fight is that way!'* he spat.

'Dugal may be glad of your help, if you just want a fight.' Tasgo growled, *'The quarry is this way.'*

With a sneer Menki pushed his horse forwards, followed by the other rider, Brad.

'And you?' Tasgo demanded of Brice. He had his hand on his sword ties, but Brice didn't know that.

'He's my clansman, sorry,' said Brice, but he sounded regretfully.

Without a word Tasgo slipped down from the horse and slapped it as he landed, and Brice was away after the others.

He looked at Danny. *'You're right,'* Danny told him. 'Kelyn, you stay here, with Cadryn. If trouble comes, ride. Fast!' he pointed back the way they came.

'You'll need Speed,' Kelly said. But Danny was already offering Tasgo a ride on Marrec's horse.

Tasgo was calling up to Cadryn as they moved away. *'I am sorry about your horse, Cad, she was a good ride.'*

'Wait here, Kelyn,' Danny repeated as they rode away.

A broad grassy expanse led back off the hill, but angled down towards a long, wooded valley. On the far side of the trees was another moorland hilltop. Any one on that would be seen by Cadryn. Danny wondered how much information he could give on that horn. Would it just call people to him?

The horse's hoof beats were muffled by soft turf, and despite the double load the horse was making good progress.

Suddenly Tasgo pointed. Startled birds were flying out of the woodland below them. The little flock swirled and turned, swooped and were gone back into the canopy. Something was disturbing them. If Tasgo was right, it was the band who had taken Moira. The turfed slope he and Danny were on would be faster going than anywhere under the trees. They would be gaining ground, getting further ahead.

What were they going to do? There were only the two of them, and over twenty of the enemy.

Dugal and the others would be coming after them through the woods. The odds were good there, and Menki and his pals would catch up with them soon. But what could two people do against so many?

Could they ride to and fro shouting, sounding like a crowd, so that the ones being chased would stop long enough for Dugal to catch up? No, that was a stupid thought.

Suddenly he realised he was looking for ways out. Ways not to have to fight. He was afraid. Whatever was coming next was going to be bloody. It had been inevitable from the moment he had said to Tasgo, 'I am going to get Moira.' He had stupidly made his own trap, and now it was closing on him.

He was afraid.

Below them the trees suddenly opened out into a wide strip of grass through which a marshy stream ran down towards the river. Tasgo pointed towards an easy run down to the trees beyond the break.

At least the horse was easier to control now. But as they turned to go down he saw behind them Kennis' brown horse Speed cantering down the slope towards them, with Kelly on its back. She was following them. Like lead in his stomach, he knew she wasn't going to turn back. He tapped Tasgo's leg with his spear, and nodded towards her.

He could feel Tasgo's anger hot against his back.

'You told her to follow us!'

'I told her not to.'

Though he didn't know the word, Danny knew that Tasgo swore. Then he pointed to a denser part of the woodland edge, his movement sharp, tight and angry.

The woods edge was bounded by a tight growth of low branches, Danny was searching for a way through, but Tasgo had pointed to where the foliage was thickest. When they got there he slid off the horse and turned to where Kelly was approaching.

Wisely she stopped short.

Danny hissed, 'It's not a game Kelly. You could get hurt!'

But Tasgo was speaking too. And he didn't sound angry.

'Kelyn, if we must fight, we shall. But you must keep these horses safe. If the enemy get Speed, then Moira is lost to us.' He was walking

towards her, and because he was talking softly, she let him come nearer. Danny was translating as he spoke. Tasgo turned suddenly and told him fiercely to shut up. So fiercely that Danny was silent.

To Kelly Tasgo said plainly and evenly. '*We must fight, and you must live. Whatever happens, keep the horses safe.*' He obviously thought she could understand. He reached Kelly and held out a hand to her. She did not take it. She looked to Danny

With one swift movement Tasgo caught her leg and yanked her from the horse. She fell towards him. Before Danny could move, Tasgo had caught her in a savage embrace, twisting her arm behind her and grabbing her hair so that she had to look into his face.

'*They will kill you,*' Tasgo snarled into her face at point blank range. '*They will rape you, then kill you. They will leave your body to rot.*' He shook her like a rag doll, and then threw her from him to the ground. Danny was so shocked he didn't move.

Tasgo wasn't in any sort of a fury though. His voice was firm but quiet when he spoke again. '*Do not die today, Kelyn. Look after the horses, and do not die.*' He turned away, towards the forest.

Danny felt as though he were not really here. Kelly was so shocked she was white. Her eyes looked huge. He wanted to rush to her, and help her to her feet, to hold her, to make it better, but he didn't. It was all distant and suddenly very simple. He told her what Tasgo had said, then, 'It would be worse than that. Keep out of the fight. Keep the horses safe. Stay alive.'

She was shaken. So was he.

The final inference was obvious. Tasgo was ready to die. This was a battle and they could both die. Twenty against two. It was obvious. And once obvious, it no longer scared him.

Weird.

He would do what he must do. He would help save Moira. If he was going to die, then he would live the last few minutes of his life to the full. He would fill it so full it would last forever.

And if he wasn't going to die, then there was nothing to fear.

Since Kelly was going to have the horses, he slid off. The horse wasn't bothered. It started grazing. It was going nowhere.

Since Tasgo was readying his shield in his hand Danny did the same.

Kelly was already on her feet, moving towards Speed, catching at the reins before the horse got spooked and moved away. She threw a hurt and angry glance at Danny before turning to the horse. Her other hand caught at the spear she had dropped when she fell.

Danny thought they would do well to get out of her sight quickly, now that she was armed.

Everything had become sharp focused and real in some new way.

Evening sunlight stroked the top of the canopy where leaves whispered. The horse chomped noisily at the grass. Tasgo ducked into the earthy scents of the shadowed forest, and he followed. The leaves closed behind them and cut them off from the rest of the world.

Once inside the forest margin it was easy going, the ground was uneven but springy, the trunks were far apart, and it was easy to duck through the low branches. It was gloomy, and shadowed with shafts of light thrown across the upper branches like green lights.

They flitted like shadows deeper into the wood, slanting back towards the clearing, where the young saplings seemed to glow with light. Here they paused, where the green leaves formed a protective screen through which they could glimpse the open land beyond.

Already figures were appearing from the trees opposite, coming cautiously into the dangerous open, and finding it empty. Then they were streaming across. Not in connected blocks, but in ones and twos, mostly mounting their horses for the open ground, but some running as if for their lives, leading their mounts.

The leaders were looking for where they could get the horses into the trees opposite, and had seen the places where animals had made tracks. Some were heading towards where Danny and Tasgo were hidden by the leaves., some further down the hill.

Was he really standing in wait with shield and spear to thrust and hurt? These were fighters, he told himself. And himself murmured back that he was not.

Suddenly a little knot of people was coming out together, in a tangled mass, as if tied together, as if fighting with each other. A sack was being thrown up onto a man's shoulders, a sack with lashing legs. His heart leapt. It was Moira! And she was no easy carry! Her arms had been tied, but her legs could still kick.

Three days they had had her, and she was still fighting back! He felt a fierce pride, and violent determination. They would free her. Now he could see her, he was certain.

The little crowd surged forward, the man staggering under his writhing load. Meanwhile Tasgo was moving towards where the enemy would reach the woods. Danny went with him, crouching low so as not to be glimpsed. In just a few moments the enemy would be bursting through the branches.

At the little stream the big man slipped. He and his struggling load came crashing down with a cry.

Danny raised his shield, and readied his spear.

Suddenly it felt wrong, so wrong.

Carrying the shield, he could only hold the spear with one hand. He could not swirl it and bring the ends into play as he had with the broom handle. All the skill he had learned was useless like this.

He realised in a flash that the shield was best against missiles. There would be no missiles now. He dropped it to one side feeling foolish, foolish to have it, foolish to be without its protection. But now the spear felt right in his hands. Fear and doubt dropped away.

He was ready.

Through the branches he saw that those nearest had stopped, dismounted and turned. They were readying their spears to throw, to cover the retreat of the others.

Dugal burst out of the far trees on foot, roaring. Danny could not make out the words, but all along the edge of the wood the rest of his team were appearing.

One of the men near to Danny made a quick run and threw his spear like a javelin. It shivered in the air as it arced towards Dugal, and landed yards in front of him.

Everyone faced Dugal. That was where the danger lay. Everyone except the man who had been carrying Moira. He dragged her out of the mud by her hair, and Danny saw his sword blade flash as he brought it up to her neck.

His words split the air.

'Come nearer and she dies!'

Everything resolved on Dugal and on the man who held Moira. Everyone was turned towards them.

Everything seemed to slow, almost to stop.

Everything except Tasgo, who was quietly moving out of hiding into the open, with a slow unhurried gait. Walking as if nothing in the world was wrong, stepping up with his sword ready, behind the man with a spear.

Danny followed behind him, heart hammering. Ten paces out into the open, twenty. They were in full view. It would only take one person to turn their head, one person to check around them.

Tasgo walked straight up behind the man with a spear. There was a spurt of blood, and Tasgo laid the man quietly on the ground and moved forward towards the one who had already thrown. The bottom fell out of Danny's stomach. He didn't want to be here. He wanted to be anywhere else but here.

But short of running screaming into the woods behind him, drawing the enemy's attention to him and to Tasgo, there was nothing else to do but keep walking. Somehow, that was what he was doing.

No one saw them. Their eyes were all on Dugal, who had not stopped. He was walking forward very slowly, his shield across his chest, and he was explaining in a loud, clear voice, exactly what would happen to the man who held Moira, if Moira died.

That man would not die. He would wish to die, but he would live on most painfully. Dugal was laying out in exact detail what would happen to him, very slowly over days, seasons, years. The bones that would break. The cuts to his flesh.

Tasgo's shield touched that of the second man, who started to turn as the sword slashed across his throat. He fell with a gush of blood, and Tasgo and Danny were still walking forward. Walking because that did not attract attention. Because they could have been part of the enemy band coming to support their leader. Walking forward, totally exposed, towards where the target of Dugal's anger was using Moira as a shield, and backing slowly towards them. There were half a dozen fighters nearby him. If any one of them turned, they would be seen.

Tasgo said softly. *'The hand with the blade. Keep it from her. Hold it tight.'* They walked steadily on in a dreamy vacuum, where no-one tried to stop them, where everyone was looking somewhere else. They were six feet away, three feet away. At any moment their target would realise who and what they were.

Danny felt Tasgo tense, then they were both leaping the last few feet. Danny let go of the spear with his right hand, swung round the twined bodies of Moira and enemy and grabbed the wrist holding the sword.

Slow motion exploded into violence. He was clinging to that hand which fought to draw the blade across Moira's throat. He was using all his weight to stop it. Behind him he could hear and see a flash of movement. His left wrist twisted his spear past the figure in front of him and jabbed behind. Sharp pain sliced across his ribs as the hilt of the spear struck something behind him.

Everywhere was a hideous clamour of shouting, the sound of steel clashing, of heavy blows of iron on wood.

Suddenly there was no resistance in the hand he was heaving on so hard and he fell backwards as a blade from behind whistled through his hair. Still falling he saw the shining arc of the blade continue towards Tasgo, who was only just turning towards it.

Danny's leg lashed out even as he fell, hit hard, and the man was toppling towards him; the blade passing harmless by Tasgo's elbow. Somehow Danny got the other end of the spear between him and the falling man, to ward off. But it failed to stop the fall. Half crushed, half smothered, his spear was stuck fast in a writhing body. Too late he remembered that one end of a spear is not blunt.

He pushed the spear sideways. And the man pivoted with the spear, clearing Danny and leaving him exposed. From his left another spear jabbed at him. A shield swung low from his right and knocked it aside, Tasgo was striding over Danny, his sword coming up short and hard under the other's shield.

Danny rolled the other way. His spear was stuck fast in a motionless man. In front of him, Moira was coming to her feet, the ropes that bound her falling off in short sections. Tasgo must have slashed them when he killed her captor. She shrugged them off and tore the short sword from the hand of the man who had held her. The fierceness of her face shocked him. For a nano-second he thought she was going to slice him in two. But no, she was turning, blade ready, to someone coming at her from the other side.

Somewhere a horse was screaming. A hideous sound.

He rolled to his feet, the whole glade was writhing with battle, paired fighters, little knots of men struggling together. How could you tell friend from foe?

A spear was lying loose. He grabbed it.

Suddenly an unearthly ululating cry filled the air, freezing blood.

A portion of the woodland burst into motion, small branches thrashing, thrumming with uncanny sound. It bounded forward, disintegrating, branches flying, into the fray. A spear thrust forward at the enemy. The woodland had come alive to destroy them.

Men froze in fear, others ran. The apparition bore down on enemy spearmen, and they dropped their spears and fled.

With shock Danny recognised the horse galloping amid the falling vegetation. It was Speed. Kelly, her hair full of twigs, swathes of leaves about her shoulders was riding him full pelt into the fray, screaming high pitched, something gothic or operatic.

Now, suddenly she was coming straight at him her spear raised to throw. Vengeance! He could hardly believe it. She hurled it straight at him.

He ducked.

He felt the wind of its passing. He heard the thunk of striking, right by his ear. Whirling he saw the enemy face, right by his own, now falling away from him, sword twisting away from a thrust.

So close. So close to being killed.

It was a body shock. Like a blade through his ribs.

Kelly was riding on, still pouring out the same eerie cry of madness, riding down the enemy, who were fleeing, like magic, into the woods.

The scene was transformed.

There were still pockets of battle, and some bodies scattered on the grass, but mostly it was fighters fleeing, or fighters in pursuit.

The enemy were fleeing, hotly pursued, into the wood. In a few moments it would be over.

Dugal was lumbering towards them out of a heap of bodies, some prostrate, others wounded. Behind him Margan was forcing surrender from those still alive, and taking their weapons.

Dugal reached Moira and smothered her in a bear hug. She collapsed into his embrace. He was kissing her head, and muttering soothing words.

Danny was shocked. Dugal was with his Gran. They were together, they shared a bed. What was he doing kissing Moira?

Moira was crying now, broken sobs that shook her whole body.

The last of the fighting was over. It was suddenly silent.

Kelly was trotting back up towards him, pulling bunches of leaves from her tunic, keeping a wide distance between her and the various figures on the field.

Danny looked at the bodies at his feet. The bloke who had held a sword to Moira's throat. The one with Danny's spear sticking out of his chest. The one Tasgo had saved him from, by killing him himself. The one he hadn't seen coming, with Kelly's spear through his neck.

He felt light headed. He felt faint. He had killed a man. He had saved a friend. He had nearly died.

Had he saved his Aunt, now in Dugal's arms?

He looked at the woods and their route from it earlier, marked by two dead men.

Tasgo was walking the field, turning over bodies. Picking up weapons. He had just killed four men.

And Moira was free.

From the woods on the other side Menki, Brice and Brad appeared, and looked about them. They took in Danny standing beside Dugal and a heap of bodies. They took in Tasgo walking the field, and Kelly riding the far side of the field. Menki said something and Brad got off his horse and started to walk through the long grass and check bodies too.

Kelly came up to Danny. She was holding the reins high, and looking at the bodies. She was very pale. Danny guessed he was too.

'Did you like the ride of the woodland Valkyrie?' she asked brightly, as Speed came to a stop not far from the bodies and the blood.

Danny could have cried.

'You are an idiot,' he told her softly.

'It worked, didn't it?' she protested. She held her chin high, as if there were a barrier between them, that she had to look over. She could have been hit by a spear. She could have been mowed down by one of their own side. But there she was, in one piece, on a horse, pretending it had been a game.

But she was looking past him at her spear, at the blood, at the man she had killed. She had saved Danny's life. He saw her suppress a shudder. Suddenly he knew she felt as he felt, undone.

He wished he could reach up and put his arms around her and say 'It's alright. It's going to be alright.' He wished someone would do that for him. Only it wasn't alright. It would never be. Or at least, it would never be the same. She had killed a man. So had he. A rational part of his brain piped up that both men had been about to kill Danny, but the rest of him knew that did not count.

Speed stepped away from the bodies, shaking his head.

Instead of offering to hold her he said. 'You had better take that horse away from the smell of blood. It's upsetting him.'

She looked back at Danny.

She said, 'Is any of that blood yours?'

He shook his head. That made him feel dizzy. Menki and Brice were picking their way over the clearing towards him. He didn't want them to see him so affected. They would take it as weakness.

But it was Dugal they went to, and looked down on him and on Moira from the height of their horses.

All Menki said was *'Did they?'*

Dugal shook his head. *'She's unharmed.'*

'Gorbeduc?'

'I didn't see him.'

Menki looked around, most of the warriors were missing, hunters and hunted in the wood.

'Are you letting them go then?'

Dugal looked around at the field, estimating the dead, and the prisoners. Moira freed herself from his arms and started wiping the tears from her face. She didn't look up the riders.

'They've paid a price,' said Dugal. *'We've got prisoners.'*

He took a horn from his belt, and raised it to his lips. It blew a great blast then lots of short staccato notes, then again the great blast. He repeated that three times. Moira's dirty face had clean smears across it where she had wiped the tears away. The dirt did not hide the fact that Dugal's idea of unharmed was not Danny's. There was a big bruise under one ear. Her wrists were chaffed raw by the ropes, and there were big circles under her eyes as if she had not slept for days. Which was probably the case.

Moira at last noticed Danny, with disbelief, and then amazement, and then concern as she saw how bloodstained he was. He tried to tell her that it was not his blood, but she ripped at the slashed tunic, and, looking down, Danny saw that he had been mistaken.

Moira bound his chest with strips from his own tunic, while Dugal blew the horn again. The dell began to fill with returning fighters.

The tops of the trees were still gilded with sunlight. It had taken no time at all.

Looking back, the rest of that day was a bit of a jumble for Danny. Some things though were crystal clear, etched on his memory forever.

Moira's face as she looked up from binding his chest. She was changed in some way. Same resolution, same clear-eyed focus, but somehow vulnerable. There had been fear in her face, he realized, recognising it in himself also.

Kelly standing by Speed as he grazed peacefully, uncaring of the chaos around him, all her attention on the horse, as if feeding on his tranquillity, as if that would blot out all the other things going on around her.

The walk up the open grassland towards the hill. He had stood by Tasgo as he knelt by a man whose blood reddened the grass around him, whose every breath seemed to be shuddered pain. Tasgo saying quietly, for his ears only, *'You fought well.'* One of the enemy. *'You did well today.'* Eye to eye as he slid the sword between his ribs, ending forever the losing battle for life. And then he had closed his enemy's eyes, and taken his spear, his belt, and the brooch that held his cloak in place.

Exquisitely clearly he remembered the peculiar rattle of spears being bound in a bundle, the softness of the fading light, the feeling of togetherness as they walked up the slope, away from the scene.

The sullen silence of the prisoners.

And now they were huddled together beneath the tree where the chariots had already gathered, and where now Margan kept watch over the dark moor. There was no fire to give away their position. Men leaned against their shields and dozed. Dugal had not left Moira's side for a second. He had wrapped his cloak round her and they sat against the trunk of the tree in which Margan kept watch. Bran Hen and Tasgo joined them there, their voices muted by tiredness and consideration.

Danny sat on his shield because the ground was damp. He had offered it to Kelly, but she had preferred a tree root. Someone had given her an extra cloak. He didn't like to think who might have been wearing it just a few hours ago. She was keeping herself aloof and wrapped in silence.

Everything had changed. Nothing would ever be the same again. He was no longer the person he had been just a few short hours before. He had killed someone. In battle, true. He had taken a life. He had fought, and he was still alive. He felt empty and strange. He guessed Kelly did too, as she sat alone and isolated.

But eventually even she had given in to the cold of night, and allowed him to wrap them both in the cloak that had so recently changed owners. She had at last fallen asleep in his arms, with her head on his shoulder. Once he was sure she was asleep he had nuzzled into her hair. She didn't smell of soap and perfume. She smelt of human being, warm and comforting and very slightly goatish. He liked it.

It was dark now and still. Most of the band were asleep already. There had been talk of riding back down the track in the dark, back to Kennis' village, but that wasn't going to happen.

The prisoners had answered all questions with no attempt to lie. They had been paid by Kuillok to help bring him a hostage or two. A small group, only three strong, was to go and watch the hill over the village, to capture unharmed any stranger who appeared on the hillside. Kuillok had been insistent on that. Whoever it was, they were not to be harmed in any way. Only Moira hadn't made that possible. She had not gone quietly.

They spoke of her with respect, though one of them made a peculiar motion of his hand every time she was mentioned, as if to ward off evil.

A larger group had been stationed at the ford again, to help bring back who-ever had been found to Kuillok. Two of them were from this group. The third was in the last group, who had been stationed at a river junction, with fresh horses where they would be easily found by the others. Then it was supposed to be an easy march to Kuillok. Except the weather, and the local farmers, had been against them. They had had to leave the easy riding of the tracks and go cross country, where recent rains had made the going difficult and rivers hard to cross.

They knew exactly where to find Kuillok, and, for the price of their freedom, could take them straight there, if they wanted.

Dugal laughed at that. *'And then you would be paid twice, first by us and then by Kuillok when you deliver us to him.'*

That was when the decision had been taken. They would not go back a night's journey to the village. They would take what rest they could here on the moor. And tomorrow they would go on, to Stonewall.

They would do this because the prisoners had told them, and Moira had confirmed it from overhearing their conversations when they thought they would make it back to him, that Kuillok already had a hostage.

Kuillok had Freya.

And tomorrow they would set her free.

Post Script

The Parisi are known from a description in Ptolemy's Geographica

The tribe are inferred to have been surrounded by the Brigantes, and with the Coritani south of them across the Humber. Their name may mean 'Fighters' or 'Commanders' though alternatives have also been suggested.

Ptolemy mentions the Parisi in association with Petuaria, which I have replaced with Cynmar,

If you would like to find out more about the late Iron Age in Britain, and the Parisi of East Yorkshire, you could try the following.

Parisi Britons and Romans in Eastern Yorkshire by Peter Halkon The History Press

Brigantia a mysteriography by Guy Ragland Phillips

http://www.megalithic.co.uk

http://www.bbc.co.uk/history/ancient/british_prehistory/iron_01.shtml

http://www.dumnonika.com/weapons-and-armour.htm

https://en.wikipedia.org/wiki/Ferrous_metallurgy#Iron_Age_Europe

https://en.wikipedia.org/wiki/Stanwick_Iron_Age_Fortifications

http://www.cartographersguild.com/showthread.php?t=19730

http://www.bbc.co.uk/history/ancient/british_prehistory/ironage_roundhouse_01.shtml

http://heatherrosejones.com/archaeologicalsewing/wool.html

http://www.teachinghistory100.org/objects/about_the_object/iron_age_horse_trappings

If you would like to delve further into the past to the bronze age, try

Coming Home by Richard Turner, Kite press or Amazon Kindle.